BOG PEOPLE

BOG PEOPLE

A Working-Class Anthology of Folk Horror

Edited by Hollie Starling

Chatto & Windus

LONDON

7 9 10 8 6

Chatto & Windus, an imprint of Vintage, is part of the Penguin Random House group of companies

Vintage, Penguin Random House UK, One Embassy Gardens, 8 Viaduct Gardens, London SW11 7BW

penguin.co.uk/vintage
global.penguinrandomhouse.com

First published by Chatto & Windus in 2025

For copyright details, see the notice on p. 307

Epigraph from *Chronicles of England, France and Spain and the Surrounding Countries* by Sir John Froissart, Translated from the French Editions with Variations and Additions from Many Celebrated MSS, by Thomas Johnes, Esq; London: William Smith, 1848, pp. 647–69.

The moral right of the authors has been asserted

Penguin Random House values and supports copyright. Copyright fuels creativity, encourages diverse voices, promotes freedom of expression and supports a vibrant culture. Thank you for purchasing an authorised edition of this book and for respecting intellectual property laws by not reproducing, scanning or distributing any part of it by any means without permission. You are supporting authors and enabling Penguin Random House to continue to publish books for everyone. No part of this book may be used or reproduced in any manner for the purpose of training artificial intelligence technologies or systems. In accordance with Article 4(3) of the DSM Directive 2019/790, Penguin Random House expressly reserves this work from the text and data mining exception.

Printed and bound in Great Britain by Clays Ltd, Elcograf S.p.A.

The authorised representative in the EEA is Penguin Random House Ireland, Morrison Chambers, 32 Nassau Street, Dublin D02 YH68

A CIP catalogue record for this book is available from the British Library

ISBN 9781784745820

Penguin Random House is committed to a sustainable future for our business, our readers and our planet. This book is made from Forest Stewardship Council® certified paper.

My good friends, things cannot go on well in England, nor ever will until everything shall be in common, when there shall be neither vassal nor lord, and all distinctions levelled; when the lords shall be no more masters than ourselves. How ill they have used us!

John Ball, radical preacher and a leader of the Peasants' Revolt, executed 1381

Contents

Introduction Hollie Starling	1
The Ossuary A. K. Blakemore	17
Perpetual Stew Daniel Draper	43
Carole Emma Glass	71
Eldritch by Mark Colbourne	97
The Spit in Your Mouth and the Bile in Your Stomach Mark Stafford	125
Yellowbelly Hollie Starling	139
The Hanging Stones Jenn Ashworth	167
The Keepers Natasha Carthew	197
I Am Hagstone Salena Godden	233
It Fair Give Me the Spikes Tom Benn	267
Acknowledgements	305
Copyright Notice	307
Credits	309

Introduction

HOLLIE STARLING

Once a year, the market town of Honiton in Devon performs the rites of a tradition thought to be more than 800 years old. Children gather in the town's public square to compete for pennies cast out from the windows above. In times past, the nobility found it amusing to watch peasants scrabbling in the dirt for the coins. Back then, it is said, the pennies were first heated on the stove. Why? Because the spectacle was much more entertaining, the desperation much more evident, when to collect them the poor had to burn their fingers.

There is power in tradition. 'The way things have always been done' carries an authority that resists scrutiny. A self-styled mouthpiece of a community's ancestors can be particularly persuasive. Take Christopher Lee's betweeded autocrat Lord Summerisle in the 1973 film *The Wicker Man*, speaking of his father and father's father before him: 'He brought me up the same way, to reverence the music and the drama and the rituals of the Old Gods. To love nature and to fear it. And to rely on it and to appease it where necessary.' His unique ability to interpret and placate this power allows Summerisle to control and guard the purity of his island. It is a trick of rhetoric not limited to fiction. In a memorial speech for St George's Day 1961, another charismatic orator invoked 'our ancestors' directly, imploring them to 'tell us what it is that binds us together; show us the clue that leads through a thousand years; whisper to us the secret of this charmed life of England, that we in our time may know how to hold it fast'. Some years later this man, Enoch Powell, would deliver his inflammatory 'Rivers of Blood' speech, carving a discursive cleft through class and identity with which modern Britain still wrestles today. Being long dead, it seems, is of no consequence; our ancestors can be summoned to aid and abet just about any agenda, especially when a touch of romantic nationalism may help to grease the wheels.

This is, I think, what thrills me about the genre that began in Britain but has become known worldwide as 'folk horror'. The menace feels so acute because real monsters *do* tread this green and pleasant land. It is a genre of obsession, and in that way mirrors Britain's perpetual fascination with itself. Dual preoccupations – a mythic Albion of spellbinding legends and glorious sovereignty, and deeply embedded systems of class and rule – mould and inform, in a Powellian echo, 'what it means to be British'. In folk horror the soil beneath our feet is seismically unstable. Our closest kin are unknowable and depraved, bound by unseen influences. As folk horror often examines belief, the very keystone of our identities, the moral

Introduction

peril is genuine. That we may be bewitched by the stirring words of a convincing populist, or fall into mass psychogenic hysteria, or take for granted ancient narratives of which we have little understanding, keeps us on our toes. Nothing can be relied upon.

Storytelling has always been one of our favourite pastimes and Britain's bursting catalogue of folklore has provided plenty of grist for the mill. It might be said that folklore, as distinct from recorded history, is a type of collective social memory. Memory, subject to glitches and distortion, is naturally imperfect; but its capacity to capture experience and emotion offers its own sort of truth. A shared repository of familiar archetypes and narratives fosters a sense of community and belonging. Stories may become amulets for regional groups and, over time, the ingredients of national identity.

Unfortunately, tradition has been invoked to defend all sorts of cynical examples of British 'cultural heritage', from fox-hunting to blackface to smacking your kids. In online spaces, folk imagery, wistfulness for unspoilt landscape and appeals to 'indigenous' pride are used as dog-whistles to further the ethnonationalist fantasies of the far right. So it is essential that we define what folk horror is, and what it is not.

More so than the gothic mode, folk horror's rules are pliable, its parameters sometimes tricky to pin down. That said, there are some elements that recur: settings are very often isolated and insular; there may be pressure exerted by some form of ancient darkness that is linked to landscape; and shared reality can exist alongside an alternative one of myth and folklore. While the rural usually predominates, folk memory exists wherever people do, and so an urban setting is not incompatible. It is very much not Christian; the 'old ways', pagan ritual and occultism may be found bristling beneath the surface. The horror element can be unsettling and uncanny; the assault can be psychological or even spiritual, rather than bodily or gratuitous (though these may feature). Supernatural elements are often present but are not required; the antagonist may reside within the rigidity of superstition or the madness of the crowd. Folk horror frequently offers incidental beauty. It is enraptured by nature. Most of all, it is concerned with a fear of outsiders and a clash of cultures.

The coinage of the term 'folk horror' is unclear, though scholar of the genre Dr Dawn Keetley attributes the first mention in print to a 1970 trade publication *Kine Weekly* in advance of the theatrical release of *The Blood on Satan's Claw*. The film, directed by Piers Haggard, forms one corner of what Adam Scovell terms the 'unholy trinity' of folk horror's origins, the others being *Witchfinder General* (dir. Michael Reeves, 1968) and Robin Hardy's cult masterpiece, *The Wicker Man*.[1] Many consider the latter the urtext of the genre, and the very best of independent British filmmaking in the 1970s.

This vanguard is often described as folk horror's first wave, even if what would become the genre's recognisable motifs were already in the water. TV productions

Introduction

such as *The Owl Service* (1969–70), *Penda's Fen* (1974) and *Children of the Stones* (1977), and the Hammer films *The Witches* (dir. Cyril Frankel, 1966) and *The Devil Rides Out* (dir. Terence Fisher, 1968), fermented a paradigm shift for horror aficionados fed up with gothic clichés. Meanwhile, delirious public information films and the BBC's *A Ghost Story for Christmas* pitched their disquieting images into Britain's living rooms.

Though the first wave of British folk horror played out predominantly on screen in the sixties and seventies, its filmmakers were drawing on literary influences much older. Arthur Machen's *The Great God Pan* (1894) was inspired by the author's terror amidst the 'strange relics' of a pagan temple in Wales. M. R. James spent the early decades of the twentieth century horrifying audiences with his fireside tales, most memorably among them 'Oh, Whistle, and I'll Come to You, My Lad' and 'A Warning to the Curious'. After the war, John Wyndham took up the mantle, his fascination with ritual and the terror of group-think particularly present in *The Midwich Cuckoos* (1957) and *The Chrysalids* (1955), the latter an early atomic horror. Inspiration may also be assumed from the haunted locales and harrowed souls imagined by Robert Aickman, Alan Garner and his many works of folk fantasy, as well as master of the occult thriller Dennis Wheatley, and in the US, Washington Irving, Thomas Tryon and Shirley Jackson's short story 'The Lottery'.

Folk horror's second wave began a few years into the new century, with particular touchpoints being the films of Ben Wheatley (*Kill List, Sightseers, A Field in England, In the Earth*), Ari Aster (*Hereditary, Midsommar*), Alex Garland (*Annihilation, Men*) and Robert Eggers's 2015 feature *The VVitch*. In literature, notable works from Andrew Michael Hurley, Adam Nevill, Sarah Moss and Benjamin Myers found much popular and critical praise. Folk horror's resurgence has coalesced around an active online community and has been supported by an explosion in zines and small presses, as well as more esoteric projects like 'Hookland' and 'Scarfolk', both reflecting a woozy nostalgia for a lost temporal landscape in post-war Britain. As folk horror becomes mainstream we have seen the aesthetics of the genre spreading out across material culture, with Summerisle inspiring the catwalks of designers Gareth Pugh and Luella Bartley, and artist Jeremy Deller's inflatable Stonehenge *Sacrilege* at the 2012 London Olympic games. Folk horror broke the billion-dollar bracket when Taylor Swift and her dancers were cloaked in ritual robes and steeped in ethereal mist during one segment of the singer's Eras tour.

More recently, folk horror's most visible examples have grappled with anthropogenic climate change. Fuelling this period of revival, then, may be the impulse in times of uncertainty to look to 'ancient wisdom' for answers, combined with the nauseous suspense of living through self-imposed and irreversible ecological collapse.

Whatever the reason for its current popularity, as Hurley himself writes in the introduction to the folk horror anthology *The Fiends in the Furrows II* (2020), the

Introduction

so-called first wave never self-consciously titled itself 'folk horror'. Our analysis of it is retrofitted, meaning those working in the genre today are at its forefront. Many of its most exciting writers are contributors to the collection you are about to read.

In *The Wicker Man*, Sergeant Howie, played by Edward Woodward, represents chastity, Protestant repression and paternalist normativity, and is set up entirely to collide with Summerisle's heathen inhabitants: godless, liberated and pleasure-seeking. In this disturbing tale of human sacrifice, an almost throwaway line in the film's final scenes has always fascinated me. Being led to the pyre, about to die, Howie thrashes amid the baying crowd, shouting, 'If the crops fail, Summerisle, next year your people will kill *you* on May Day!' The brief look of panic on the face of Lord Summerisle betrays an overlooked dimension of *The Wicker Man*. The whole project a confection of his industrialist grandfather, Summerisle does not actually believe in the 'Old Gods' in whose honour he has constructed his cult island; the story is kept alive so that his idiot peasants do not turn on him and storm the gates of his tropical mansion. They perform their brutal ritual not because they are savage and unenlightened, but because they have been socially engineered. Distracted so as not to notice they are scrabbling in the dirt for hot pennies.

Inequality has always been a part of Britain's fabric,

with the possession of land and wealth hereditarily preserved. If folk culture is the memory of human experience, it is reasonable to expect these divisions to bubble up in our stories and traditions. Medieval England found this so self-evident as to have turned it into a joke; each year a 'Lord of Misrule' was appointed from the peasantry to poke fun at his betters during the Feast of Fools. Because of course: a member of the underclass given fleeting impunity to masquerade dignity and power over nobility, what could be more absurd?

In *Workers' Tales: Socialist Fairy Tales, Fables, and Allegories from Great Britain*, Michael Rosen brings together some of the fantastical narratives that informed the foundations of the labour movement. It's not as unlikely a combination as it first appears; to the uninitiated, a public speaker delivering a tract by Karl Marx or Rosa Luxemburg could well be too abstract and dry to inspire action. But by using the formats of children's literature, stories familiar to all, the inequalities and hypocrisies of the British class system could be revealed plainly. Such was their effectiveness that many of these narratives found their way into publications like the *Clarion*, William Morris's *Commonweal* and the *Workmen's Times*. Keir Hardie used such stories up and down the country while campaigning for his Independent Labour Party and ended up being a prolific writer of them himself.

Many of these fables centre the rural labourer and indentured serf, the indispensable agricultural workers whose toil made the industrial revolution possible. The

Introduction

sunlit pastoralism of academy art and highbred poetry promoted the peasant experience as one of simple living surrounded by bucolic symbols, making a pretty image of something that has held critical significance to centuries of ordinary people: the harvest. It was the harvest that governed the whole year, a calendar event which brought with it the annual reassurance of survival. When a person's chances in life are sealed by an accident of birth it's no coincidence that it is the pitchfork that has become the most familiar totem of the angry mob.

In folk horror, meanwhile, class narratives may be overt or covert. We see this most often in differing claims to the ownership of land. Idyllic and isolated rural communities are frequently depicted as deeply connected to the land and its traditions, a kinship that is underestimated by meddlesome outsiders soon to meet their end. Alternatively, the rural working class may become victims of dark rituals or manipulations by malevolent entities, reflecting themes of powerlessness and vulnerability in the face of forces beyond their control. Indeed, throughout history the poor have suffered indignities both natural and unnatural, whether *force majeure* or being indentured to a lord or via religious suppressions of personal liberty. Widows and suspiciously unwed women have especially met with persecution, and the scold's bridle and other ways of shutting people up have cast a long shadow in the folk imagination. Behind each example you don't have to look hard to find a vested interest. It is a deep and murky well.

All this makes folk horror supreme in exploring revolt. The genre gives anthropomorphic voice to an earth assumed to be inert. It grants magical powers to the most downtrodden, wretched and witch-hunted. It finds the uncanny in the clash between different socio-economic worlds. It offers up a high-born sacrifice on a sea of pitchforks. Folk horror narratives may also explore the impact of economic decline on rural communities, as external pressures force them into desperate acts or dark pacts to survive. Out of desperation of grinding poverty, yes, but sometimes by unleashing a glorious flex of collective power.

Of course, history is written by the literate. The vast majority of our forebears are lost forever, not even present in the marginalia. But if we look hard across Britain's landscape, we see evidence of ordinary people persisting, and resisting too. The Chartists, who sensed the power of Calderdale's ancient Basin Stones when they gathered there in the summer of 1842 to foment their general strike. The folk balladeers, whose music has a strong history of protest and rebellion, and which proliferated widely because its style is easily learnt without requiring literacy. Apocryphally, the megaliths of Stonehenge are said to have been erected in honour of Boudicca, whose low-born followers wished to ensure that a symbol of their defiance against the Romans would stand for all time.

There are echoes in our calendar too. May Day, the fire festival of the agrarian calendar, a day of feasting and indulgence, was once so closely associated with the folk

Introduction

figure Robin Hood that illegitimate babies conceived on the day were known as 'sons of Robin'. These boys often grew up to be outlaws, which originally referred to someone who had run away from serfdom. Of course, many now know May Day by another name: International Workers' Day.

Remnants like these remind us that equality is a cause that requires active participation and visible representation. The Lord of Misrule was permitted to lampoon his real-life lords within the bounds of entertainment, but what if there was no 'commoner' to take on the role? A 2024 report by the Sutton Trust found that young people from socio-economic disadvantage are systemically blocked from earning a living in the creative sector,[2] with research from the Creative Industries Policy and Evidence Centre finding that fewer than one in 10 arts workers comes from a working-class background.[3] When art speaks from the same few overrepresented perspectives, culture withers. The contributors to this collection do so as a refusal against the project of marginalisation, and to force reflection on just whose interests are vested in maintaining a system of feast and famine.

Post-Farage Essex is the chosen hellscape of A. K. Blakemore, where the shifting sands of contemporary divisions encourages one woman's slide into bone-cavorting deviance. At the country's westernmost extreme, Natasha Carthew's Cornish islanders fight to endure as guardians both of a disused lighthouse and an unearthly secret. Like cautionary tales of campfires old,

Mark Stafford's mirror-world Dorset reminds us why we should never eat the food of the faery world, however tempting. In 'Carole', a clutching, mud-bound horror of loss, Emma Glass takes us on a pilgrimage through devastating terrain right to the bog-riddled borderlands. Unstable earth marks the very centre of England, a fitting stage for a familial psychodrama examining the ritual roles we so often create for ourselves, in Jenn Ashworth's Pendle Hill requiem. Hauntology, folk horror's sister genre exploring phantoms looped in time and place, is the brooding premise to Tom Benn's psychogeographic music-hall spectacle located in a 'Hellmouth north of Halifax'. My own story, 'Yellowbelly', the slang term for a person from Lincolnshire and here a tidy short-hand for male gutlessness, takes working-class fetishisation to tasteless ends. Rising from the ashes meanwhile, and proving folk horror needn't be rural, is Salena Godden's young Londoner witch and her talisman of revenge. Lastly, the winners of the *Bog People* competition for unpublished working-class writers: Mark Colbourne's retrospective of tragedy-blighted 1970s folk-rockers Heptagonal Sons, and a queasily flavoured tale of fraternal chest-beating from Daniel Draper. Both are presented here in print for the first time.

A note on class. The most recent large-scale study into class in the UK, conducted by the BBC in conjunction

Introduction

with Manchester University and the London School of Economics, determined that 'the working class' is today more complex than traditional definitions used by sociologists in the twentieth century.[4] After many decades of demographic change through de-industrialisation, global migration and a greater percentage of women entering the workforce, the old yardsticks of home ownership, occupation and education level have become too simplistic. Self-identification, meanwhile, brings its own challenges and limitations. For the purposes of this collection contributors were asked to consider if they grew up in circumstances of low social, cultural and economic capital and/or asset wealth, and that regardless of their current circumstances and lifestyle that they could write authentically from that point of view. All contributing bog people, including me, have been paid equally.

Defining class may be complicated and often fraught, but that some of us exist in significantly different realities to others is as clear as day. The project of uplifting the world's poorest has stagnated, while Oxfam's most recent survey of global inequality predicts that the world will have its first trillionaire within the decade.[5] In the UK today, 4.2 million children live in poverty.[6] Such extravagant injustice demands our sustained attention. In place of explanation, we are spun fables about the working poor being indolent, told that striking for above-inflation wages and labour protections is grasping and uncivilised. Space is ceded for bad-faith political insurgents speaking in mimicked concern for Britain's future, warning any compassion towards refugees and economic migrants invites a river of blood; or for a serving prime minister to suggest that global pandemics are 'just nature's way of dealing with old people'.[7] Stories are still being used to incite, to divide and to kill.

The great unwashed has always been an inconvenience, the grubby workers' hands on the wheels of commerce an understood necessity, though an unsightly one. Those vested in the maintenance of capital-driven systems of control have worked hard to distract from one of history's most abiding truths: that there are more of us than them. So often in folk horror narratives we see a culmination of an aberrant individual or group suppressed by the multitude. In this moment it is the perfect genre to glimpse an exhilarating role reversal, to provoke a change of regime. To conjure together a Feast of Fools that endures beyond dawn.

With *Bog People* we excavate the mud-bound relics and restore the great unwashed. In its pages we recognise the countless dead unnamed by the chroniclers of history; the poor, but also women, people of colour, marginal identities, the voices of the colonised, silent and suppressed. Together we will relearn the disruptive potential of stories to upend fortresses of power. Stories of reaping and sowing, stories that turn the staid soil so something fresh can grow from it, stories as sharp as a guillotine blade, stories to persist for all time.

Hollie Starling
London, May Day 2025

Introduction

NOTES

1. *The Wicker Man* (1973), directed by Robin Hardy, screenplay by Anthony Shaffer inspired by the novel *Ritual* (1967) by David Pinner. Produced by British Lion Films.
2. 'Social Mobility: The Next Generation', Sutton Trust, June 2023, www.suttontrust.com/wp-content/uploads/2023/06/Social-Mobility-The-Next-Generation-Lost-Potential-Age-16.pdf
3. 'Fewer than one in 10 arts workers in UK have working-class roots', *Guardian*, May 2024, www.theguardian.com/inequality/article/2024/may/18/arts-workers-uk-working-class-roots-cultural-sector-diversity
4. 'Huge survey reveals seven social classes in UK', BBC News, April 2013, www.bbc.co.uk/news/uk-22007058
5. 'Inequality Inc.', Oxfam, January 2024, policy-practice.oxfam.org/resources/inequality-inc-how-corporate-power-divides-our-world-and-the-need-for-a-new-era-621583/
6. 'UK Poverty 2024', Joseph Rowntree Foundation, January 2024, www.jrf.org.uk/uk-poverty-2024-the-essential-guide-to-understanding-poverty-in-the-uk
7. Quote: Sir Patrick Vallance, Coronavirus public inquiry, BBC News, October 2023, www.bbc.co.uk/news/uk-politics-67278517

The Ossuary

A.K. BLAKEMORE

A. K. Blakemore is a poet and novelist based in north Essex. Her novels include *The Manningtree Witches* (Granta, 2021) – winner of the Desmond Elliott Prize for Best Debut Novel, and shortlisted for the Costa First Novel Award and the Royal Society of Literature's Ondaatje Prize – and *The Glutton* (Granta, 2023), shortlisted for the Dylan Thomas Prize. Her full-length poetry collections are *Fondue* (Offord Road Books, 2018) and *Humbert Summer* (Eyewear, 2015). Her work has been widely published and anthologised, appearing in the *Poetry Review, London Review of Books, Guardian* and *White Review*, among others.

MONDAY

The ossuary of Saint Andrew's Church, in north Essex, contains one of the largest collections of ancient human skulls in the United Kingdom. It is open to visitors from eleven in the morning to four o'clock in the afternoon, Monday through to Saturday, April to September. During this time, it is staffed by volunteers from the local community. Well, one volunteer really. Or so the vicar, Father Daniels, jokes. She is an eighty-year-old woman. A retiree, named Shirley – always Shirley, never Shirl – Lister.

Every morning of the 'tourist season' – such as it is, in this mildewed and flaking coastal town – whether rain or shine, Shirley Lister arrives at Saint Andrew's in her neat, comfortable slip-on shoes at precisely 10:45. She opens the ossuary, round the back of the church, with the spare key she has been entrusted with. She will find, laid out tidily on the fibreboard desk at the entrance: a small steel lockbox for the cash float; a sheaf of glossy pamphlets in a plastic container; a box of tissues; a broken chunk of brick with which to wedge the heavy door open when it's warm out; a little metallic bell of the kind found on hotel reception desks, which can be used to summon Shirley to attendance (though this has never really been necessary); and a laminated sheet of A4 paper displaying the price of admittance. It reads:

£4 ADULTS
£2 CHILD (TO BE ACCOMPANIED AT ALL TIMES BY AN ADULT)
£3 PENSIONSERS, STUDENTS & ALL OTHER CONCESSIONS

('St Andrew's Church Ossuary' scrolling across in a font the vicar had chosen – *Blackadder ITC*, which seemed fitting.) Shirley supposes that 'other concessions' means the unemployed. The *between jobs*. The idlers. Truth be told, in all her six years of volunteering at Saint Andrew's, it's never come up. Pensioners – or 'pensionsers', as the price list would have them – doubtless form the majority of their daily traffic, padding round the room from bay to vaulted bay of the tarnished, gap-jawed skulls with a quiet reverence. Polyurethane handbags and lipstick on their dentures.

Students? They come in every now and then. Primarily the 'gothic' type, so-called. That's how Shirley thinks of them, though it's probably not what they'd call themselves these days. She's not up on the lingo, and nor would she wish to be. In long fringed skirts and stacks of silver rings. Little enamelled badges of rainbow flags on their backpacks. Trying to take pictures with their mobile telephones – always encased in glittering, bumpy plastic – so that Shirley must clear her throat and tap the sign. *So* disrespectful.

The unemployed? Well. *When hell freezes over, perhaps. Why spend £3 of your giro on heritage when it could go towards a pack of cigarettes, or an ugly tattoo?*

Shirley Lister is getting older now. And so the *now* seems to slip out of view, sometimes. Pocking and bubbling like the skin on milk. She likes the ossuary, not only because the demographic of its patrons corroborates her pre-existing prejudices, but because it is peaceful, and still. She likes the routine of it. She sits here, day after day, on her stiff plastic chair, and watches the world go by. In sun and in rain. The world, she is sorry to report, seems mainly made up of absurdly fat women with plastic shopping bags and nose rings, immigrants and spotty children exhaling clouds of lemon-scented vapour.

She turns her phone off when she arrives at the ossuary in the morning and doesn't switch it on again until she gets home, around five, and begins heating up her supper on the hob. Nets over the kitchen window getting dirty again, greying.

An alert flashes up on the screen: a missed call from Nathaniel. A little later, Shirley rings him back. The first episode of *Springwatch*, on mute, and the cat in her lap.

He asks about her day. She tells him, in so many words, that she is sorry to say the world seems mainly made up of absurdly fat women with plastic shopping bags and nose rings, immigrants and spotty children exhaling clouds of lemon-scented vapour. He calls her a racist. Her only son.

Well, she answers. She's got a fridge full of insulin, if she ever does decide to end it all. It's not as though anyone would care, she says. It's not as though anyone would miss me.

You're a fucking vile woman, Nathaniel says. *You know that?* And then he hangs up. On the screen, a juvenile goldfinch parts its little beak, and flits from bough to bough.

TUESDAY

Her knees know when the weather will be bad. Noon, and not a single visitor yet. It's the rain that's keeping them away, of course. The April shower riffling through the leaves of the big sycamore in the churchyard, and the metallic, rolling sound of distant thunder.

Sat at the desk, Shirley takes out the KitKat she has in her handbag to keep her glucose levels up, in case of emergencies. She ought not to eat it really, but after yesterday's phone call with Nathaniel she feels she owes herself a treat. Nibbling on a wafer, she thumbs through a glossy pamphlet. *The earliest remains,* it says, *housed in St Andrew's charnel date from the fourteenth century. It is estimated that the collection consists of the bones of over two thousand individuals.* She has this all by memory now.

A 1998 project by osteologists based at Essex University provided a demographic analysis of all the skulls on the shelves,

The Ossuary

revealing a higher proportion of male than female skulls, but it is unclear where most of the individuals housed in the charnel originated. A scarlet starburst on the corner of the second page offers a smug DID-YOU-KNOW: *Medieval peasants sometimes kept parts of their dead relatives' bodies around their homes. This was thought to help attract good luck for the surviving members of the family!!*

It's not just the bones that intrigue her, but the words that go with them: *talus, de-flesh, calvarium, sub-adult*. For cold beauty, they almost match the bones themselves. With twenty minutes to go until closing time, Shirley has them all to herself. Brushing the crumbs from her pleated skirt, she rises to her feet.

Within the ossuary, the bones are arranged in arched bays, along shelves carved deep into the pale stone from floor to ceiling. At the apex of each bay, a single skull; then two; then five; then ten, as the shelves widen, to accommodate as many as twenty-five at floor level. Although it's the skulls that draw the most admiration, they've other bones kept in the ossuary too. A long iron trough filled with thigh bones, bleached and bulbous at the ends: a classic bone, the femur. The kind of bone a puppy dog might slobber over in a cartoon. Shirley has always found the pelvises and scapulae particularly appealing, orchidaceous and palely fluted. The vertebrae have a pleasingly ergonomic sort of quality. They put her in mind of a set of stacking resin cocktail glasses her great-aunt Barbara bought her as a wedding gift in the late sixties, now up in the attic.

The finger bones and foot bones, however, she can take or leave. Piled together, they don't look like much of anything besides a pile of gravel.

The skulls are undeniably the stars of the show, and for good reason. They've got character. All are jawless. Most face outwards, their shadowed eyeholes directed at the room. But some, seemingly at random, have been turned into the wall. As though in punishment. Or as though they're sulking, even – presenting to the viewer only a hump of yellow-white parietal bone shot through with slender hairline cracks.

Many, though not all, have three-digit numbers painted or inked like eyebrows above the supraorbital, in cursive Victorian handwriting: the remnants of an attempt at inventory, initiated by an ambitious nineteenth-century vicar, and never repeated since. Others are partial, or cracked, or otherwise malformed. Shirley has always admired 389, particularly, as a perfect specimen: the colour of white chocolate, with a smooth and delicately protruding maxilla that seems to betoken chastity, and eyeholes neither too deep nor shallow. Shirley has named her – and she feels certain 389 was a her – Isabel. 216, whom she calls Valentine, is, on the other hand, a more piquant sort of fellow, with a gaping cavity where his nasal bone should be and a swashbuckling dent in the centre of his forehead. Then there is 341. Richard. The baby of the bunch, whose cavernous sockets appear to express some great and unresolved sorrow (while the pin-prick holes within these hint at *cribra orbitalia* – an iron deficiency brought about by poor nutrition, the pamphlet has informed her).

You come to know them, after a while. To feel you'd be able to tell one from another through touch alone. And Shirley Lister does touch them, on days like this, when there is no one there to see her do it. Back at home that evening, taking off her face, she wonders what her own skull looks like, beneath the sagging, rouged flesh. Sagging and rouged. That's what her home is, too. She used to take pride in it – that's the way she was raised. *Things* mattered, appearances. This ought to match with that. Avocado bath sets, apricot and cream shag. She feels that the love that women of her generation bear for embellished cushions and frilled toilet-tissue covers, so commonly derided, ought not to be mocked, and is somehow connected, in an abstract sense, to their robust moral fibre.

Nathaniel, who studied psychology at Birmingham University, has insisted it is something to do with World War Two. A craving for control among ex-evacuees, expressed through commitment to co-ordinated soft furnishings. *A childhood filled with upheaval makes you want to nest.* After he'd said this, he asked her if she remembered the first time she'd seen pictures from the death camps.

What a thing to ask. Those ugly photographs.

Well, do you?

Shirley had thought about it. *No, I don't.*

But she wanted to give him something. *I remember when Kennedy was assassinated. I was doing the ironing. Your uncle Brian was sat in the corner of the kitchen.*

WEDNESDAY

Among her acquaintances, and the very few people she might, at a stretch, call *friends*, her volunteer work has been a source of curiosity – and sometimes, she senses, suspicion – since the very month she started at the ossuary. Ruth, from her book group ('It's all rather *morbid*, isn't it?'), or Elaine, with whom she used to attend doll's house and miniature fairs at suburban exhibition centres ('Oh, God, Shirley. It'd just give me the heebie-jeebies.') But she doesn't get out so much anymore. There's her legs to think of. And anyway, everything, even a coffee and a muffin at the café in town, is so expensive now. And a teacher's pension doesn't go very far. Not after money on the prepayment meter, cat food and her regular trim and blow dry. It's down to the line most months, and no doubt she'll be even harder up now the new lot – or, should she say, the *old lot* – have got in. No more triple-lock, and taking away her free television licence – and for what? To pay for these Somalians and single mothers to stay in plush hotels. She can't remember when she last stayed in a hotel, and here we are, putting up the world and his uncle in the Holiday Inn just as long as it bloody suits them. (Nathaniel in her head: *Single mothers? What do you think it was that you were?*)

And now Jennifer won't let her see the children, all because she voted for 'that man'. It's silly, really. Childish. People used to be made of sterner stuff. They used to be able to disagree. Look at her own father – he'd drink with all sorts down The Swan. From skinheads to transvestites, and never blink an eye.

Anyway, they send her postcards, when they go abroad. What friends she has, or had; Nathaniel and Jennifer. They send her skulls. All sorts of skulls, from paintings in museums across the world. She has three, in fact, of Van Gogh's famous *Skull of a Skeleton with Burning Cigarette*, which isn't a favourite, as it reminds her of her father. The shading on the brow-bone, like the skull is frowning – too human, too fleshly, somehow. She has a whole set of Holbein's *Ambassadors*, where the skull is stretched at the bottom across a lush, geometrically patterned carpet, and, unless you peer at it from a certain angle, it looks as though the two handsome Tudor dandies are stood either side of a long wooden pole. From Nathaniel's last trip to New York, Pieter Claesz's *Still Life with a Skull and a Writing Quill*, in which she was pleased to notice something of Valentine's empty-eyed insouciance in the titular cranium. That Belgian fellow, James Ensor. He painted skeletons getting married, skeletons going to nightclubs and bars, skeletons dressed up in soldiers' uniforms and fighting like dogs over a pickled herring. Vasily Vereschagin's *The Apotheosis of War*, where large black birds flock over a mountain of bones, and clot in the branches of white and desiccated trees.

Shirley's favourite of all the skull postcards she has been sent over the years, most now sun-bleached and fading on her fridge-freezer, is *Garden of Death*, by Hugo Simberg. Here, three skeletons in black cassocks tend to flowers – star-shaped and bell-shaped, blue and ochre red – in a sepia-tinted garden. At the very top of the picture, a meandering path leads away, between the roots of trees, to a place beyond the honeyed realm of these deathly horticulturalists. It must be hell, Shirley thinks, that the path leads to. Or else just the *nothing* in between the two extremes. Because, whether Hugo Simberg had meant it that way or not, his garden of death looks to Shirley like a very heavenly sort of place. Just looking at it, you feel like you can hear the bumblebees browsing between the flower beds. And no one there is speaking. No one there ever says a single word. All you would hear, if you stood there, among those eternal gardeners, would be the swish of the skeletons' heavy black cassocks, the trickle of watering cans, and the thrum of insect life.

On Wednesday evening, as Shirley retrieves a fresh cartridge for her insulin pen, she lets the fridge door swing closed with a thwack and stands there, looking at this postcard, until the sky outside goes from bright cerise to brown to a polluted black. The offshore wind turbines twirling, ugly and ruby-eyed, out at sea, visible through her netted window.

This is when she decides.

THURSDAY

Thursday feels like the first real day of spring, as she buttons up her jacket on her doorstep and heads out on the ten-minute walk to the station. The fizz of new life under the tarmac and broken stone. The regenerative energy is infectious. It doesn't even dampen her spirits when she sees, at the crossing, yet another ragged front garden being smothered in concrete. Bad for the bees. Bad for drainage. And just so *gauche*. A labourer in muddy boots, sat on a crate by the mixer, peers up from a milky cup of tea to catch her disapproving glance as she walks by. Who is it that lives at number 46, again? The Irish family? Or that awful fat woman who goes about in flip-flops all the time, draggled bits of hair extension clinging on for dear life. The things women do to themselves these days, and willingly. A spicule of memory lodged in the corner of her eye as the 98A rolls past, pushing puddle-water up onto the pavement: she can't have been much older than fifteen and riding the bus back from school. A busy bus, so she was standing in the aisle. A shrivelled old dear with Silk Cut breath and a fur pillbox hat leant over, tapped her shoulder, and told her with a sympathetic smile that her slip was showing beneath her skirt. Such embarrassment she had felt! Her cheeks burning. And all over a half-inch of polyester on show – *her underthings*. But now she sees young girls who can hardly be older than she was then, out and about in clothes so tight they look painted on. Leggings, bra tops. Those tiny, tawdry 'knickers' that barely deserve the name emerging from the waistbands of jeans that appear to her to be made up more of rip than of denim. Pretty girls as well, sometimes. Wearing get-up that would make a whore blush. Down on the seafront, chomping through stick-rock and throwing empty cans into the waves.

But look, Shirley, she tells herself, returning from her reverie, *you can't keep nature down.* It does what it wants. The puckered yellow buds of dandelions squeezing up through the cracks in the slabs. (Shirley Lister recognises no dissonance in her appreciation of the natural world's endless capacity for change and the terror that the similarly protean quality of human culture inspires.)

The town's a mess, but you can look past it on a morning like this. The filth and the squalor gilded with the ormolu of the coming summer. Wasps pecking at the rubbish piled next to the bins, and the junkies at the station with their jackets tied round their bony hips. The doors open to the platform with their customary trill, and on she gets. The train is quiet: commuters, mostly. The smell of cheap cologne and cheaper coffee, sweat on rayon. No one else gets off where she gets off, which she supposes is a metaphor.

All quiet all day at the ossuary. She sits at her desk with the door propped open. The scent of summer and the budding sycamore. At around two in the afternoon, she's eating her sandwich – cheese and ham on white bread – when the vicar comes by. Hurriedly, she swallows a half-masticated mouthful and sweeps the crumbs from her skirt, but Father Daniels seems unperturbed. *You can close up early if you'd like,* he tells her. *Don't think we'll be getting anyone in today! Such gorgeous weather out. Everyone's probably got better things to do than poke about in the dark with the dead people,* he chuckles. *Why don't you go and enjoy the sun, Shirley?*

The Ossuary

And she hates him, with his thinning chestnut hair and his earring and his *just call me William* and the rock band T-shirts he wears to the church youth group (The Misfits? *Crass?* Well, indeed). But she smiles, and nods a curt assent. As he lopes back towards the porch, she closes up and locks the door.

The windowless skull chamber is absorbed in an absolute darkness. And there Shirley stands, for several minutes, with the remains of two thousand human beings, and her hand resting on the heavy brass key. They are there, she knows, somewhere in the shadow. Their unbreath stirring the very fine hairs on the back of her neck.

Carefully, she lets her arm drop and takes a step backward. Gingerly, she feels her way round the edge of the visitor's desk, until she is standing in open space. Stretching out her hands, left and right, she finds only the empty air, and the silence of the grave. Like being at the pictures, she thinks, during the day – that timeless, vertigo-inducing feeling when you step outside again, and find the world a different colour to the one you left. She turns – twirls, even – on the spot a few times, before catching herself. In her mind's eye, she reconstructs the shape of that most familiar room, that room she knows better than any other. The position of the desk, the radiator, the fire-extinguisher hanging from its bracket on the wall, the shelves of skulls – then gets down to her knees.

Shirley crawls through the dark, until, reaching out, her fingertips brush against the chicken wire mesh that unobtrusively covers the shelves, ostensibly guarding its residents from theft (a rash of skulls went missing back in the early 2000s – a few, the vicar has told her, with obscene jollity, *ended up on eBay*). The wire feels chill to the touch as she slides her index finger through the aperture. A centimetre, then a centimetre more, until she feels the bone, powdery with dust. She caresses along a series of indents, and ragged, pointing outcrops – the very bottom of a fractured maxilla. Up she goes to the nasal cavity, like an overturned heart. One finger buried in each space where the nostrils would lead, where the breath would pass into the body. Like gripping a bowling ball. Next, she caresses down the cheekbone, and at last, to the eyes.

Sliding forward, she removes her hands briefly to wipe the dust from her fingertips onto her skirt, before reaching back in through the wire. A centimetre, then a centimetre more, until she feels something warm, and plush, and pored, and very slightly waxy. It's not bone she feels beneath her fingertips, but a hermetic, living flesh. She doesn't scream. She doesn't even shudder. There's an uncanny sense of familiarity, in fact, to the face she feels there, behind the meshwork.

The first day of spring. The eyeballs give out under her touch like the juicy flesh of an overripe plum.

FRIDAY

These rhythms, these habits. There must be a reason we end up doing the same things, day in, day out. Hardening into a way of life, like the mineral sealing on the lip of a mollusc. An English thing? A human thing, she thinks. Necessary in a dangerous world. The way the skin hardens when it's held close to something burning. The way the bone calcifies around a break. Her dressing gown of mint-green terrycloth, which she wears when she lets the cat out of the back door in the morning. Her blouse and pleated skirt, which she will be wearing by the time he's screaming to be let back in again. Her thermos of milky tea, which she drinks on the 10:10 train. Her navy-blue Marks & Spencer handbag, that contains a Tupperware box that contains a sandwich. When. When does it happen. You have things – things you look forward to, things you do, things you collect. Until it's all like chalk in the mouth. Classic FM. Porcelain ornaments. *Only Connect*. Crochet blankets. Take the arcades down by the seafront, scrawled all over with phosphorescence, strung with candyfloss like bulging sacks of medical waste. Skittering gulls and the smell of pollution rising off the sea. She used to love those places. She used to love men with tattoos. Serpents rearing on their ropy necks and HATE inked on their hairy knuckles. Popping gum in her cherry-red mouth and penny after penny in the slot machine. Now the flickering of their marquee lights makes her so anxious the feeling is physical, like a punch to the stomach.

    She once, on a hot August evening in 1963, gave a policeman a hand job beneath the boardwalk. Now the only company she can bear is that of the dead.

But this morning, she must share it with two young Asian men. They arrive at the ossuary around noon and pay the £3 student concession rate. She hands them each a pamphlet and sits back in her seat with an evincive lack of curiosity as they gaze around the dim-lit room. *Let me know,* she says, *if you've any questions about our collection.* It still gives her a little ripple of pleasure – such as she seldom experiences, these days – when she says it like that: *our collection.*

They do not have any questions. In the periphery of her eyeline, she watches as they make their way around the room, in their duffle coats, occasionally exchanging a few hushed words. After a little while, Shirley sees the shorter of the pair produce his mobile phone from the pocket of his jeans and readies herself to issue a tart reproof. But he keeps the screen angled downward in his hand, jerking at it with his thumb a few times. She watches them, oh so carefully, from the corner of her eye. The shorter man gently nudges his friend with his elbow, and then tilts the mobile's screen in his direction. She can see it. She can see it from where she sits – on the screen, a melange of peach and flesh tones that rhythmically shudder, merge and throb across the tiny screen. It is. She can see it. She can tell. It is a pornographic video.

She feels the blood prickling up her throat as the two young men chuckle under their breath and jostle closer together. When the taller of the pair shoots a glance over his collar towards where she sits, she jerks around like a cracking whip to stare directly ahead, turned mute, her eyes watering. God, how humiliating. What filth and ugliness there is in the world. This is the problem: it forces you to reckon with the shame that oughtn't belong to you. Forces you to hold the shame, like someone else's ugly baby. It beats you down into the corner, laughing all the while. Her embarrassment and discomfort is an aspic, soaking down and around to hold her in suspension. What should she do? Her own mobile is in her pocket. She could take it out, switch it on, and send a text message to the vicar. Easily, she could do this. And yet not easily, no. For what could possess a person, to view pornography at a British Heritage site? What possible gratification could they derive from doing so? She is flushed and she is sweating. She feels the nervous perspiration on the back of her legs soaking through her tights and her skirt, sticking her flesh to the hard polypropylene of her chair, and feels that she might very well vomit.

Still. Be still, Shirley. Like one of those quiet and big-eyed creatures in a forest, who waits until everything is dark, and silent, before it sticks its nose out to snuff at the indignities of the violet night. No strength left in her to set herself against the corrosive flow of the world's spite. She will let it bite her unloved flesh away, until she is only clean white bone.

The young gentleman puts his phone away now, back in the pocket of his duffle coat. She listens as the pair of them perform a last, perfunctory circuit of the skull-room, and make their way towards the exit, where she sits. No acknowledgement, or nod of appreciation. No *very interesting, thanks.*

At five o'clock she closes up the ossuary as usual and walks back to the station through the balmy afternoon. The sleek train, in its livery of red and white, pulls onto the station platform. She chooses a carriage that appears empty, but soon discovers she has made an error. A few minutes into her journey, she hears a mumbling voice from several seats behind her. The reason the carriage is empty is because it contains a man who is patently insane. Raising herself in her seat, she peers back to look at him: a crumpled shape in a dirty combat jacket, his head moving in a disquieting, jerky way against the window. He murmurs and whispers to himself, a fleck of spittle in the corner of his beard. And then occasionally he shouts – obscenities, nonsense. Even, occasionally, a string of enigmatic words that might be charitably construed to be a prayer. His fingers clenched around a sagging roll-up cigarette that he tries to bring up to his twitching mouth. She sits stock-still again. Frozen in fear.

You can do it, girl, he says, to the empty seat opposite. *You can do it. Cunt. Cunt. Cunt. And the shepherds was speaking among themselves. Cunt. Write to your Member of Parliament. Fuck.*

Through the window, she can see the Channel. She can see the stony shoreline, and the little beach huts painted in their plastic unicorn colours. She can see the wind turbines rearing high from the offing, and an unwound skein of tarpaulin dancing beneath the emerald effulgence of the big ASDA sign on the edge of town.

You can do it, cunt. Fuck. Fascist. Fascist cunt.

The Ossuary

SATURDAY

On Saturday morning, Shirley opens the kitchen door to let the cat out. He prevaricates, weaving himself in and out her ankles for a minute or two before he pads down onto the patio. He rolls over, exposing his soft tangerine-coloured belly to the sun. Then she goes upstairs to put on her face. When she leaves, the cat is calling to be let in again. Scraping his claws uselessly at the narrow gap beneath the door, where the pale green linoleum is peeling up. She puts on her jacket, and leaves him there, mewling.

A short and uneventful journey, which is how she likes them. In the station car park, a traffic warden inspecting tickets lifts his hand to tilt the visor of his cap as she passes by, the gesture so conspicuously old-fashioned she could allow it to augment her neuroses if she chose. Which of course, she does. For old times' sake, if nothing else. Outside the newsagent, she stops beneath the awning to check her makeup in her compact mirror. She does not look, to herself at least, unduly elderly today. She has taken great care with her appearance, in fact. Tonged her hair and worn a brand-new blouse, wisteria-blue sateen. A memory: something Nathan used to say, when he was a teenager. Coming down the stairs, dressed up for a night on the town. Looking like a queer, more often than not – and so she would tell him. *They'll take you for a queer, they will. Don't blame me when you end up in hospital.* Cravats and eyeliner. Like the angular boys striking poses on the covers of his records. Admiring himself in the mirror on the landing at the bottom of the stairs, securing his plastic clip-on earrings from the charity shop: *Dress every day like it's the day you're going to die.* She knows it was difficult for him, growing up without a father. You don't need to be bloody Freud, do you?

And if she was a bad mother, as he says – well. Too late to do anything about that now. Today she is floating, moving as though through water. All is softly coloured. Powder-lemon in the morning. Her handbag heavy over her shoulder, and softly clinking with each footfall. Her deliverance, her weightless freight – a three-month prescription's worth of Humulin M3. In the middle distance, she can see the spire of Saint Andrew's, the pale ragstone glittering above the roofs of the terraced houses. The ossuary is closed to visitors on Saturdays – but not to her. It will be the easiest thing in the world to slip in unnoticed and lock the door up behind. There are no alarms, no security cameras. She will be with them. They will all be together, silent as boulders. Silent as chemicals.

Although the circumspect company of skulls appeals, there were other considerations. She didn't want to do it at home. Too much labour involved. She'd have to hoover, dust the skirting boards, clean out the fridge-freezer, bleach the nets, do the windows, change her bed, fish the hair out the plughole in the bathtub.

Couldn't have them saying she didn't keep the place well. Whoever *they* are. The paramedics, she supposes. Yes. Just the thought of them, those men in heavy black boots and fluorescent jackets – opening up her kitchen cupboards and seeing the cracked and tea-stained mugs, tutting at the cobwebs in the corners she can't reach – fills her with a glowing shame. No, you've got to do things in the proper way.

Shirley takes the long way round to stop by the Post Office on the way. A short line. A woman with a pram and a scraggly ponytail, stinking of nicotine. An elderly gentleman in cargo shorts, his swollen feet overhanging his leather sandals and varicose veins livid on his pale calves. One letter, first-class delivery. She sweeps her thumb across his name, scrawled in biro across the manila envelope. *Goodbye*.

And it is now, her final duty discharged, that she allows herself to feel it fully. Freedom, as she steps from the artificial light of the Post Office into the spring sunshine. With the letter tossed into their post-sack, there can be no takebacks. The intention is declared. It is *real*, what she is doing. The needle, the drugs. *Garden of Death*. A fresh breeze blowing down the High Street carries with it the scent of the sea, and Shirley Lister so light in spirit she feels like it could carry her away, like a crumpled lottery ticket. Across the road, a metal sign, attesting to the availability of ice-creams, squeaks on its metal frame. It is an impact from behind – a shoulder – that knocks her down and into the gutter.

The acid pain of a skinned palm on the pavement as he wrenches at the handbag strap. She reaches out a hand, but he is stronger, faster, and more desperate. He pulls it from her grasp, and then he runs. Laid out there on her belly, she watches as he pelts away down the road, past the minicab offices, the vape shop, the arcades. Her vision swims, and the dirty combat jacket flapping out behind her assailant seems to stretch into a cassock, trailing behind him into the guttering. It is as he steps into the light that he becomes fully fleshless – a stamping, dancing, rattling skeleton – then two, then three, fleeing on a rainbow road of blinking marquee lights, down towards the wrinkling sea.

Thirty minutes on, Shirley Lister is admitted to Clacton & District Hospital with a severe concussion which an MRI reveals to be an intracranial haemorrhage. She slips into a coma before surgery can be attempted.

SUNDAY

No post on Sundays, and rail replacement buses all the way means it's early afternoon by the time he arrives at the hospital. A nurse in maroon scrubs leads him into the room and smiles sympathetically as he draws back the curtain and retreats into the corner.

Nathaniel barely recognises her. What surprises him most is the smile. Her flesh sunken, the lips drawn back from the teeth. Like a skull resting on the pillow. He recalls their conversation at the beginning of the week: *You're a fucking vile woman. You know that?*

He won't say sorry. But he does sit down, and, reaching out, he takes her cold, limp hand in his.

Perpetual Stew

DANIEL DRAPER

Daniel Draper is an award-winning writer from Derbyshire who has been published online, in print and in audio form. He's inspired by the uncanny and macabre of the everyday, folklore and its development over time, and the stories we tell ourselves to just get through the day. He tries to squeeze in writing short stories and novels around his day job, and while he may not always manage it, he always finds time to read. You can find his work at www.danieldraper.uk, where he finds self-promotion difficult, but not impossible.

I haven't seen my brother in over fifteen years, but now he's here, sat on my settee. The question of who'll eat the stew hangs between us. It's a fetid, rotting question, fermenting with each passing minute, yet we've both managed to politely ignore it so far.

Instead, he's welling up and clutching a mug as he makes small talk with my wife like he's never been away. Like it matters to him that Dad's dead when he hasn't stepped foot in this village for a decade and a half.

We're not close, me and our Gareth. You'd think we'd have loads in common given he's only a couple of years older than me. We grew up in the same house, in the same village, with the same parents.

It's not the gay thing, either. I've got nothing against that. Gareth's as bent as a three-bob note, Dad would say. But nicely and with a smile, not being homophobic or anything.

It's Gareth's smugness that keeps us apart. Thinks he's better than the rest of us because he left the village as soon as he could.

Not that Dad would hear a word said against him, mind.

Not that Dad's hearing anything no more.

That's why he's back. Eyes full of tears while he grabs Jane's hand.

Our Gareth's got the energy to cry you see, because he hasn't been dealing with the funeral. Hasn't had to register the death or sort out the wake. Hasn't wanted to throw his phone across the room every time he reads the word 'condolences'. Gareth hasn't been trying to explain to his daughter that Grandad's gone. Hasn't been up in the middle of the night as his wife whispers that if he doesn't drop it about that bastard stew she'll leave him.

He does look well though, I'll give him that. I'm glad he's looking after himself.

He's brought our Joanne a present, a wooden bracelet – made of twisted cypress, pine and cedar, apparently. Bit odd for a seven-year-old. Our Joanne's far more easily bought with some felt tips. Still, Jane fawned over it like he'd brought home a fatted calf.

He puts down his drink.

He's only been back an hour and he's already sucking up all the air in the room.

'You stopping at Dad's?' I ask him.

'Yeah,' he replies. We exchange looks. It's not Dad's anymore. It's ours. We haven't spoken about it, communicating exclusively via solicitors, but Dad's house has been

Perpetual Stew

willed to us both. His solicitor's put forward an offer to buy out my half in cash. I'm yet to respond.

I don't know what Gareth does for work, but it's something inner-city that pays through the nose. I don't even know what city.

It wasn't that I didn't want to stay in touch, but round here when someone leaves, they've left. They've abandoned the rites. They've made a choice. Least we can do is honour it.

'It's been so long,' Jane says, like it's news. I suspect it's Jane that's kept in touch with him. Told him about Dad's prognosis. Pair of 'em were thick as thieves until he moved away. I find myself jealous when I think of their friendship.

'Dunna set me off scraightin',' Gareth's voice chokes.

He's talking like Dad on purpose just to wind me up.

'No, come on, it's proper to cry,' she says, putting her arm round him and shooting me a death glare.

I haven't cried yet.

'Oh we can do without me sat here all maudlin, J,' he snivels back. 'There's time enough for that.' He smiles at her. Brown-nosing. It's the first indication that he's going to stay longer than a few days. 'Who's got Joanne?' he asks.

'She's at me mum's,' Jane says. 'She's going to have her tonight and bring her to the funeral tomorrow.'

'Is Dad's body ...?' he asks as he looks at me, voice cracking again.

'Yeah,' I reply. It's in his dining room, on the table, au naturel. It's how we keep our bodies before we burn them.

Gareth might have left the village, but he sure as shit still knows the rites.

'Who's got the stew?' he asks me, wiping his nose on his sleeve.

Jane tenses and gives me a searching look.

'The Hamblins,' I reply. Calmly. But I'm not calm am I? I'm raging. He's dancing around the subject, waiting for me to speak. My mouth is dry.

'Going to be weird seeing it again tomorrow,' he mutters. 'Have you explained the stew to Joanne?'

'Bits,' I say.

I think of Dad. I think of how every time it was our turn to keep the perpetual stew on the stovetop, he'd say the same thing. *Right, lads*, he'd say. *Touch that pot and I'll belt pair of you so hard you not be able to sit right 'til Christmas.*

That's stage one of learning about the stew. Your dad picks it up from the Jenkinses', then it stays on your hob all day and all night, and then it goes to the Hamblins'. You get a few years older and learn it goes around what's left of the old families in the village. As a kid it was just a pot of gloop. There'd be a gamey wet soil stench for about a month that would linger in the curtains for far longer. Dads spoke about sacred duties and how it's been on a simmer for longer than your little head can imagine, while mums raged at the gas bill.

'Does she know what's going to happen tomorrow?'

Gareth says, waiting to take apart my answer to find fault, no doubt.

'Bits,' I reply.

She knows Grandad's naked body will be burned. She knows the songs we'll sing around the pyre with the rest of the nine families. She knows that some of the grown-ups are going to eat the stew.

'Is there something you need to tell me, Steven?' Gareth asks. Smarmy git. Using my full name because he knows it rankles me. He was the same as a kid, prodding and poking with his silly little comments, trying to get me in trouble with Dad.

He's always been entitled, but it's the smallest thing, the tiniest arch of his eyebrow when he sips his coffee, that sends me over the edge. I feel a flushed indignation roll over me, like people get when they're six pints in and are about to deck someone.

'Yeah there is,' I say, not stopping so he can't throw in a joke or stupid comment. 'Tomorrow, I'm going to ask the elders to acknowledge me as the head of the family.'

A beat.

'Are you now?' he says, smirking, like he already knew. Always smirking like he knows something I don't. My entire life, he's cast a shadow I can't seem to escape. Always wiser, knowing more. Dad's fucking favourite.

'It's been done before,' I start to say, and he stands up to interrupt me.

'During emergencies. Wars. Just because you stayed here doesn't mean you get my birthright.' He's stood like he's ready to punch me. The same violence in him from when we were kids. Everyone's best mate until he doesn't get what he wants, then he turns nasty.

'You forfeited that birthright when you left.'

'The fuck I did,' he spits. I can see Jane glowering, but it's best we have this out now rather than causing a scene tomorrow.

'I don't see the stew sat on your hob for a month at a time. Haven't seen you at a single stew exchange in the last fifteen years.'

'Details.'

'Everything's fucking details, Gareth. This whole community would fall on its arse if we ignored details. I've done my duty.'

It's not until Jane puts her hand on my arm that I realise I'm shaking. Gareth gets up and stands in front of me, his face an inch away from mine.

'Listen to me, you little shit,' he hisses. 'You don't know fuck all about duty.'

His coffee breath falls on me in waves as I feel my ears go red with shame.

'So I'll tell you what's going to happen tomorrow,' he continues. 'We're going to release Dad's body back into the earth, and his spirit into the heavens. And then we're going to have some snap and listen to all these fuckers tell their little lies about how nice he was. Then *I* am going to eat the stew.'

I feel myself shrinking, back in my box, a squirmy little boy again.

Perpetual Stew

Jane clears her throat.

'Gareth,' she says, 'I've explained this to him,' and the softness in her voice hurts me more than anything our Gareth could say or do.

It's night now. I'm lying in bed and the house feels empty without Joanne. The only sound is Jane's breathing as she sleeps. I've been shut off all evening, dissociated. Gareth and Jane colluding like that, it makes me feel like a kid again, the third wheel hanging around his brother's best friend, hopelessly in love with her.

She might have married me, but it's always going to be Gareth first for her.

I feel sick.

I keep thinking about my grandad's funeral. I was only nine, so our mum was still alive then. She put me and Gareth in our smart clothes. School trousers and a proper shirt. Court clothes, as Dad'd say. I don't remember Dad crying, and I don't remember Mum giving him any grief over it either.

Grandad's pyre stood at the top of the hill that marks the edge of the village; on the opposite side to the old pit works. The other heads of families had built it in the week between the death and the funeral.

Gareth told me to watch Grandad's eyeballs. He said they'd pop when they burnt. He'd seen it in some Italian horror film.

The eyeballs didn't pop. Not in the way I was expecting. They leaked. I remember being at just the right height to see Grandad's irises collapse and a thin milky liquid ooze down the side of his face.

We keep their eyes open, no clothes. It's important we look at death honestly, release our attachment to our bodies. While we sing, we imagine ourselves on the pyre, even though it's only the heads of families that are granted the honour nowadays.

Grandad's eyes took a while to burn, but his wiry hair vanished instantly. After a while, his blackened skin split as charred muscle and fat leaked out into the ashes at the bottom of the pyre, eventually leaving nothing but bones.

And then the wake.

The wake's where the heads of the families eat some of the perpetual stew. Then the new head of the family makes a sacrifice to replenish it. At Grandad's funeral, Dad hacked off his middle toes on both feet.

It's funny, the smell of the stew never makes you think of cannibalism, even though I suppose that's what it is.

Each family does their sacrifice differently. The Hamblins always sacrifice a chunk of the thigh, and the Gillespies tend to go for a bit of belly fat. Every head of the Jenkins family since the dissolution of the monasteries has gone without their left little finger – a sanctimonious protest at the new religion. You'll never know anyone keep a grudge like a Jenkins.

The rest of us tend to do something different each

Perpetual Stew

time. Grandad would never tell us what he put in the stew. Said it was morbid to talk about it.

While I was watching Grandad's eyeballs, Gareth was scanning his body looking for a missing part: his sacrifice. He wanted to be the only one of us to know what Grandad had put into the stew. Even as kids, he'd hoard knowledge, that sing-song 'I know something you don't know' regularly driving me round the hat rack.

All of the remaining nine families stood around and sang to the sky. We sang about return, blessings for the ground on which we stood, the usual.

Tomorrow, Dad'll be naked on the pyre, burnt away until he's nothing but bones, and the only bit of flesh that'll remain will be in the stew.

The cycle continues.

Dad's pyre's burnt itself out, and we're at the miners' welfare club for the wake. It was quite beautiful actually, seeing the sun rise above the fire, the old songs carried away with the smoke. Pete Jenkins officiated. Dad always thought he was a pompous twat.

The other heads of families have brought their token offerings to me and Gareth. Traditional gifts, mostly. Jane's great-aunt Judith, head of the Wrights, gave us a lovely shawl she'd knitted for our Joanne that had a twisted circular branch motif embroidered on it.

Jane's still not talking to me. Says I'm being pathetic.

Says it goes against everything we stand for, usurping Gareth like this.

I disagree. I think fucking off for money and to cavort amongst outsiders and then reckoning you can waltz back in and become head of the family is usurping.

Everyone else at the wake seems to be having a decent enough time. There's about a dozen pensioners sat with their dominoes out along one side of the wall, while a gaggle of kids lean along the other side on their phones. The bar's being propped up by Pete Jenkins and some of the other family heads. Jane's sat around a table with some of the other women, deep in conversation with Judith.

It's not exactly a roaring turnout, but then I guess we are quite insular. You can count on one hand the people that aren't from the nine families.

I suppose from the outside it looks like a normal wake. Beige walls at odds with red and brown carpets around the edge of the room while young kids run and skid on the vinyl flooring in the middle. The buffet's laid out across the stage which'll host bingo again come Tuesday. Always the same setup, be it for a kid's birthday, wedding, fortieth, fiftieth, retirement, funeral. Every do of your life.

I'm sat hunched over a pint of tepid lager with a plate of tinned salmon and cucumber sarnies cut into triangles.

I can hear our Gareth holding court, telling everyone how it's true, he's moving back to the village, into Dad's. Settling down. Might try to find a husband.

I hate how easily he moves through the world.

Perpetual Stew

The serenity I felt seeing Dad off this morning has evaporated.

Joanne runs over to him and starts hanging on his arms, begging him to play. She looks so grown up in her frock. Reckon it won't be long until I can't easily pick her up.

I'm so absorbed in my thoughts that I don't notice Judith coming over until she nicks one of my sarnies. I've a lot of time for Judith. Even though it's Jenkins what runs things, she's the oldest head of any of the families, and the only woman. I've never thought of it until now, but she's the one that's eaten the most stew.

'Carol make these?' she asks through her second mouthful. 'Always puts too much vinegar in, does Carol. Bet she goes through more vinegar than Hobson's chippy.'

I flatten my mouth in an approximation of a smile.

'You've all on filling up on that, Jude,' I say. 'In't stew due within the hour?'

'Gi' over, it's not like it's a bowlful. It's ceremonial, Steve. Just a nibble. And anyway,' she nudges me with her shoulder, 'it in't all that. I swear at Dobby Gillespie's wake I got a bit of gristle in mine. Probably one of them Taylors – every sod knows they put a bit of rump in, dirty bastards.' She nudges me again and chortles.

'What did you put in then?' I ask.

'Me tit,' she says straight away. 'Mum passed right around the time of my cancer. Had Jenkins's dad as my surgeon for my mastectomy, so we kept some. Not that you could've fed the five thousand with it, mind.'

I look at her properly for the first time. Judith Wright had always been an old lady, even when I were a kid. She had short grey hair and sharp, keen eyes. But cancer? To have her body turn on itself? To take that and make something beautiful out of it?

'I never knew,' my voice is meek and boyish.

She turns to me.

'Why would you? It were before you were born. Besides, there's plenty you don't know, love,' she smiles. 'What's your Gareth going for? Toes, like his dad?'

My breath catches in my throat. Everyone's waiting for him to take up the mantle. Slot right back in and claim his place. Nobody's even asked me what I'd put in, even though I've known since the first week Gareth left. A chunk out of my forearm, something visible.

'Dunno,' I mutter, 'Dad always said he liked the idea of "dipping a toe in". Made it feel less . . . permanent, I guess.'

'Less permanent?' she says, raising her eyebrows. 'Chuffin' Ada, Steve, God love your old man but he weren't half daft. Less permanent! That stew's been on the flame since before England. Twelve families made a pact—'

'—and while that stew still cooks, all stays safe,' I finish. 'I know.' I go back to my pint as I scan the room. Though I can't see him, I can feel Gareth's presence. 'Reckon he might go for something else jokey?'

'What do you mean?' she asks.

Perpetual Stew

I take a long gulp.

'Y'know, he might "lend a hand", or "put his best foot forward"?'

'Or drop a bollock,' she says, winking.

'Judith!' We both chuckle before turning back to watch the room in companionable silence while she picks at my plate.

Back in sight, Joanne stands on Gareth's shoes as he holds her hands to make her walk like a marionette. Even at seven, I look at her and think she could bring her fist down on this village and crack open a valley. The very first time I held her I thought *stalwart*. The word just dropped into my mind like a stone into water. Stalwart. Hours old, and I already knew.

It was a relief, to hold her and feel her strength. I knew then that she'd be the head of this family after me.

I watch one of the Taylor women interrupt them, taking Joanne by the hand off to the toilets. As the door swings open I can see Jane in there with the other women, all stood around, talking. I mean, I know women like to go together but it's nigh on all of them in there.

It feels quite empty in here now. I start scanning the room for the heads of the families and it's clear that it's nearly time. No doubt Jerry Hamblin's gone to fetch the stew. I don't see Jenkins or Hobson either.

My palms are getting sweaty. I loosen my tie.

'This it then?' I croak.

'Yeah,' Judith says, not unkindly. 'Steve . . .'

'Don't, Judith.'

'Don't "don't" me, Steve,' her tone hardens. 'I know it's unfair. I know it hurts. But . . .'

'But what?'

'Stay the fuck out of that back room.'

'I've every right to say my piece, Judith.'

She softens. I'm not stupid, I know full well Jane's told her everything. I can feel the same pity and patronising air from her that I get off Jane.

'It's a can of worms you're opening, love.'

'Well on my own head be it.'

'It's not on your head though, is it? It's our Jane and Joanne what'll have to deal with it.' I don't know what she means, and I resent her cryptic clues aimed at shutting me down.

Seeing Jane and the other women come out of the toilets, she gets up, taking the last sandwich with her. She bites into it.

'Jesus wept, these really are foul,' she chunters as she walks away, seemingly unaware that it's her fifth.

I see her stop and say a few words to Jane before she makes her way into the back room with the other heads of the families. I can't see Jane's face, but I can read her posture. Unnaturally still. On edge. She's normally expressive. She does everything fluently, gracefully. Always has.

It's like her and Judith have something planned. I feel the guts drop out of me, looking at her. My Jane. Truth be told, I thought there'd be an issue once we'd had

Perpetual Stew

Joanne. About the stew. The sacrifice. Everyone says they understand, that it's not just hacking off body parts and eating them, that there's honour in it. But it's different when you know it's coming for your own daughter. For you. Maybe that's why Jane had seemed so relaxed about it, if she'd always known Gareth would come back . . .

No, I can't start this. I can't lose my nerve.

I down the last of my pint and get up to make my way to the back room.

Joanne rushes up towards me and cuts me off.

'Dad, can I have a Coke? Uncle Gareth said he'd get me one but he's gone to the old-people meeting.' I fish out a pound coin and hand it to her. 'A pound? That's not enough,' her voice condescending. The briefest flash of rage zips through me – she sounds so much like Gareth.

'It's all I've got,' I tell her, moving her to the side out of my way.

'You have your card,' she says, pouting.

'I'm not giving you my card, young lady.'

'Swap you this for it,' she takes out the bracelet Gareth got her. There's an uncharitable corner of my heart that's thrilled Uncle Gareth's gifts can be traded out for a half-pint of pop.

'Do you deny the natural order of things?' she says suddenly in a rehearsed monotone.

'Too right I do, Joanne,' I say. As if the natural order of things is her seeing off fizzy drinks all afternoon, and before I can ask where the fuck she got that question from, she's off. She stomps in a strop towards the pensioners, no doubt on her way to charm them into giving her what she wants.

I head to the back room to do the same.

The back room itself is unremarkable. Three trestle tables in a long line. Nine of those metal chairs that look like their seat and back have been made with old red carpet. The stew is in the middle of the table, in its giant pot. The table's set with small bowls and spoons like a kid's party.

Pete Jenkins is at the top of the table, then the other heads of the families sit in two rows down the sides. Judith to Pete's right, Jerry Hamblin at his left. Then Hobson, McGough. Taylor, Gillespie, Baker. The folk what run this village, sat together about to break bread. And then of course Gareth at the opposite end. The newcomer.

Their idle chitchat stops once they see me.

'Steve,' Pete reproaches, 'what are you playing at?'

'I need to say my piece.'

They all look to Gareth.

'Let him,' Gareth says. I expect him to look angry, but he just looks amused.

'Well,' I begin, unsure if my gamble will pay off.

'Well,' Pete replies.

'I should be the head of our family,' I say, straight to the point. 'And it's not because I stayed and made a home here; it's practicalities.'

Judith keeps her eyes fixed on Gareth, while the others

try to avoid looking anywhere. I address myself to Pete and Pete alone. I haven't even told Jane my argument, a rationale that only came to me last night while I couldn't sleep.

'Gareth's gay. And he's childless.' Pete goes to speak, but I keep going before he can chime in. 'Look, we're already three families down. And alright, that's taken eighteen hundred years or whatever, but we're taking a risk in letting him continue the line if he doesn't have children.'

'Steve, it's not a eugenics program. We don't breed for heads of families,' Pete snaps. 'If Gareth decides not to have a family, then the line ends.'

'How is that fair when I'm right here?' I blurt out. 'How does the line end when there's literally our Joanne running round begging for some pop?'

'Irrelevant,' Pete says. 'And you haven't even got a son yet, Steve.'

Judith looks at me. She seems upset. My neck feels really warm.

'What if he has HIV? In the stew?' I sputter. A low blow, but I'm scrambling. The other heads of families look at me like I've got three heads. I swear Hobson's even about to laugh.

'And what?' Gareth says, his voice cold, clipped. 'It's not the nineties, Steven. Undetectable means untransmittable, you ghoulish ignorant fuck.'

'And besides,' Pete interrupts, 'for you to come in here and think we don't know what we're doing? That pot, young man—' He's nearly shouting now. He stands up and slams his hand on the table, a cheap thing that buckles under the force. '—That pot contains the meat of this village going back beyond the black plague.'

I've properly fucked it.

'Eyam might have barricaded themselves in for a noble death, but I swear to you not a single rat takes a step in this village without our nine families knowing about it.'

'I just thought—' I try to say.

'No, you didn't think. Twelve families made a pact, and while that stew still cooks, all stay safe.' A small chorus of *aye* echoes around the table. 'Do you think we don't understand what threatens us? Steve, that stew's been going uninterrupted for hundreds of years. Luddites smashed their looms and that stew still bubbled. We had the birth of the Industrial Revolution, then all the coal ripped out the fucking hills to power the bastard thing before being left to rot once them pits shut, and that stew still bubbled.'

'And through them "once in a generation" floods we get every year,' Judith adds.

'And them,' Pete says. 'The stew persists. We know what it takes to protect this community, Steve. This land. For you to try to disrupt that? And then pretend it's out of concern? If he were here, your dad would belt seven shades of shit out of you.'

He sits back down. His breathing is forced, and even though he's red in the face I can make out the spider veins across his cheeks.

Perpetual Stew

I know Pete means it as a dressing-down, as a way to shame me into backing away, but all he's done is remind me what's at stake.

I know all this, everything he's saying, because my entire life is in this community.

I tell him.

He's unmoved. There's a light twitch in the corner of his right eye.

'It's been done before,' I say to the others. Not one of them has the decency to even look at me. Spineless, the lot of them. They'll follow anything and everything Pete Jenkins says.

'It has,' Judith says, finally. 'But, Steve, I am asking you to step back.' She sits up straight, every word deliberate. She reminds me so much of Jane outside, poised. She's got a bracelet in her hand. 'Do you deny the natural order of things?'

'I'm saying I'll do whatever it takes to make me the head of my family, yes,' I reply instantly, and the sting immediately goes out of the room. There's a few more relaxed shoulders, and they begin to make eye contact with one another.

Gareth doesn't change. His posture is still ramrod straight, eyes fixed on Judith.

'Gareth?' Pete asks, his face blank.

Gareth snaps out of it. Incensed. I suspect it's the first time in his life he hasn't got what he wanted immediately, without pushback.

'You fucking idiot,' he seethes.

'It's what Dad would have wanted,' I say, and he jumps up, storms over to me. He pokes me in the chest with his index finger, hard. I wince, and then boil with rage at him seeing me wince.

'What Dad wanted?' Flecks of spittle land on my face as the other heads of family get up to separate us. 'Ever since I were born Dad told me to fuck off and live my own life, to go and do what I wanted while I could, because the second he died I'd be back here to become the head of this family.' He jabs me again and I feel hands grabbing me, dragging me back before I can swing for him. 'You've got no idea what you've done, Steve,' he shouts.

I struggle free and try to catch my breath. My thoughts scramble. I'm trying to come up with a justification for why this is a lie, for a world in which Gareth and Dad haven't spent my entire life shutting me out.

'Is it unprecedented?' I ask again.

'No, but—'

'But nothing. I am head of this family,' I say.

Judith places her hand on my chest. I see the glisten of tears beginning to form in her eyes.

'Tonight at midnight then,' Judith says, 'you'll both meet us at the pyre for a test. By dawn it'll all be settled.'

The heads of family take their leave, all heading back out into the wake apart from McGough and Taylor, who lift either side of the giant pot for the return journey to Jerry Hamblin's stove, neither any emptier or any fuller than when it arrived. Gareth says nothing as he leaves, leaving me to think. A test. Well, whatever it is, there's no way on earth Gareth knows more than I do.

I'm not worried.

◆

Back home, that night, Jane's sat at the kitchen table. She looks a sight, sat there crying in her dressing gown.

'You still have a choice, you know?' she says.

'Like hell I do,' I snap back. I'm coiled with nervous energy as I put my boots on.

It's gone half eleven already, and whatever silly little hoops Judith and the others need me to jump through won't wait.

'It's not yours, Steve. It's never been yours. And if you take it, then what? Our Joanne has to eat you once you die? Our Joanne has to—' she stops, overwhelmed at the thought. 'If I'd have known you'd end up like this, I'd have—'

'You'd have what?' I whisper back, enraged. 'Never had Joanne? Never married me? Never moved into this house I pay for? What, Jane?'

I don't mean it, I don't mean any of it. But I don't understand why everyone is acting like I'm the one in the wrong.

She blows her nose. She takes a bracelet out of her dressing-gown pocket. I already know it's made of twisted strands of cypress, pine, cedar. The same as Joanne's, as Judith's.

'Fine, Steve.' She's barely audible. 'I am asking you not

to go to the pyre. I am asking you to drop it. We can end this all now. Do you deny the natural order of things?'

That question. Again. I don't know what Jane's playing at. Or Judith. Good grief, even Joanne's wandering about talking in riddles. I'm sick of it. Each of them clutching those bracelets like talismans and asking their little question as if it's an incantation.

It's high time they got over their superstitions.

'Yes.' I'm emphatic. 'I'm doing what's best for all of us,' I say, kissing her forehead. She leans into me with her eyes closed.

It's a gorgeous night and the air has the thinness of late summer. I make my way down our street, through the square and up the hill. I don't know what I'd expected when I got up there, but a naked Gareth surrounded by eight robed figures is not it.

'Strip,' one of the figures says, clearly Baker.

'What the fuck?' I say, laughing, but nobody joins in.

'Now,' Gillespie says from beneath his hood.

I take off my jacket. Deep down I reckon this must be some kind of humiliation ritual, probably something the Jenkinses have picked up through their generations of medical school. I take off my boots and place them on top of my jacket. Jeans, jumper, socks. T-shirt, boxers.

It might be a nice night, but it's a bit nippy to be standing stark bollock naked at the top of the hill.

Perpetual Stew

The eight take down their hoods.

'Steven. Gareth,' Pete begins. 'We find ourselves at a crossroads. It's sad, though not unprecedented.'

'You've shown yourself to be selfish, Steven,' Judith says, her voice carrying the authority of all of them, all of us. 'By prioritising yourself over our community, our traditions, you've shown you cannot be trusted to know the truth about what really protects us.'

'I know all about the stew,' I blurt out. 'We all know!'

Muffled laughter comes from behind me. McGough?

'You do not know,' Judith booms. 'And you do not have the humility to find out.' She's shouting now. 'Everything is connected, Steve. Everything. You've denied three of this community's women. You've made your choice.'

I have no idea what she's on about. I can feel the cutting night breeze make its way over my goosepimpled back as I scrunch my toes into the soil.

'We offer you both to the gods, old and new,' Judith bellows. The hooded figures repeat her. 'To the earth, the sky and all who dwell between.' I feel hemmed in by the sound of the family heads.

Gareth has his eyes closed. Breathing deeply. Preparing himself. I try to catch his gaze, to see if he knew about this. In the midnight breeze, stood with no clouts on, it starts making sense. How can a stew protect you? It's the symbol of it, the effort of it, that protects you. The constant reminder of what it takes to keep a community going. To simmer and replenish.

I want it all to stop. I want to make amends. Apologise.

'To protect, to settle, we return to the foundational family schism. To Cain and Abel,' Judith continues.

Fuck. No no no no no. It's him or me, isn't it?

'We love you both, and we're so sorry it has to end this way,' she says, her voice quiet, remorseful.

Oh God, I've been so presumptuous. So arrogant. Of course it's more than a bit of stew. It's a god damn cult. It's a god damn fight to the death.

I swear I can smell cypress, pine, cedar.

Gareth opens his eyes and picks up the large rock that's been laid out in front of him.

There's one in front of me. It's about the size of a human head.

'It ends now. Fairly.' Pete puts his hood back up. The other family heads do the same. One by one they each turn their back on the circle we're in.

'He who survives will become the head of your family,' Pete shouts. 'While he who dies shall contribute to the stew. Wholly.'

Gareth locks eyes with me, holding his stone. I can't make out his expression, whether he's sorry, whether he's willing to refuse.

'Twelve families made a pact, and while that stew still cooks, all stay safe,' they say.

Gareth says aye.

I pick up my stone.

The family heads begin to sing.

We begin.

Carole

EMMA GLASS

Emma Glass is a Welsh writer and nurse. Her debut novel *Peach*, published in 2018, was longlisted for the Dylan Thomas Prize and has been translated into eight languages. Her second novel, *Rest and Be Thankful*, is currently being developed for a film. Published by Cheerio in 2024, her third novel, *Mrs Jekyll*, was longlisted for the Dylan Thomas Prize and shortlisted for the Gordon Burn Prize.

You need to go home.

The solicitor is trying to lead me from the courtroom with his arm around my shoulder to steer me but my legs won't walk. The coroner's assistant insists that the witnesses and journalists and the spectators wait to stand until we leave so we won't have to face them. But hearing them whisper is worse.

Poor child.

Poor woman.

Just take your time.

My legs are stiff with sitting, muscles and tendons tense with the agony of waiting. Wait is over but blood won't flow. Nick has to take my hands in his and walk backwards to pull me away. He stoops his shoulders to bring his face close to mine and he says come on, Carole, love, we need to go now. He pulls one limp limb towards him, then the other, until my arms are too far away from my body and if my feet don't stump up the space between I will fall.

He pulled me towards him this way for years, when we were dancing or when I didn't want to walk up the hill. But he didn't really have to pull me, I would have gone anywhere with him. One day he stopped reaching for me; his arms stayed at his sides and I watched him do his backwards walk into open arms, someone else's arms. I called to him, but he never came. My voice is soundless.

I'm so sorry, Carole.

So sorry.

Condolences, Carole.

My condolences.

The frozen fingers that wrote the findings of fact reach out for mine but I don't grasp, mouth still open; Nick sticks his hand out instead, shakes hands with the coroner and says thank you and I can only hoarsely manage to say what? The solicitor holds out a tissue and when I don't take it from him he tries to wipe my face.

Come this way.

You need to sit down.

Someone sits me down. A table with three empty chairs. Nick stands by me but won't sit. The solicitors won't sit. They are talking to the coroner in low tones; I can't hear them and I don't want to. The coroner has drawn her conclusions. The inquest is concluded. We are concluded. We.

Nick has his hand on my shoulder. He says Carole, I need to go now, I need to –

Home, I say. You need to go home.

Yes.

Carole

Home to Sarah and the baby.

Yes, he says.

His lightest kiss lands on the top of my head.

I nod woodenly. Either my neck or the chair, the table or the floorboards are creaking, all at the same time. Nick walks away, as he should, and I stay still. In this empty room, at this empty table, I am a splinter in the wood.

I will stay here. Others like me will sit in this chair and I will sit with them. Smoothing into the frame. This old chair won't be comfortable but I will be their comfort. Someone who knows. Someone who has been in their shoes.

The solicitor in his squeaking patent leather shoes comes for me. Fetches and carries me. I didn't know it was part of his job, but then I realise there is no one else to do it and this hollow place is holding onto me. I have to find my grip.

You need a taxi.

No, I'll walk, I say, voice still not coming out of my moving mouth.

Here we go, he says.

He picks up his briefcase with one hand, and with the other opens the door of the black cab that has pulled up. He takes my hand and squeezes it to put feeling into his words. He says, I'm so sorry, Carole, it's not the outcome we hoped for, but at least now perhaps you can find some closure.

Closure. I am bundled in the back of the cab and the door is closed.

Where to, darling? Fella said Deptford? Is that right? Gasp out a little 'yes'.

No no no no no –

Black cab, I don't have any money.

I remember the handbag strapped over my shoulder, my jacket with pockets inside and out. Empty except for balled-up tissues. I unzip my bag and feel around for my battered purse, broken clasp and peeling pleather. It flops open. I flip between a couple of cards; no cash, not a single coin. One old, folded and unfolded receipt, thick yellow paper with indigo price punched on, indentations still felt.

Clarks

BLK PTNT SHOE GRL UK 10	£10.75
VAT.	£0.00

18/08/95 14:37
This is not a VAT Receipt
Clarks
Surrey Quays
Shopping. Leisure. SE 16

Your first pair of school shoes.

Fingers going over it, trembling and then touching the edge of your photo. There you are. Whole world in 4x6 inches. Grinning, glossy as the day it was taken. Touch it to my lips and tuck it back in with the receipt.

Oh God. I can't pay.

Driver drives. If I meet his eyes in the mirror I won't

Carole

be able to do it. I slide across the seat. Look for the handle, which way does it pull. We're slowing to a red light. I take a deep breath and dive for the door, slip out and slam it shut. Sorry! I cross the road behind the cab and walk quickly in the opposite direction. A horn is blaring and maybe he shouts after me but the sounds are consumed by the congestion. I disappear down a street where they no longer reach me.

Feel bad about it. I have never done anything like that before in my life. But then I don't ever travel in taxis. Too expensive and nowhere to go. Other than walking to work, when I worked, and school until you didn't want me to walk you anymore. Twelve and old enough, with a friend.

Walked in all winds and weather, didn't we?

What if I had learned to drive?

What if we could've afforded a car and I had driven you to school. You'd have missed the downpour, you'd be safe and sound. We'd be singing along to the car radio and wiping the condensation off the windows with the sleeves of our coats, wipers going, scraping the heavy rain away, peering out of the windscreen to avoid the potholes full of water.

We'd be home by now.

I think about it all the time. The rain. It drips on my head like on the roof of a house. But they said it didn't work like that. It wasn't because you were soaked through all day, wet socks and shoes, the lining of your skirt sitting damply against your thighs; even the tails of your tucked-in shirt were wet. Your usually bouncy ponytail saturated, stuck flat against the back of your head and dripping to a point, a paint brush dipped, dripping watercolours down the back of your neck, the cheap red sweatshirt dying the white collar pink. Terribly hard to wash and make white again; terrible to think that's what I was thinking about as I picked your clothes up off the bathroom floor as you were soaking in the bath, your last bath. I wish you'd let me wash your hair.

I'd be home now, if I'd stayed in the taxi. But with no money to pay the driver, no money to pay the rent or arrears, no one to welcome or be welcomed by, there is no home. Without you there's nothing to do but walk.

The day is long and hot and I didn't even realise. I undo a couple of buttons to loosen my blouse at the neck and take off my jacket, flipping it over my arm to walk, and when I realise I won't need it any more I hang it over a fence post. Maybe someone will come along and take it, wear it to an interview or a funeral.

I walk through the streets past rows and rows of houses, big and small, fancy, cheap. I find Nick's house somewhere in the middle. The blinds and windows are open. I hear gentle music, a woman singing, Sarah singing to her daughter who is in her arms. Nick is sitting by them, shirt collar open, tie undone, drinking a cold beer. He looks sad and happy at the same time. He doesn't regret us, he won't forget us. I know this by the way he looks over Sarah's shoulder, to your photograph on the shelf, same red sweatshirt, different day, a happy day,

Carole

your smile and your hair curling around your temples. I blow him a kiss, knowing Sarah won't mind.

I walk down the high street to the supermarket. I see Mo through the window. He's sitting on checkout five, my checkout, and has lowered the seat so his knees don't knock the till. He scans a net of oranges, a carton of milk. He is chatting to an old man, scanning the shopping slowly to give him time to pack. The receipt is long, a big shop. Mo leaves the till to help the man with his bags to a plastic chair in the window where he can wait to be collected. When the man is seated and the shopping bags are tucked into the corner, Mo looks up and sees me. He gestures for me to come inside but I shake my head and mouth sorry, pointing to a watch on my wrist I'm not wearing and pointing down the street where I'll rush off to for no reason at all. He nods and smiles and turns back to his work.

Where I am standing, Nick stood holding the hand of a little girl. Even with the sun streaming in, I could see him, beaming at me from my stool behind the till. I had to shade my eyes to see who he was with; a little girl, waving, jumping up and down with excitement. And I gasped and started crying when I realised it was you. Your father had taken you for a haircut. A thick fringe, ridiculous. You looked like a little mushroom.

I saw the world from checkout five. On the busiest days, Jessie would come over with tea in a polystyrene cup and a knowing look for me and say well everyone has to buy toilet paper from somewhere. And she was right. Regulars coming in for their weekly shop, going fat to thin or thin to fat, babies growing into children old enough to choose their own breakfast cereal, the elderly who I worried about if one week they didn't come. Mr Norman was the only customer I knew who died and he was very old. You met him once; he tried to put a pound coin in your palm but you started crying because his hands were so wrinkly. You were only little. Every year without fail we'd get a Christmas card from the family who ran the Chinese takeaway across the road.

They'd take me back if I asked, I'm sure they would. Eight years and never a day off sick. Except for when you threw up whilst rehearsing the nativity play at school. You were a snowflake and you took your role very seriously; you were spinning and spinning until the silver tinsel on your costume came loose and your fish fingers and beans came up. The school rang and Jessie put an announcement over the Tannoy: CAN THE CASHIER ON CHECKOUT 5 PLEASE COME TO THE MANAGER'S OFFICE? I was almost sick myself, so worried – what had happened to you? They were really good about it.

They were good to me last year when I rang them from A&E, when it looked as though you were just being kept in for observation. Mo said Paula would work extra that week, as it was so close to Christmas, and told me not to worry. They were good to me. Two weeks' pay. Mo and Jessie came to the funeral and said just come back when you're ready. I'm not ready. Sitting on checkout five, people would be so kind, they'd want to say something, sorry or how beautiful you were and how sad it is and how am I coping and how nice it is to see me and is there anything they can do. I'll never be ready, so I walk away.

Down to the river. Boats go by, people drinking rosé wine on upper decks, laughing in the light summer evening. Tourists trail across the bridges, queue for attractions, for cold drinks and hot dogs, queue to cross the busy roads, queue for anything. The sun begins to set by the time I reach Chiswick roundabout. We've been this way on a coach before. A few days away in Paignton. A bucket and spade on the beach, Mr Whippy and raspberry sauce dribbling down the side of a cornet. You had toothache and a temperature.

My feet are sore from the stupid black leather shoes I bought from the charity shop to look smart. As if anyone would've noticed what shoes I was wearing to court. I could've gone in pyjamas and it wouldn't have made a blind bit of difference. I take the shoes off and stuff them between the slats of a storm drain. The motorway tarmac feels smooth beneath my stockinged feet. Car headlights illuminate the nylon. They go by fast, but give me room, a semicircle of acknowledgement, a toot of the horn. We each have a share of the way to go.

The night air is light; I am only aware of the breeze when cars go by. My hair ruffles, the sweat on my blouse is blown cool against my skin and there is a small sound. Not cars, not night, something else: a voice. It could be mine. I breathe, think, speak freely. Of you, of our love, your father, us getting older, it all getting harder. You wanted to know everything. You wanted me to show you and I'm afraid I didn't know anything. You'll see it all from where you are now. I see you blinking down at me from the stars.

I count six lanes on the roundabout. The sky is pinking into morning, so I break out into a run; I run with my arms outstretched to signal to the cars who dance around me. I wave little goodbyes to them as we head in our different directions.

The A303 is quiet. I am in the company of birds only. They sing, but I hear the voice too and this time I know it isn't me because I am only listening. I follow the voice, eyes up and open, but I put my foot down on something wet and soft and I shudder. I look down and cry out loud to see my toes in the tiny splayed feathers of a white baby barn owl. Oh no no no no. Oh no. I scoop it up. Its little face, closed eyes. It could be sleeping but the blood from the broken wings has seeped red into the body and there's nothing to be done. I walk with it in my hands for a couple of miles until I find a soft mossy place to lay it down. My tears have run out some of the red in its plume.

Goodbye, baby.

I leave the sadness behind me. It is only nature.

Moon guides my miles. Sun sees me swallowing the distance between then and now.

✦

Carole

There is a commotion up ahead. I see people, lots of people, a coach pulled up on the side of a bank. Elderly ladies and gentlemen stepping off the coach with cameras around their necks, sunglasses and hats, walking sticks, having terrible trouble shuffling over the grass. One man says there isn't even a proper car park. One woman says oh look at all those hippies. She says it with dirt in her mouth.

Stonehenge is surrounded by an enormous dancing circle. People of all ages holding hands and turning towards the sun. A hand reaches and I am pulled into the circle. We turn until we are dizzy. There are many voices singing, but I hear one above them all. With the bright summer sky shining, the movement, the soft grass under my feet, I can try to smile. One of the old folks throws their stick at the stone, kicks their clompy orthopaedic shoes off and grabs my hand, whooping and turning in age-defying motion.

A man named Owen asks me if I want to camp with a group who plan to stay close to Stonehenge for the foreseeable future. He holds onto my hand, looks deeply into my eyes and says he can sense my power.

No thank you, but it's nice of you to ask.

The driver is leaning against the coach smoking a cigarette. He's chuckling and shaking his head. He says half of them are sulking on the bus and the other half, well, I might have to leave them here!

Good luck! I say, stepping back onto the road.

BOG PEOPLE

Tarmac is heating up. I walk on the grass where I can. A cardboard sign propped against a windscreen of a parked car in a lay-by says:

LOCAL STRAWBERRIES
AND
CHERRIES
£2.00

Cherries are my favourite but I never bought them from the supermarket. Even with my discount they were too expensive. But you spotted some in the market at the end of one stinking-hot day and they were practically giving them away. A carrier bag full – two kilos for a pound, more than we could eat in a week, so we made jam, put them in brownies, our lips stained red for days.

The chap sitting on a deckchair by the open boot of the car gets up when he sees me, lifts his sunglasses onto his head.

Hello, love, it's hot out here today. Are you on your own?

Yes, I'm on my own, I say.

I want to buy some cherries, but my hands fly to my face when I realise I've left my bag behind, swung off my shoulder in the dancing circle with the druids. Your photograph. I left it. I start to cry.

Oh no, come here, love, what's wrong? Come here, sit in this chair, have a rest.

I nod and sob and sit.

Carole

There, there.

Would you like some strawberries, the man asks.

Some cherries, I say.

I want some cherries but I've left my bag and I don't have any money.

Don't you worry about that, he says.

He takes a big plastic punnet of cherries from the car boot and puts it in my lap. Dark red jewels. I look up at him and say thank you, that's very kind.

It's my pleasure, he says. But there is something you could do for me, in return.

I glance at him, worried he'll ask me to do something I haven't done for years and don't really want to do, not even for cherries.

Oh no, love, don't worry. I was going to ask you to mind the stall whilst I nip into the woods to do my business. Didn't want to risk leaving the car and someone nicking it. But you seem like a nice woman – you wouldn't nick it, would you?

Maybe just the cherries out of the boot, I say, laughing. Don't worry, I can't drive.

He laughs and says well, this is working out very nicely. I won't be long.

He walks off into the bushes, which a few steps in becomes dense with trees.

I take ages choosing my first cherry. I pop it in my mouth and let the juices flow, sucking the flesh. I can't remember the last time I tasted anything, let alone something so delicious. I suck the stones and spit them out and by the time the man comes back, I have a little mountain of them, dry in my palm.

Thank you for that, he says. Did anyone stop?

No, I say, only two cars have driven past.

It's early yet.

I should be going, I say, shuffling my bottom out of the deckchair and standing. Thank you for the cherries.

My pleasure, he says again. Take some more with you, for the road?

No, thank you. Goodbye.

Bye, love.

I hear him calling out a few moments later, where are you going?

But I don't know, so I don't tell him.

Many cars slow down, drivers wind down the windows and ask if I need assistance or a lift.

I had forgotten how kind people can be.

I say no to all and walk through the night. It moves with me. I hear snuffling badgers in hedgerows, owls hooting gently, the soft pad of my own feet, and the voice all around, guiding me off the road and into a field, blue grass in the moonlight. The voice sings me to a safe sleep.

Wake up in rain. My poor, wet girl. Will it do to me what it did to you? Soft rain, deceptive, dropping pattering pearls on the leaves of the trees. The sky is grey,

Carole

crowded with cloud. In search of shelter, I walk through the field until I see a copse on a distant hill.

Fences fall away, the fields now a wide wild stretch of moor. The copse never gets any closer so I give up and set my sights on a boulder where I can sit and look over the world.

The rain stops, the sun shows, another night comes dark and flowing with energy. I don't sleep; I feel my way through the landscape, the trees that reach and catch my shirt sleeves, holding on to me, saving me from slipping on mossy roots, the unfriendly gorse keeping me at a distance, saying don't step here, stopping me from tearing my feet on its throne of thorns.

Stars alive, alight, I wish you could see them; I think you can. I never brought you to nature. Greenwich Park was the closest we got. We thought it was fresh air. Your lungs, fuzzed and furrowed, uninflated. No air entry, they said. Pneumothorax. Pneumonia. I didn't understand what they meant. Exacerbated by the damp in the flat. It ravaged the walls. Did I try to keep it clean? How dare they. Infection. Aspergillosis. It ravaged you too. I can't see you that way anymore, grey like mincemeat. I look for you in the wild flowers; there you are smiling sunny yellow, pink and red, standing tall and swaying in the summer breeze.

I see rocks ahead, a boulder with smaller stones surrounding it, a shady tree, the greenest grass I've ever seen; I run towards it, breath catching as the earth turns upwards and I'm running up a hill. Almost there and then –

Wet, cold, mud up to my calf. Squelching. My feet are stuck. I try to lift my legs to climb out but I'm stuck, sinking fast. I slid into it so quickly, I never even saw this puddle, pond, bog. Is it a bog? God knows. I search for a branch, a rock, anything I can grab onto to pull myself out but there's nothing in reach, not even close. The boulder and the tree are shimmering a few feet in front of me. My feet feel so far away. Sinking into another world. No bottom to touch, suspended in sludge, the harder I strain to pull away, the stronger the suck. I bend my knees. I flap my arms but any movement makes the water lap, the mud swallow.

The sun is high and scorching my scalp. I raise my hands to cover my head and sink a little deeper. There is a thick brown film forming over the bog and I wonder, if it dries up enough I might be able to crack it and climb out, but that will take a long time. I'm waist-deep now. All I can do is wait.

HAVE YOU SEEN MY DOG?

She's in front of me, waving madly. Her body blocks the sun; the blotting out of the light sends blotches dancing in front of my eyes. Her arms are multiplied, a manic millipede.

MY SPANIEL! HIS NAME IS SCOOTER! HE'S RUN OFF! HAVE YOU SEEN HIM?

I think for a moment. Foxes, badgers, hares, no spaniel.

I'm sorry, no. But I did see some hares to the south of here, perhaps he went off that way?

OH!

Carole

Her arms drop, her shoulders sag. The bog slurps, fancying her. I stay still.

I guess I'll try south then. Thanks. SCOOTER!

Sun blinds me as she starts running away.

Drowsy, I begin to doze. I dream of baked potatoes, perhaps because I am baking in the sun. I hear you ask me if we have to have baked potatoes for tea again and I say yes, they are good for you and delicious and what if I cut up sausages to go in the beans with cheese on top and you roll your eyes. I don't know where you learned to do that.

Excuse me?

A cough, a throat clearing.

Hello?

I open my eyes, squinting at first, forgetting where I am. Boulder, tree, bog. A young man in shorts and hiking boots.

Yes?

Do you know the way to Okehampton?

What?

Do you know the way to Okehampton? I thought it was north from here, but I think I'm lost.

His cheeks are bright red with heat and embarrassment.

I'm sorry, I'm not from around here either, I say, gesturing to my soggy surrounds.

No, of course, he says, face purple now. Sorry. Do you need some help?

It takes me a while to hear him, to understand the question and decide whether help is what I need. The doctors offered help, the solicitors offered help. Help. Did they?

It's kind of you to offer, but I'm not sure how you can help me. I'm really very stuck.

The bog belches in agreement, air expelled drawing me inward, another inch.

The man scratches his chin.

I could throw you a rope and you could grab it and I could pull you, or we could tie it around your waist?

Do you have any rope?

No, he says. No I don't.

Don't worry, I say. I've been here a while now and do you know what? It's more comfortable than it looks.

He laughs hesitantly.

The muddy water is cool and it's almost a relief to not have to think about my feet. I don't really feel them now.

How long have you been here?

Honestly, don't know, I say.

Would you like one of my sandwiches? he asks.

He sticks a toe out to test the ground, touches it to the very edge of the bog and sits down cross-legged. He reaches into his bag and pulls out a flask and foil-wrapped parcels.

He unwraps one of them.

Ham and mustard, he says.

On brown bread?

Yep, he says.

You're a couple of slices of tomato away from perfection, I say, smiling. My favourite.

Catch!

He tosses a foil parcel to me. I'm not particularly

Carole

hungry but the chew of the bread, the zinging mustard in my nostrils, brings me to my body. I fold the foil into a little hat to keep the sun off my scalp.

What's your name? he asks.

Carole. What's yours?

Jack, he says.

It's good to meet you. What's in Okehampton?

Molly, he says, smiling with young white teeth.

I see, I say, grinning back.

Actually, he says, maybe you can help me with this. I want to ask Molly to marry me, but we're quite young, see, and I think she'll say no because we're quite different; she grew up on the moor and, well, I don't know where the bloody hell I am but I thought that if I could get myself to Okehampton, she would see that I'm not bloody useless and then she might say yes?

My heart melts into the muddy water and the first of my arms is swallowed up.

How old are you, Jack?

Twenty-four, she's twenty-five.

I got married at your age, I say.

He says, yes, but no offence, Carole, that was a while ago, wasn't it?

I suppose so, I say, head nodding, tinfoil tinkling.

Do you think it's a mad idea, he asks, frowning.

I think it's mad that you came onto the moor without a map, but then who am I to judge? I say, shrugging with one shoulder.

Listen, life is short. If you love her, you should ask her

to marry you. Life is short, but it's too long to spend without love.

His mouth is a concentrated line and he nods.

I think you're right. I think you are very wise, he says.

I shrug again and this is a mistake: the movement makes a bubbling and a gurgling, a big groan and my other arm is gone. Everything up to the shoulders.

Oh God, says Jack. I wish I could help you.

It's okay, I say, and then I shush him.

Can you hear that?

He stands up. He looks around. He listens.

A breeze blows the tinfoil off my head; it skims the surface of the bog and lands next to Jack's feet.

The wind?

No, the voice.

He shakes his head.

Sorry, I don't hear a voice.

I hear it louder now. And I feel it. In the water.

Carole, he says, smiling. I'm going to do it. I'm going to ask Molly to marry me.

I smile back. I hope she says yes.

He starts packing up his bag, careful to pick up every scrap of rubbish.

Right. I'm going. I don't quite know where I'm going, but I am going to find Molly, I'm going to ask her and then I'm going to come back and tell you what she says! Bye, Carole!

Goodbye, Jack.

Carole

I watch him skip across the moor. His whooping laughter bounces off the boulder.

What are you, Bog? Why do you want me?

Cool water laps at my throat in response. It isn't slowing, no matter how still I keep. Sucks me like a leech. I lift my head up and look around; one last glimpse of the moor, the valley beyond, rocks and trees, blue sky, birds, then looking directly into the sun I fill my lungs, last full of fresh air, a breath big enough for us both, like I breathed at your bedside. You went under and now I go with you.

I let the water in. Fill up and sink. Thicker than water, seeping, silken, like melted chocolate. Instinct is to wave my arms, kick and push to the surface, but it's all too heavy for that. Pulled down deeper, but it's not dark down here and it's not quiet. The voice speaks loudly into my ear.

It's you.

All the colours of the world: your hair, your eyes, your red school sweatshirt, your pink fluffy dressing gown, flannel pyjamas blue and full of stars.

The sounds of you; your laugh, the sound of you breathing. I reach out and touch you.

You're here, you've been waiting all this time. I pull you close and wrap you in my arms.

You rest your head on my breast and hear my heart. It sounds like you.

BOG PEOPLE

We are still.
    Held by the cloying mire, tangled in the pulsing peat.

We   will   stay   here.
Alive by
        love
                and the l i f e s u r r o u n d i n g us.
We
    will
              l i v e
                      f o r e v e r.

Eldritch

MARK COLBOURNE

Mark Colbourne lives and works in the Black Country, West Midlands. Occasionally, he sits down and tries to write, usually swaying between the silly and sinister. His short-fiction scribbles have appeared in *MONO*, *Open Pen* and *Coup of Owls*, among others. He has been assured that he is not what you are currently looking for.

In 2012, the album *Eldritch* by Heptagonal Sons turned forty years old. To mark this anniversary, *Cult Sounds Monthly* commissioned the journalist Simon Payne to produce a critical retrospective of the work and its ongoing influence.

The article was never published.

Simon Payne remains a missing person.

ELDRITCH – FORTY YEARS OF MYTH

By Simon Payne

In the autumn of 1971, when Heptagonal Sons began work on what would become their second and final album, they were already a band out of time.

The pomp of prog was ascendant, whilst the counter-cultural gambits of acid and psych rock were riddled with burnt-out casualties and wayward experimentation. Folk music had either relented to the demands of popular entertainment or retreated to its traditional environment. For a struggling group of pot-happy long-hairs, any prospect of success must have seemed no more substantial than the dreams bound in a three-skin reefer threaded with the finest blends of Moroccan hashish.

And yet, although that album unequivocally failed to trouble the charts, the mystery that surrounds its gestation, the intricate beauty of its songs and the tragic legacy which remains have all contributed to the record enduring as a respected cult concern. As *Eldritch* enters its fortieth year, it seems an apposite moment to revisit its spectral melodies and intricate construction, to commemorate the musicians who birthed its eerie majesty, and perhaps – just perhaps – to lay some old ghosts to rest.

Heptagonal Sons formed in 1968 when bassist Ken Walker and keyboard player Guy Spondley-Feathershore were dismissed from the Top 40 act Georgie Wolf and the Straw Houses, following a disagreement with Mitch Mitchell of the Jimi Hendrix Experience regarding two crates of brown ale. Spondley-Feathershore recalled the incident as 'regrettable', whilst Walker went on record to assert that Mitchell was 'a right prick' and Georgie Wolf believed 'the sun shined so brightly out of his own arsehole that he didn't have to stick a shilling in the meter'. Suddenly unemployed, the duo roped in two similarly circumstanced musicians, Dave Matherley and Charles Kitson (drums and guitar respectively).

Initially, the vision for this tentative grouping belonged to Spondley-Feathershore. Born into a wealthy family with aristocratic ties, he styled himself as a musician's musician. His fleeting success with the Straw Houses had only convinced him that pop was a game he had scant desire to play. In a 1992 interview, he told *Record Collector Magazine*:

> *Jesus, all those teeny boppers jigging about on* Ready Steady Go . . . *what did any of it mean? I was an artist, with art to create. I had this sense of a curtain being drawn across the sixties and knew the time to make my statement had arrived.*

The precise nature of that statement, however, proved somewhat elusive, and it wasn't until late in 1968 that a way forward was revealed.

Neal Caruse had skirted around the fringes of the folk scene for at least two years before crossing paths with Spondley-Feathershore. Raised in rural Norfolk, Caruse moved to London after attracting the attention of Andrew Loog Oldham, the manager of the Rolling Stones. Performing as a solo artist or within short-lived collaborations, he became predominantly renowned for his prodigious drug intake and, seemingly washed up before he had even set sail, appeared destined to languish as an also-ran. In her 2005 autobiography *A Debutante in*

Swinging London, Jane Shestonal briefly recalls watching a pre-Heptagonal Sons Caruse share a bill with a then unknown David Bowie:

> *Neal was so handsome that he should have commanded the stage, but he could barely command his own faculties. Groping though an LSD nightmare, he knelt beneath the spotlight and screamed for twenty minutes until some sympathetic soul guided him back into the wings. Pat tapped me on the shoulder and quipped, not unreasonably, that this was why the working class shouldn't venture down the rabbit hole.*

There are no records of either his sobriety or performance on the night Caruse first encountered the fledgling Heptagonal Sons. One can only assume that his light shone somewhat brighter than on the evening Shestonal so colourfully evokes, as Spondley-Feathershore immediately asked him to become their singer.

With the key personnel in place, momentum quickly gathered. Early gigs led to a deal with Harvest Field Records – a folk-orientated subsidiary of EMI – and a debut album, *Raking the Soil*, was released in the summer of 1970.

Unfortunately – and establishing a theme that would come to encapsulate their career – the band were derailed by events beyond their control. 1969 had birthed King Crimson's *In the Court of the Crimson King*, and Spondley-Feathershore, after doggedly pursuing what he believed to be a distinct musical direction, was distraught that he'd been beaten to the punch. In the *Record Collector* interview, he describes first hearing that album:

> *I honestly couldn't believe it. It felt like McDonald and Lake had grabbed both my arms while Fripp was hoofing me in the balls with a steel toe capped boot.*

By the time of its release, *Raking the Soil* appeared dated and tame – a record which neither pushed the boundaries nor played to the crowd. Reviews were lukewarm and sales poor. Defeated, Heptagonal Sons retreated to lick their wounds.

And really the story should have ended here – countless careers have been derailed by an indifferent public or ephemeral tastes. But this setback only served to shift the dynamic within the group, and the role of Heptagonal Sons' leader and chief songwriter suddenly found itself falling to Neal Caruse.

In a 1994 Jethro Tull profile, Stevie Hollands (Harvest Field Records A&R, 1967–1974) references this period:

> *The label was full of whimsical hippies and nonsense noodling, to a man public-school educated and all off their rockers. It was dire. None of them knew anything about the real world. I suppose amongst that shower there was only Heptagonal Sons who were worth their blood. Around then it seemed like they were onto something. Obviously that didn't pan out, and there's some pretty*

unfortunate ends to some of their stories, I know. But at least they had a direction. At least the flame was allowed to burn before it got snuffed out.

Over 1970 and into the following year, Caruse chiselled into shape an audacious anthology of songs and, in October 1971, the band decamped to Sussex's Claverley Hall Studios with producer Andrew Port to record what would become *Eldritch*. It is an album which, to an enlightened minority, embodies the stuff of legend. David Pajo considers it a 'masterpiece'. Ed O'Brien and Warren Ellis are known fans. In an early interview, even Richard D. James acknowledged its structural and sonic influence. And yet it is inextricably bound in mystery and entwined with disaster. So let us now take this record and critically revisit all seven tracks in order, interpret the orbiting myths and consider the fates of those involved.

Track 1 – Winter's Call

Eldritch was released in March 1972. Spring was an incongruous season for its stylings: the album was made in and for winter. The music is chill winds and dark nights, rain shimmering in the moonlight whilst mist rolls across the moors. We are in a world of abandoned stone abbeys, of rural tracks cut through coarse fields, of still and silent woods with harsh, bare branches closing in a lattice above our heads ... All of which is signalled from the very first second. As the CD spins in my stereo, a

Eldritch

Gregorian chant emerges – almost inaudibly – from the right-hand speaker. Further voices join this call, a revolving chorus of the other band members and, presumably, a multi-tracked Caruse. Although the volume builds, the lyrics remain obstinately indecipherable. Even the language lies beyond recognition. Is this a forgotten tongue? A string of idiosyncratic neologisms? Perhaps even a strange joke? At 3:42 – as the suspicion mounts that this bizarre a cappella is all the record will contain – a reversed crash cymbal announces the arrival of instrumentation. As the chant spirals, the rhythm settles into a relaxed but tight groove as Spondley-Feathershore turns to a church organ to complement the sound.

Atop this swirling foundation, Charles Kitson grabs the opportunity to demonstrate his talent, unleashing a guitar solo constructed entirely of *feeling*, fingers combing the fretboard and uncovering the melody like a palaeontologist softly brushing away millennia of dirt to reveal some perfectly preserved skeletal specimen. The notes are a rising wave that never actually breaks and, as the listener anticipates the crescendo, it becomes unclear quite where the vocals end and the guitar begins.

Compared to some of the overblown pyrotechnics of the period, Kitson was a player of nuance and restraint. He was an established session musician before joining Heptagonal Sons and cut his teeth in numerous mod bands during the mid-sixties. Unlike Spondley-Feathershore, the other band members were from unprivileged backgrounds, and for Kitson music was definitely a job rather than some route to fame or the accomplishment of any creative aspiration. He was – in the kindest sense of the epithet – a *journeyman*, albeit one duly noted for his competence. By all accounts, he had little interest in rock's more cliched excesses, which makes his drug overdose in 1973 even more bewildering.

I earlier asserted that *Eldritch* is an album for winter. I feel it only pertinent to declare that, as I write and listen right now, it is a biting-cold afternoon in early February. Outside, I can see a grey sky preparing itself for night. A breeze cuts across my garden whilst the trees sway in submission and I adjust my jumper as the temperature drops. As 'Winter's Call' winds to a close, I'm doubtful my surroundings could have a more suitable soundtrack.

Track 2 – The Maze

With the near-ecclesial echo of 'Winter's Call' still reverberating, the sudden snare drum crack which heralds 'The Maze' has the impact of a gunshot. There is barely chance to catch one's breath before Dave Matherley initiates a galloping 4/4 beat. The enormity of the sound is sensational, and recognition must be given to the producer, Andrew Port, for so successfully capturing this force. One can only imagine what heights he may have scaled behind the desk (a Martin? An Eno? A Visconti?) had he not taken his own life so shortly after the *Eldritch* sessions.

Four bars in, the rest of the band launch into a riff which lurches towards heavy metal. For someone familiar with their first album, or perhaps lured into a false sense of hypnogogic security after 'Winter's Call', the brutality of the guitar and bass would certainly arrive as quite the surprise: a drop-tuned dirge which announces the extent of Caruse's ambition. Heptagonal Sons are no longer a band who can be pigeon-holed. Indeed, the power on display here suggests that Heptagonal Sons are no longer a band who can be *ignored*.

Caruse begins to sing – vocals rapt with a conviction and strength regrettably absent from their debut. The opening line, 'The cattle all march to slaughter, fires begin to burn', certainly turns one's head and, over the subsequent seven lines, Caruse continues in apocalyptic vein. A chord progression ascends into the chorus as Caruse howls, 'You are all lost in the maze, my friends.'

It would be a brave man who'd dare to disagree.

Following this, we are treated to another of this record's copious flashes of genius. Caruse, as the songwriter, must presumably take the credit here. Whilst we – an audience schooled in the recognisable tropes of Western pop – would naturally assume a return to the verse, we are wrong-footed by the early introduction of an elaborate middle-eighth. Already off balance, the listener is then sucker-punched by what follows: a 4/4 riff which drops the final note, commencing the following rotation one beat too early. The pattern continues with each repetition before eventually turning back on itself. Despite the technical temerity of the timing (the drumming in this section alone would be worth the price of admission), our ears – raised on the melodic structures of the Beatles and Beach Boys – are simply unaccustomed to a trick of this calibre. Where is the second verse? Where is the chorus? And how, with this mutating riff which approaches some manner of demented call-and-response, do we ever hope to get back to the original song?

And then the penny drops: *we* are in the maze. We are lost, swerving around corners, sprinting down corridors, blindly feeling through the dark to find a way out. This isn't a middle-eighth: it's a labyrinth, and we are trapped within it.

The release arrives without warning. In what should be the central point of a chord progression, the song suddenly tilts back into its initial, brutal riff. The change is a strangely liberating sensation: like emerging into open air and once again drawing breath. And yet that air has a flavour: something is different; something *has* changed. A chorus follows the verse, but with Caruse adjusting the lyrics to 'You have left the maze.' It seems that we have found our exit, but where has this led us?

It's a question that the album review in *Sounds* was disinclined to address. An unfavourable write-up described 'a muddle of half-baked ideas, falling apart with a lack of focus'. Obviously, I disagree, although I can imagine how an unprepared critic would have been caught off-guard. It is an entirely different beast to the band's previous work, and cultural history is littered with instances of prodigy being either ignored or condemned at the time of their birth.

Eldritch

Scanning through the press archives, it does sadly seem that the *Sounds* scribe was not alone in his opinion. *Eldritch* suffered from universally lacklustre reviews and this was undoubtedly a key factor in the record's commercial failure. All one can do, I suppose, is consider an alternative history – emerging from the maze but through a different door. What if the album had been a hit? Would the lives of those involved have been shunted onto another track? And would this mean they'd still be with us to explain the work they produced?

But, of course, they are not. And so, in their absence, I sit here – in my empty house, in the room I used to sleep in before my wife moved out – trying to unravel what they were attempting to convey. The album is cloaked in the unknown; it has the structure of a puzzle. As night descends, I cannot help but think that it's down to me to figure it out.

Track 3 – Heretic

After the pummelling head-spin of 'The Maze', 'Heretic' retrocedes into what, at the time, would have been considered more typical terrain. A finger-picked acoustic guitar (played – as the sparse sleeve notes inform us – by Caruse himself) steers a gentle melodic progression whose tone suddenly shifts with the introduction of a diminished fifth – otherwise known as the devil's chord. Over the past forty years, this has been a commonly employed ruse and yet – both at the time and considering the preceding chord sequence – its arrival here is genuinely disconcerting. The listener is paradoxically thrown back and drawn in. Whatever we imagined this song was going to deliver, Caruse appears determined to prove us wrong.

A light, percussive floor tom, strummed second acoustic guitar and rhythmic bass add flesh to the bones as Caruse presents a potted history of rural Albion. Images are conjured of gallows and gibbets, of bonfires and Saxon villages, of a life beholden to the seasons' change. The song itself, even despite that jarring diminished fifth, is not unpleasant, although both the lyrics and vocal performance create a nebulous sense of foreboding. The nearest comparison I can draw is to Mr Fox, who released two well-regarded albums (the eponymous *Mr Fox* and *The Gipsy*) on Transatlantic Records during the early seventies. Caruse would have certainly been aware of their work and, although I'm unable to verify whether they actually shared a stage, it is entirely probable – if not quite a fait accompli – that the paths of these two acts would have crossed.

Halfway through, Caruse closes his narrative as, with the lift of a key change, Spondley-Feathershore glides in on a pub piano. The band shifts gears and we find ourselves on a familiar folk-rock footing.

As the more vocal of the two band members who survived the 1970s, most of our insight arrives from Spondley-Feathershore. Although an inarguably talented pianist, he retired from making music after *Eldritch* was released. Using the contacts he'd established – and undoubtedly mining the influence of his well-connected family – he moved into artist management. A successful career included an early hand in Dr Feelgood and an instrumental role behind the scenes of the New Romantics. Tragically, he died of a heart attack in March 1997, exactly twenty-five years after *Eldritch* was released.

In 1992, he noted that:

> *I suppose you could say we were a failure. In terms of sales . . . of fame. But I don't know. I think Neal set out to do exactly what he wanted to do, and in that regard it was a success. He realised his vision. I just hope, wherever he is, that he's happy.*

Track 4 – A Séance

By this point, it would be obvious to even the most casual observer that a lyrical theme has emerged. 'A Séance' is the final song on the record's first side, and it feels like an appropriate moment to pause and reflect on precisely what Caruse's preoccupations were.

In the aforementioned interview, Spondley-Feathershore recalls that the lyrics were constantly changing, with Caruse making revisions even in the studio. Claverley Hall is a secluded stately home with an oppressive gothic styling and I must confess that – as I imagine Caruse within its walls, pen in hand, making those eleventh-hour edits before entering the vocal booth – it is hard to believe this setting could have failed to bear an influence. A writer will naturally absorb his surroundings. Even as I type away now, with the evening merging into night and the suburbs subdued, I am assailed by the sense of quiet, of solitude . . . by the introspection this inevitably provokes.

So exactly what was Caruse trying to communicate? Darren Shields, in his otherwise comprehensive 2007 folk retrospective *Crank Up the Hurdy Gurdy*, dismisses *Eldritch* for failing to comply with the conventions of a folk record. Whilst not a criticism *per se* (and arguably a valid point – *Eldritch* is some musical miles from 'All Around My Hat'), it does excuse any detailed analysis of Heptagonal Sons' work. Shields cannot, however, ignore them entirely, and has this to say regarding Caruse's muse:

> *Comus were not the only band exploring the darker reaches of both one's own psyche and what we might term as the spectral. Heptagonal Sons, on their second album,* Eldritch, *waded even further into these waters, with lyrics rich in pagan references and openly addressing the occult. Their singer, Neal Caruse, was something of a troubled man, and his interest in magic and ritualism was freely indulged on this record.*

It is hard to disagree with this last point, especially as the ballad-like 'A Séance' swings into life and Caruse sings of standing at a hilltop altar to summon down demons from the skies. Rum stuff, although the real surprise is that he pulls it off. Something like this could easily be dismissed as comically theatrical, but Caruse delivers with such conviction that the effect is actually rather chilling.

Although, if candlelit pentagrams and the reading of runes were the only lyrical focus then even an intensity of performance would fail to carry the song. In my opinion, the genius of Caruse's writing is the extent to which he exposes his emotions, occasionally cracking the door ajar to allow a tantalising glimpse of what's really happening. As the second verse closes, his voice retreats to a broken croak, a defeated whimper: 'And when you left me, I was left with this ... This heart is broken, so they'll have no heart to take.'

No archives exist which detail Caruse's personal life. The music press of the time was primarily concerned with music, and he was neither famous nor rich enough to warrant inches in the society write-ups. If we take the lyric at face value (and we have no reason not to) then it appears he dwells in the furrow of a broken relationship – something to which we can all relate. Heartbreak is the perennial preoccupation of pop and it is woven through *Eldritch* like ley lines through our land, hiding within couplets and metaphor, embodied in the strum of a minor chord or descending piano motif.

I write this as someone recently separated. My wife moved out – an estrangement I cannot claim as amicable, although I'm acutely aware that this article is an unsuitable theatre for all the gory details. But I wonder, therefore, if I'm currently more receptive – more *susceptible* even – to these songs because I share something of

Caruse's experience. Despite recording in a studio resembling the set of a Hammer Horror film, despite the darker imagery of folklore and an occult history that flavoured these songs, I wonder if Caruse is ultimately singing about love, and how we are supposed to manage when that love is taken from us. How do we fill the void? What powers can possibly heal the pain? When our world is shattered, what circling dangers will exploit those cracks to try and seep inside?

The song gently fades away. The stereo hums and the house around me echoes with a still and empty silence.

Track 5 – The Line of Seasons

As track 5 begins, I reach across for the compact disc case (shamefully, I cannot claim that my copy of *Eldritch* is a first-pressing vinyl edition). The album had a limited re-release during the early-nineties glut of record companies attempting (quite profitably) to make everyone purchase records they already owned. The artwork in the CD booklet, however, does replicate the original sleeve. It is a photograph of the band standing in a muddy field. The five musicians face the camera, dressed in earthy tones and sporting beards. Nothing is noted about the location or when it was taken, and the background reveals no distinguishing topography. The picture is credited to Nic Hooper, who was a jobbing photographer around this time. A Google search suggests he died in a car accident in 1975.

Eldritch

Neither glamorous nor artistic, the image could even be considered somewhat slapdash – the result of a harried record-company employee scrabbling around as the print deadline drew near. And yet I think the sleeve perfectly represents the music. By its very nature – the anonymous landscape, the blending of colours – it becomes a further mystery. Here are these young men in this untraceable moment – we cannot read anything from their eyes, we cannot hear the beat of their hearts. All we have is the work, and we must understand it as best we can.

'The Line of Seasons' opens what would have been Side 2. As my CD glides from track to track, I imagine getting up after the needle rose at the end of 'A Séance', stepping across to the record player and flipping the vinyl, starting all over again. It is a surprisingly ruminative image. I close my eyes and allow the moment to guide me, shepherded by a bass and drum groove which would not have been out of place on some of the more contemplative Stax releases.

Groove is an essential ingredient of *Eldritch*, and it's genuinely surprising how much swing and sway these songs boast. I have already trumpeted the drumming of Dave Matherley, but his rhythm-section partner Ken Walker also deserves a fanfare. Walker's style is informed by R&B and even approaches funk. We are far removed from the plodding, root-note pulse of traditional folk. Ken Walker also warrants a special mention as he is the only band member who has not been officially pronounced dead. (Matherley drowned whilst trying to swim across a stretch of the Thames in 1974. An inquiry noted he was sober, fully clothed and apparently on his way to a bank appointment. The ruling was death by misadventure.)

Unfortunately, Walker *has* been missing for over twenty-five years. Through Facebook, I found his daughter and chanced a prospective message to enquire whether she knew of her father's whereabouts or would be willing to talk about the album. It would be indiscreet to quote her reply, but appropriate to relay something of the sentiment: Ken Walker's daughter hasn't heard from her father since he left the family home in the late 1980s. She has serious concerns about his mental health and has come to accept that he is most probably dead. Finally, if she ever receives another query about this 'fucking record' then she will hunt down the person asking and embed the CD somewhere medically implausible.

With the trail cold, it seems I won't be fortunate enough to talk to any of the people who actually made *Eldritch*. I lean into my disappointment as 'The Line of Seasons' climbs into its final refrain. Lyrically, we have been taken on a four-verse tour of spring, summer, autumn and winter, and this structure only births another question that will remain unanswered: why did Caruse choose this route through the year? Why not end the song with the optimism of spring or glory of summer? Winter is a recurrent theme. We're constantly returned to the darkest, cruellest time of year – but why?

As I lose myself in this, trying to read what nestles between the notes and gather the allusions and references,

Eldritch

I can imagine my wife's reaction. Why do I have this obsession with music? Why do I spend so much time sitting in this spare room poring over album sleeves, joining dots and making connections? The guy who played guitar here produced this and co-wrote that? And so on and so on. It never ends. It's not a puzzle, she would argue. There's nothing to solve. It's just *life*. It's just what happens.

And this is my life now. This is what happened. She left me . . . she left me and I'm all alone.

Track 6 – The Gate

Track 6 opens with an Eastern influence – an acoustic guitar riff structured around a Persian scale atop a chiming piano and percussively brushed bongo. Melodically, the muscles are flexed again: one is quite in awe of the versatility on display. Caruse takes his cue and, with a croon not dissimilar to Robert Plant in his more controlled moments, sings of a traveller arriving at the walls of an unnamed city to stand at the eponymous gate. His origins are uncertain, but we are informed that 'he has been called, he has been summoned, and he is waiting to be let in'.

The song has a curious flavour and a shiver steps down my spine as I listen. Perhaps it is time to tackle the aspects of this album that are regrettably not concerned with music. *Eldritch* is infamously and indelibly linked with catastrophe. I'm sure there are those of a certain disposition who would even claim it was cursed. A little logical consideration obviously rubbishes such a notion, although the events that befell those involved do seem spectacularly egregious.

Across my desk and multiple tabs of an internet browser, I have the spread of my research into Heptagonal Sons: the sparse Wikipedia page, the music press cuttings and scans, references from books and blogs penned by enthusiasts. The producer, Andrew Port, hanged himself in the woods near Claverley Hall. Charlie Kitson died of a heroin overdose the following year. Dave Matherley drowned. Ken Walker is missing and presumed dead. Guy Spondley-Feathershore suffered a heart attack alone in his home.

Now, obviously people die. It's our ultimate and inescapable fate: we get old, we get sick; accidents happen and misfortunes strike. But when the deaths are listed as above then ... well, then what exactly? Is it simply unfair? A series of tragic vicissitudes? Or is it something else? Something that we need to consider?

The final, unresolved link in this morbid chain is Caruse himself. He disappeared the very week that *Eldritch* was released. This was disastrous. As previously mentioned, reviews had been indifferent at best, but his absence meant the band were forced to cancel both their immediate tour and an appearance on *The Old Grey Whistle Test* – exposure that would have considerably raised their profile. (As an aside, their slot went to Vinegar Joe with a performance of 'Rusty Red Armour'. The band featured Robert Palmer, who died of a heart attack aged only fifty-four.)

Details of Caruse's disappearance – in a pre-internet world – are unfortunately thin on the ground. The *NME* reported that he lived alone and the police had been alerted by his management after numerous no-shows. Nothing had been intimated to his bandmates or friends. There were no leads or sightings and the story drifted out of the papers. To be blunt, Caruse wasn't famous enough to capture the public imagination, and his case was quickly forgotten. At the request of his extended family, a death certificate was issued in 1979.

So where did he go? Spondley-Feathershore, in every interview he gave after Caruse's disappearance, swerved this question when it inevitably arose. Was his reticence out of respect or genuinely because all he could offer – like the rest of us – was speculation? I am obviously unable to say, but if this was suicide then where's the note? If foul play then where's the body? If Caruse ran away to a new life then for what reason? His drug issues are documented. Unsubstantiated rumours allude to an association with sex cults and communes. Ultimately, what happened to Neal Caruse is a mystery, albeit one whose key I cannot help but consider is held within this album. I can almost imagine his voice telling me that there is something here to divine, something that I need to understand.

And so I listen to the record; I trace the CD case in my hand like a puzzle box, focusing on his face as he stands alongside his band. I try to decipher the lyrics and search within the sound. I enter *Eldritch* with head and heart until it absorbs me. Here I am – behind the walls as something knocks at the gate, something that wants to come inside.

Track 7 – Ritual

All great albums should close with an epic song – a rule to which *Eldritch* is no exception. A riff which, once again, veers towards hard rock (albeit via a detour in the direction of Pink Floyd) opens atop clattering drums and droning keys. The mood is crepuscular, and the hypnotic power of the mid-tempo repetition captivates. It is a full two minutes before the vocals arrive, with Caruse picking up the story from the previous song.

Should *Eldritch* be considered as a concept album? It's a contentious point which depends entirely on your definition of 'concept'. There is no overarching plot or character – or at least none that has either been recognised by a critic or asserted by the band themselves. And yet, as previously noted, there are recurrent lyrical themes and a definite sense of atmosphere. The songs lead into each other and feel like entirely different beasts when individually lifted from the context of the album. Whether this qualifies as conceptual is, I think, open to interpretation. I will, however, assert that *Eldritch* is intended – and therefore should be taken – as a *complete* work.

Caruse sounds desperate. As he sings of opening the

Eldritch

gate to brace himself against the storm, his performance even approaches the deranged. Not in the sense of the frantic – no, a singer of his aptitude is far more nuanced than this. Instead, his voice quivers between fear and awe, guiding the listener as he stands on the precipice of this new world. The band launch into the chorus and Caruse squints into the elements. Slowly, a dark shape emerges from the gloom . . .

It is here when we get to the most notorious moment of the record – at least amongst collectors. The original pressing (and the CD release, in keeping with a desire for authenticity) contains ten whole minutes of silence. At the time, this was immediately assumed to be an error and subsequently rectified. However, the band have confirmed that this was entirely intentional. Caruse had, apparently, insisted the song would be incomplete without this section. Presumably, the record company thought that this was simply the end of the album and allowed the master tapes to pass through to the pressing plant.

It is a disconcerting experience: a sudden dead, continuous silence in the middle of a song. Even though I've been expecting it and sit with the temptation of a skip button on the stereo and the foresight that in precisely ten minutes the song will begin again, it feels discombobulating. But to experience the album completely, it's something I have to endure. The house around me creaks and strains – the ambient uproars which emerge when the hustle of the modern world is numbed. It allows space to think: about the past, about how we are alone, about how we are hurt, about the *purpose* of what we are listening to.

Eldritch has seven songs. There are seven classical planets. Seven notes of a diatonic scale. Seven chakras and seven elements: earth, fire, water, air, above, below and within. There are seven points of an elven star. A heptagon, of course, has seven sides. *I think Neal set out to do exactly what he wanted to do,* Spondley-Feathershore said. *He realised his vision.* But what exactly was that? As I sit here in my empty house, deafened by the silence, the dots begin to join. Caruse created this structure because it was required: the song is exactly what its title claims – a ritual. The album before it is an order of service, a heretical set of sacraments. Everything is aligned, everything has a purpose, everything has been planned. Jesus Christ ... people were playing Black Sabbath backwards to hear messages which didn't exist when all along the real thing had been captured by this ignored and forgotten band.

Music has power. I doubt that anyone reading a magazine like this will disagree. Music can help or heal, it can provoke and inspire. We turn to it when we are sad or happy or bored or excited ... And yet, for some of us – for people like *me* – music not only soundtracks our lives but also consumes them. We trade records and seek out trivia, we obsess about labels and B-sides, we fixate on people we will never meet and moments we will never know. But what if, even with all that passion and mania – perhaps *because* of that passion and mania – we missed something? Something that Caruse uncovered? Music is an energy, and rituals are invoked with energy. Sex, sacrifice, an oblation . . . they need fuel, they need order. This is how they work. What if music has the power to do this?

The song returns without warning. It should be startling, but my body doesn't seem able to react. A chorus follows the verse and leads to a lengthy fade-out. 'I give myself,' Caruse repeats, chanting the words like a mantra and, finally, I think that I understand. I can see what happened to him. I can imagine what happened to everyone around him and why. He was devoured by what he created. He called something that shouldn't have been called and used this record to invite it into our world. He gave himself and left this album behind for others to follow . . . an insidious gift; an endless cycle of offering. The temperature drops as an acrid smell creeps across the room.

I can feel it now. It's behind me, inching closer, patient but predatory. It has come. The ritual has worked – Caruse's ritual fed by my energy. I stare at my computer, not daring to turn around and acknowledge its presence, because that will make it real. And this *can't* be real. Surely? So I keep typing these words, my eyes unblinking, my fingertips on the keyboard. Hot breath warms the back of my neck as a cold hand rests upon my shoulder.

The Spit in Your Mouth and the Bile in Your Stomach

MARK STAFFORD

Emerging from the UK small press/underground comics scene, Mark Stafford (@marxtafford on yer socials) is the co-creator of the graphic novels *The Bad Bad Place*, *Lip Hook* and *The Man Who Laughs* (with David Hine) and *Cherubs!* (with Bryan Talbot). He's also the sole creator of hundreds of pages of comics and illustrations, as well as numerous beer labels, theatre posters, record covers and at least one library mural. He was selected by the British Council to work on two projects in South Korea, has exhibited art in squats, galleries and the ICA, and is the long-standing and loosely defined cartoonist-in-residence for the Cartoon Museum in Fitzrovia. A collection of solo works, *Salmonella Smorgasbord*, was released by Soaring Penguin in 2023.

Yellowbelly

HOLLIE STARLING

Hollie Starling is a Lincolnshire-born writer working in London. She is the author of *The Bleeding Tree: A Pathway Through Grief Guided by Forests, Folk Tales and the Ritual Year* (Ebury, 2023). Her essays and short fiction have appeared in various print and online publications. Starling runs the page Folk Horror Magpie on social media.

'They said not to worry about picking up me exam results cos the local factories always needed girls to work the machines.'

It's such a batshit thing to hear while you're balls deep that for a second I think I've imagined her saying it.

'Still a ways off for my littlest, but *god* it's a mare just getting her to go in sometimes. Non-uniform day today but she were point blank refusing this morning, says all her clothes are nunty. Proper bealing, asking us why she dun't ever have ote new. Turning into a right stroppy little madam, that one.' That *ote* had done it: her accent is definitely up here, not Fens way. 'Course I never see a penny off their dads, but I love 'em to the moon and back.'

I pause and shift my weight onto my shoulders, her narrow body motionless underneath me. 'It's like me mam said: "Money mayn't bring me happiness but it would bloody help me look fer it on a nicer street."' She looks up at me and smiles widely. Her two blue eyes are like blowtorch points.

This is properly putting me off my rhythm now. I didn't pay this much money to be this soft two minutes out the gate. It feels a bit wrong, but there's no use. I put both hands over her mouth and pummel like a Jack Russell on a settee cushion until I'm over the line, then I wipe off and check the website:

Lulah: the only fully customisable personal companion.

I run my eyes over the familiar blurb: *Designed with world-beating machine learning, Lulah gives a hyper-realistic . . . Market-leading AI utilised to maximise your self-care requirements better than any . . .* There's nothing much in the FAQs so I scroll back up to My Account and log in.

Listen, I know how it sounds, but right off the bat let's get this straight: I'm not some neckbeard Reddit deviant with an all-caps manifesto on his hard drive. You can get Lulahs with all sorts of adaptables: external plug-ins and what have you; silicone accessories in mad colours, dimensions that should be illegal. No thanks. Mine is as nature intended her. Legs are on the longer side but medium height, medium build, sometimes glasses even; the 'girlfriend model'. None of that weird cartoon shite. What some lads are into is honestly disgusting. I'm not like that. It's just been a very stressful time.

Fuck's sake, I'm going to have to ring an actual number, aren't I? Seriously, what year is it?

On the bed, Lulah has rolled over and seems to be examining Mum's address book. I swat it out of her hands. The slimline navy pad goes flying and lands behind the adjustable tray table as the phone connects. I'm actually surprised anyone picks up.

'This is . . . ShenYuan Systems.' The customer service agent is chewing something. 'What . . . can I help you with today?' His accent's English, maybe Essex. But I guess it makes sense to have global distribution centres.

'Yeah hi. I have your Lulah Q3-Xi Zhu Series 8 Smart. It's been nearly a week now and she's . . . It's. Speaking. Too much. Strange stuff, I don't know how to describe it, but stuff about being poor? Or something?'

It's weird how you can hear someone smiling over the phone.

'Alright, mate, no worries. You got a screen in frontya? Do me a favour wouldya and log into your account for me? Then go into Learning and Language? Yep. Then you have Other Settings? Scroll down to the bottom and there's a menu called Authenticity. You got it? Right, in there is where you have your Identity Controls, it's like a series of adjustable slides. Betya anything that Regional is all the way up, yeah?'

It is.

'That's it. So. When we take your place of birth, school years, all that, to get your Formative Worldview? You must of hadya FW down as one of your Intimacy Intangibles. Thing is, right, these designers all the way in China don't get it, the variety of different regions we got over here. This is *finely attuned machine learning*, a large language model hoovering up whatever behavioural input it can find to mimic human speech patterns. And there's a lot of stereotypes on the old web ain't there? Crank Regional all the way up and you have her selling matches and talking like a chimney sweep. Or in your case ... Where is it you said—'

'Lincolnshire. Humberside.'

'Okay, okay, let's have a look under the hood. Right: yeah, I can see here they took the Humber region datasets from oral testimony, interviews with munitions women at RAF Coningsby, looks like some 1960s sociological studies; demography of the family, gender, mobility ... An ONS report into industrial decline in former fisheries, urban deprivation and excess child mortality 1994 ... Wow okay, this data pool goes back a ways. "From the British Library collection of ethnographic wax cylinders: antiquarian and folklorist A. G. Pryne records the agrarian traditions, calendar festivals, et cetera, of textile workers near Sleaford, May Day 1886."' Well anyway, have a dick around with those settings and you should stop hearing about sausages or whatever. Have fun, mate.' A click.

I toggle Regional down to 50% for now and look over the other options. My cursor hovers over Independent Expression. Hmm.

You might reckon otherwise, but when I spent the bulk of my inheritance on Lulah, I was after something more than just the obvious. Bit of conversation, you know. It's been a rough month. I can see now that the thing with Pia was in its death spirals a good while before I left UCL, though it wrecked my head when she ended it for good.

Yellowbelly

One thing I don't miss since we broke up and I moved up to Mum's house is this way she had of not really talking *to* me. Especially when we were around other people. *Oh my god when he goes 'orr nurr' or 'I an't dun ote' I love it! SO funny!* She'd be laughing away and I'd be stood there next to her, and I'd know it was meant like an instruction, though I never really knew what for. With Pia it was like everything I said needed a little correction, a little tidy. *Remuneration not 'renumeration'. Yes it's unpaid but it'll be worth more to you as experience, you really should consider it.* Until it felt like it wasn't my way of talking that needed the correction, but me. Really, that cut-glass voice of hers should have told me from the off that I'd never meet her dad. Anyway, with Lulah I just wanted something easier, someone who got it. 'Connection' or whatever. A lass I could talk to.

Lass. Funny. Being here it's so easy to slip back into words like that.

Speaking of connection, here's Gideon calling and I remember the broadband through here is shite.

'Hold on one sec,' I say to the screen, though it's still showing his university avatar because the blind fuck has to relearn how to turn the camera on every single time. Which is lucky because I manage to catch the jumpscare in my own background before he notices: Lulah sitting bolt upright on the end of the bed. I can see the peach fuzz that covers her arms standing on end, and I am distracted again by her amazing detail. She is stock still, staring at the awful yellow wallpaper. When I was a kid, I would never go in Mum and Rick's room alone because the pattern looked like eyes and mouths.

'Just taking you somewhere with better signal,' I say as I carry the laptop down the hall and kick open the door to my old room with one foot. In the past couple of weeks I've tidied up a bit, shoving the boxes and boxes of Mum's pills on top of the bathroom cupboard, but there are wedge pillows and big tubs of creams and, like, washing assistance stuff still piled around, and I angle the screen so that only the bookcase is in view. Mostly it's my old books and comics from when I was a kid, Mum being too sentimental to chuck them, but he shouldn't be able to see from that distance.

'Aha! There! Can you hear me well enough? Sorry for the racket, we're having a wee spruce-up on the gable end.' Dr Gideon Horton is my old thesis supervisor. A very noted if oblivious anthropologist, with big red cheeks from a creeping brandy dependency and small misty eyes from cataracts. He only uses 'wee' when he's talking to me, I've noticed. He's not Scottish and he hired me partly on the basis of my *extraction* – his word – to catalogue the oral folk tales and kinship ballads of old Lincolnshire and the Fens, and so he must know that neither am I. I would guess it was a wild stab at cheery provincialism when we met that he doesn't feel he can course-correct now.

He tells me about the folk song transcripts he wants me to go through, most of which he couriered over earlier this week. He has decided that the time is right for a book, unrelated to a colleague in the department recently publishing a foiled hardback on neolithic Britain's 'psychic landscape' that had gotten 'Book of the Week' on Radio 4 and a cover quote from Stewart Lee. About twenty-five box files are sitting in Mum's hallway. *My* hallway, I mean. Applying the Aarne-Thompson-Uther folktext index to everything inside is going to be a massive task.

'As I say, this will be a tremendous string to your professional-development bow, but it's just a case of wading through I'm afraid,' he says, as though the research bit of a research project is not the main body of the work but just an unfortunate bit of faff (worth more as experience!). I had wondered about a collaborator credit but I already blew my shot reminding Gideon of the principle of minimum wage.

'Oh! There's one in particular that you'll ... Hang on now, where did I—' In his deranged clicking Gideon turns his mic off, and for a few seconds I watch him flap his wet gross fat lips like a hooked fish.

I switch my sound off too. 'Right away, master, and those boots look overdue a licking – may I?' and we both shrug and grin and wave bye at each other.

There had been no furlough for us postdocs during lockdown and afterwards our undergrad teaching contracts got worse, from fixed term to zero hours. Admin for the faculty and the bit of bar work I picked up was the same: demented hours that I couldn't decline when they needed me and fucking crickets when they didn't. Tell me how anyone is meant to manage London rent on that.

Being 'home' and rent-free means I can just about survive while I weigh up what to do next. As well as research for Gideon I have a data-entry gig with the council, which I only got when I took my PhD off the application and resubmitted it, before very quickly finishing a full pack of Tyskie and kicking a dint in the gas box. Grubbing for minimum wage is not where I'd expected I'd be at thirty-three, to put it mildly. Sometimes the boredom of inputting letters and numbers makes my vision swim at the edges but it's good being able to work remotely, plus I needed the free laptop since I had to hand mine back to UCL. Anyway, it means I don't have to live off toast. And when I feel like I want to flip a table at least I have stress relief from Lulah.

Where *is* Lulah?

The big light is on in the front room. I drop the laptop back through to my work desk and then follow the glow downstairs. I find Lulah sitting on the carpet, both legs kicked out to the side. Books are strewn everywhere. On the telly Jack Nicholson is reclining on a big bed and being all randy in a silk robe.

'What the fuck is this?'

'It is a DVD format recording of *The Witches of Eastwick*, a 1987 American supernatural comedy film directed by George Miller and based on John Updike's 1984 novel of the same name.' Lulah beams up at me, eyes like disco lights. I didn't know she could do that, put a DVD in the player, read stuff. Put knickers on. She has a book open in each hand. *The Yellow Wallpaper and Selected Stories* and something called *Cronehood Rewilded: Becoming Daring, Defiant and Disorderly in your Triple Goddess Power Era*, each with pages dog-eared. On the bookcase there are dust rings as if things have been moved and I notice a few books with upside-down spines. Has Lulah been down here before?

I run my eyes over the shelves. A keyring of a black cat next to a candle shaped like the torso of a pregnant woman. A wooden dish with a goose feather and bundle of twigs inside. Mum's collection of pagan shite: tarots and planets and crystals, collections on myths and legends, and especially historical accounts of witches. She always loved that stuff. Last time I was here, before she took the turn, she had been on a family-tree kick and was bouncing off the walls that she'd apparently found our ancestral link to the 'famous witches of Belvoir Castle' down near Grantham. It was nice seeing her so happy so I didn't say anything, but it had to be a second cousin or something, since the mother and sisters were all tortured and hanged.

At Lulah's feet is a pile of scattered papers that must have fallen from the mantlepiece. Bills, appointment letters, some bits from Macmillan, a stack of cards from my auntie Jill in Wales. I pick up a clipping that had been cut out of the newspaper. It's about a study that found that men were seven times more likely to leave their wives than the other way around if one of them got cancer, and written on it in blue biro so hard it has torn the page is: PIG PIG PIG PIG.

I take Lulah by the wrist and push her upstairs, and it's leisurely but disciplinary in nature shall we say. She can't be wandering about the place, what if someone looks in? No more weird comments though, just kind of whimpers, which I actually don't mind.

I detach the pelvic compartment and wash it out in the bathroom, and when I'm back I see that she has curled up in bed with the covers around her shoulders. She looks all cosy and cute, like a girl from a Disney. Subtle freckles, natural makeup, nose a little upturned at the end. I get into bed beside her. Her head feels warm on my chest and her skin smells like Skittles, and I nearly jump out my skin when she starts spluttering:

'Lincolnf. Lincolnffshh. Li—'

I follow her gaze and burst out laughing.

My desktop background is a page from Francis Grose's *A Classical Dictionary of the Vulgar Tongue*. A funny line about Lincolnshire from the 1796 edition of his 'provincial glossary of local proverbs':

> *Lincolnſhire, where the hogſ ſhite ſoap, and the cowſ ſhite fire.*

She's pronouncing it wrong because she's reading it as *f* and I have to explain the 'long s' to her, from the typesetting tradition. All that web scraping and data mining and here's something I know and she doesn't.

'What does this sentence in the book mean?' She says that word – book – with the vowel as flat as a roof slate.

Buhk. The Regional control is still scaled down to 50%, but that accent seems to be deepening again.

I explain that it is an old saying that alludes to the practice of cleaning clothes in urine and manure, and having to burn cow dung for want of better fuel, i.e. those Lincolnshire types are literally shite poor.

She laughs hard at that and I'm glad I toggled up Amiability.

'Were you shite poor? When you were a child, in this house?'

'Nah. Well, I don't reckon so. Not that bad anyway, not like now with the food banks and the energy bills and everything. Fridge were full, lights were always on. I was a happy kid; never bothered me about being an only child either, this street used to have tons of kids on it. Playing out every day after school. But yeah, I guess we didn't go on holiday. Or have ote new. And I never liked my mates coming round here to be honest, would always want to go play at theirs.'

Later on, that was more to do with Rick though. I tell Lulah about him moving in, how things changed. Even Mum's voice changed.

But however she let Rick speak to her, Mum always stood in between him and me. He had a big thing about her wasting his money. Certain things would just set him off. He hit the roof whenever she got me Robinsons Fruit & Barley though the own-brand was cheaper, because I could tell the difference. 'Pink Drink, we called it. I'd have it in my *Space Jam* tumbler with some of them Nice biscuits when I was off school poorly. She said it were medicine.'

Mum did stand between me and Rick when I was younger, at least. But over the years he wore her out. I remember the first time she said it and realised she was speaking to me: 'Maybe it's best if you just go, love.'

So I did. Even though Rick called me applying to uni 'a joke' and said that I was too big for my boots. Went around telling everyone that I thought I was better than them. And the truth is, I did. I've never said this out loud to anyone, but I did. Spending your entire life in one town, fuck all to it. Neither of them ever left this place. Well I suppose he did, didn't he, in the end.

A bloke built like a catering fridge who still felt he needed to belittle people, control what they did and said to feel like the big man. Being like Rick is the worst thing I can imagine. But then somehow, in one way, I guess I am. I speak my shame very quietly into Lulah's neck.

'Like, I know, it's bad. I feel really bad. That I only came back the once after she were out the hospital. She looked so different. I couldn't stop thinking how fucked up it was. Like, we all have these certain number of years, and she just *wasted* so many. Wasted them on feeding and cleaning up and looking after a bully. I couldn't look at her. I left too.'

Robinsons. I actually saw a bottle knocking about in the top cupboard when I was looking for the Bisto the other night. It can't have been from all the way back then. She must have got it in more recently, hoping I'd be visiting soon.

Yellowbelly

Lulah looks so intently at me that my throat catches. But I don't need to talk anymore. It's nice, this, lying close together. I know it's an old-fashioned phrase, but it pops into my head then: the comfort of a woman.

I sleep and my dreams are flashes of the mundane and perfect: Mum pegging out the washing, me zipping between the breezing sheets on my Tonka truck, when it was just the two of us, how it should have been. When I wake up I feel lighter than I have in weeks. I stretch out in the feeling's strange glow for a minute or two, inhaling the morning. Then my gut tightens. Ah right, that's today isn't it. My summons.

After yesterday's wanderings, I think it's best to confine Lulah to upstairs. Mum never took off the old babygate at the top of the landing, installed after I once sleepwalked down the stairs and right out the front door and was almost down to the Fighting Cocks before Mrs Kettlethorpe from the Costcutter saw me and nudged me home. Rick gave me earache for that, because something I did while literally unconscious was obviously me playing silly buggers to wind him, specifically, up. The babygate had only been used since for draping over sheets that wouldn't fit in the airing cupboard, always propped open because it was tricky to undo even with adult hands. Lulah has a good grip – *powerful, sustained and intuitive* as per the specs, a claim supported by my extensive end-user testing – but I doubt the hydraulics in her fingers are dextrous enough. I briefly consider buying a lock for the bedroom door but depriving her of a bathroom makes me feel weird, though I know that's daft. Upstairs will do.

The summons is to the council offices, so that my supervisor there – a man I've never met but whose *lovely stuff* and *happy days!* replies to my sparse contact implies a blokey familiarity that has not been earned and that I have come to resent – can tell me off in person. The data-entry job in the housing department. I collate metadata on our clients for internal stats and FOI requests, stuff like that – all identifying info removed first, of course.

The town hall offices have recently been renovated like a sort of municipal brain-trauma ward, all big blobs of colour and tactile sofas. Across the length of one wall is a quotation: *Work gives you meaning and purpose and life is empty without it.* Stephen Hawking, apparently. Mad that there's fifty flavours of 'meaning and purpose' when you're from a family of Oxford academics but not even vanilla whippy when you ask at the window in the Job Centre.

My supervisor introduces himself and I nod to the wall: 'A little *"arbeit macht frei"*, that, in't it?' He smiles in a way that is really just tightening his lips and I don't think he has any idea what I'm on about as he leads me down an over-lit corridor that smells like soup. He is younger than me and actually looks a bit yellow to be having to do this dressing-down, as weak as it is clearly going to be. Almost feel a bit bad for him.

'We can see several occasions where your computer has been left idle for long periods.' Bossware. I probably should've guessed. I took the job thinking I would get as much of my own work as possible done while on their clock. The dates he gives are all while I've been doing Gideon's reading and, okay, fine, spending time with Lulah. It's through gritted teeth but I do a bit of a grovel: my mum's only recently died you see, and I've been finding it tough, mental health, etc., etc. I'll absolutely get on it.

'Alright! Lovely stuff.'

Back at home, I order a mouse jiggler. Another miraculous Chinese-made bit of tech; by nudging the cursor to move one pixel at a time the screen remains 'active' and fools any surveillance software. Well not any, only the most simplistic, but this is Lincolnshire County Council, so.

A delivery guy pushes it through the letterbox before the sun is even up.

I open the new spreadsheet I've been sent. I should probably get in a few solid hours of actual work before I plug the jiggler in and call it a day. The list runs hundreds deep and truth be told I can't remember what all the colour coding means without having to scroll back up to the top. Then I realise something. This is more information than I should have access to. This looks like the master list, with all the identifying details. Of course I have a look through, for absolutely no reason than to exercise an illicit power. A name jumps out. I have to Ctrl+F to find her again.

Laney Beelsby

Every part of me that is in contact with a surface begins prickling and warming like nettle rash. At the same time my insides rush cold and I can taste pre-sick. Gippy, Mum would have said.

Dependants: 3

Referral: Refuge @ CrisisLineLincs

It has been years but Laney is still the only girl that ever meant anything proper, if I'm being honest with myself. Lasses were always standing around in packs back then, hair scraped back and faces sour, gobbing at any of us who tried talking to them, but not Laney. She let me ask for her MSN name without laughing at me, and she never told her mates the stuff I told her on there. Laney had all these allergies but she had a way of turning things down while still making Mum feel that whatever she'd baked was amazing. The point of one of her ears was flattened and a bit fucked up, after a dog bite as a toddler, but rather than hide it she'd put a piercing through it, which for some reason drove me wild. For weeks I went around absolutely made up that she was my girlfriend, but on our three-month anniversary, holding gloved hands at bommy night on the common, I realised for the first time how happy I was to be *a boyfriend*. How good a guy I must be, to have won her. That was love, and I finally got why everyone made such a big deal of it. It was great, but it didn't stop me being sick of everything else. So sick of always *wanting*; wanting to get out of this place and just *do something*, whatever the fuck, I didn't care, just get on with the terrible head-rush of the real world, to become someone worth something. Laney really believed I would, and I really believed she would be there with me in every version. A person seeing me not as I was but how I one day would be, *that's* what I assumed love was. It took me years to realise that wasn't a given.

When I applied for my BA in London, I just assumed she'd come with me. Laney wasn't like the rest of the people here; she was really smart, obsessed with books, knew about politics, was actually curious about the world beyond the A180. But no. I couldn't understand it. Still can't. No one who isn't a complete dribbler likes their hometown that much.

We were sitting on the bin shed in the front yard at her dad's, and before I closed the gate behind me I told her if she stayed up here she'd just end up working at the veg-packing plant, pregnant by some twat who turns out like Rick, and she'd never do a single interesting thing with her life while she aged like milk and waited to die.

And oh, look who was right? Looks like that's exactly what she's done to herself. Three kids and nowhere to put them. Begging for help now, when all she had to do was *listen*.

I highlight her name and delete the row. Then I minimise the spreadsheet and open My Account, go back into settings and search for Obedience.

'Lulah, come here.'

'Right away, master, and those boots look overdue a licking – may I?'

Hello.

I close the curtains.

My energy takes me a little by surprise. It's like a dulled craving suddenly restored and ravenous; the *thing* bit of me awakened and pounding. After that time we fall into something of a pattern. Lulah is perfect. She is a Victorian street waif looking to keep out of the workhouse – *surely there's a speshul agreement to be 'ad between ourselfs, Constabul?* – or a clumsy kitchen maid who has broken a candlestick and *please sir* just won't manage if I took it out of her pay; or has come ruddy and illiterate from the fields to the sweated industries and is surprised by but cooperative of the foreman's interview process; or a school-leaver caught waitressing cash-in-hand and anxious of her Universal Credit claim; or a young widow pleading to the magistrate to merit the mother's desperation behind her petty theft; or a lovely dew-scented shepherdess gone to ruin, reclined and sun-dappled among the lambs and ewes, and as I come I whisper into her hair: *We'll leave the baby on the church steps.*

I can't believe how quickly a week passes, but eventually there is no more food in the house, and so I put the sheets on a hot wash and nip out to the Tesco by the garage.

When I get back, I find that Lulah has cleared some boxes of Mum's stuff to the side and is dancing in the middle of the bedroom. She is wearing some of the things she came with, shorts and a sort of strappy top, but she has one of Mum's big scarves wrapped around her shoulders and the tassels fly about as she twirls. She has her eyes closed but somehow I know she knows I'm watching. A series of half-twirls followed by a little hop, her hands coming up to meet above her head and down again. I recognise the folk dance from a stock of archival footage on the BFI website that I was looking at yesterday. Backlit by the sun setting in the window it looks like Lulah's hair is on fire. The colour is 'cinnamon mocha' and falls just below her collarbone, so not like Laney's at all, or not after she cut it like I saw on Facebook a few years after I moved away anyway. She dances like a little kid, and I think suddenly of bouncy castles and a slice of cake wrapped in a paper towel to take home, sunbaked and sleepy and hanging on Mum's arm. I should really remember to shut the laptop when I'm away.

This past week I've let things slide so I stay up until it's nearly light out, annotating and filing the folk traditions of Lincolnshire past, and I forget to set an alarm.

The ping from my laptop wakes me, and I push my palms into my eye sockets and run my tongue over my teeth to unstick my dry lips. It's an email from Gideon:

> *Very hurt that you missed our zoom this morning, but I expect I shall get over it in time. Softened somewhat by the occasion to talk with your very lovely wee girlfriend. Always fortifying to find that there <u>are</u> young people interested in the tapestried heritage of this little mongrel isle of ours! Anyway, deep in the recesses of the*

oast-house I found that folk song, copied below. Thinking chapter 4? Lots to say on Boudicca + the Iceni in Lincolnshire (raped in war etc.) and this example is probably the conclusion to the erotic reveries of some young Romantic's visionary Albion rather than a trad. fieldsong – still, amusing no? Sending as I think you'll get a kick. If you could apply Aarne number etc. and file please.
Speak on the morrow!
G.

Jesus fucking Christ, Lulah took the call?

I scan the song. There are many verses, separated by a chorus of non-lexical vocables; when everyone is meant to join in the *fa la la*, that sort of thing. The tone is funny, a bit bawdy. The story is about an idealistic young Briton, a picaresque figure who dreams of improving his lot. Believing himself to possess the only wit among them, the youth steals his family's herd of milking goats and trades them with the Romans. His father is so ashamed both by losing his livelihood and of having a collaborator for a son that he drinks himself to death. Displeased by his family's ingratitude the son leaves, parlays his gold into other ventures and grows to be a rich man. As a wealthy merchant he travels the empire for many years, forgetting completely his lowly beginnings and even the town of his birth. One day the man unwittingly returns to the town and beholds the most beautiful women, three sisters, that he has ever laid eyes upon. He demands that each of the women marry him, raping and killing two for their refusal. Before she dies, the third sister warns that her estranged brother will avenge them. With her last breath she reveals his name – Melyn Boll, or 'yellowbelly' – and the man realises that the sisters he has raped and killed are his own.

That chorus again, and I realise it's not in my head but coming up the stairs. So she worked the gate out too then.

Yellow, yellow, yellowbelly . . .

There is one final verse and I read it over quickly before I go down. I find Lulah squatting on the kitchen counter, humming the same tune while she rifles through the top cupboard, jean shorts straining at her hips. Consciously or not I take the seat at the table with the best view.

'Now then!' Her back is to me and her head is buried in the cabinet, which makes hearing this Humber greeting from her even more disorientating. 'I geddit now,' she says, 'why yer bin poring ovver all them old stories, mekkin all them lists, collecting and comparing and what not. Tekkin trouble ter figure which type belongs with which. It's dead interesting.'

After all her characters in our role-play scenes I am surprised to hear this voice again. Now it is even more pronounced than before; true yellowbelly North Lincs, though I haven't touched her controls. 'See I reckoned people were just people, but all those songs and legends and reports and memories, well *apparently* there's all these different *types*. Especially types of lasses. Maid, May Queen, spinster, shrew, hysteric, domestic, charwoman, land girl, pattyslapper, biddy, bint, old bag. Sprite, succubus, sea-witch, cunning woman. Prude, fallen, loose, intact. *So* many words! "Vernacular", in't it? Words "of the vulgar tongue", like your book with the Long Ess.'

She closes the cupboard door and turns to face me.

'Vulgar, alright. Tsk! I found that word you call me most, the four-letter one beginning with the Long Ess.' She smiles and two dimples appear in her cheeks. 'Does it mean the same as "Laney", that other word yer call me? Yer say it in the same way.'

I start to get up from the chair and she holds out a palm.

'Settle, petal, am just jesting.'

Her feet hang off the counter and I notice that her soles are scuffed. 'Anyway, I din't know ote about it, my type that is, so I borried your computer and had a little neb. I found many like me. Often inside, often alone, submitting often. Some just lasses from old stories, some real but long dead, some right there on yer computer: the long list with all the colours.'

She brings her knees up to her chin. 'Looks like my type are keen to be bonded together, and then there are different words fer us. A gaggle, a coven, a waiting list, a refuge.'

She speaks brightly but her face now seems vacant of all the new expressions I've watched her develop since I opened the box a month ago. She begins humming, eyes closed, face to the Artex. The sound is lovely. It must be improvised; I don't know how she could know the tune, but she sings the short lines I just read upstairs, after Melyn Boll realises his terrible mistake.

> *'Dread, what's this that I have done?*
> *Profaned my sisters, all and one.'*
> *Then wielded he his own flint knife*
> *And ended he his infamed life.*

Lulah hops off the counter and walks towards the table. In one hand she is carrying a willow-patterned plate. Why is it you never see these plates in shops? Does every mum just get issued with a set? She sets it down and takes my hand, and then she brings her face in very close to mine. I expect the heat and smell of breath but there is nothing. Maybe she had it all along, or maybe she powered Obedience down to nil while she was on my laptop, but either way her strength is suddenly insane. My wrist is very close to snapping.

'Summatup, lovey? Eh, I reckon I have your folk type down an' all, if yer want ter know it? It's a very old type and a dead common story. Yonks ago it were like, kings and landowners and witchfinders and fact'ry bosses and law men, but it goes all the way through to just normal lads like yourself. Men from the same stock, men that should be brothers. So long as he has a little power over the lasses around him, dun't matter if that power is total and, like, "upper-class", or the mean petty snide type, the women get tret the same one way or another. Lotser stories in this subgroup have endings I din't understand. Endings s'posed ter finish off a story, but these had bad endings for the wrong characters. Were getting me right dowly, to be honest with yer, love. It were only today I finally heard a story with a different ending, and it has a dead nice tune an' all.'

Her eyes burn hot blue and she is no longer talking to me. ' "Profaned his sisters all and one." *ATU type 3031B: domineer, defiler, deficient son; dies by his own hand.*'

I only notice it now, a plastic cup of Robinsons Fruit & Barley on the table in front of me. Pink Drink. It has left a water ring on the top of a short letter I did not type or print. And on the plate placed next to it, heaped like mint imperials, are the rest of Mum's pills.

They always needed girls to work the machines. Her fingers are at my mouth, prising and then locking as she feeds me the first.

The Hanging Stones

JENN ASHWORTH

Jenn Ashworth's first novel, *A Kind of Intimacy*, was published in 2009 and won a Betty Trask Award. On the publication of her second, *Cold Light* (Sceptre, 2011), she was featured on the BBC's *The Culture Show* as one of the UK's twelve best new writers. In 2019 she published a memoir-in-essays, *Notes Made While Falling*, which was a *New Statesman* Book of the Year and was shortlisted for the Gordon Burn Prize. Her latest novel is *Ghosted: A Love Story* and her new memoir, *The Parallel Path*, is published by Sceptre in 2025. She is a fellow of the Royal Society of Literature, an honorary fellow of Newnham College, Cambridge University and a professor of writing at Lancaster University.

Little Fell House gave a poor welcome to its off-season, unofficial guests. It was a low-fronted farmhouse with small leaded windows and a steeply pitched tile roof. The Lancashire moorland in which the place hunkered was no better. Future guests who would find the place on TripAdvisor, book themselves in for a night or two and expect to enjoy cycling and bird watching in peaceful rural surrounds, would get nothing but rain, a view of the harvest remnant rotting in the fields and the stink of lame sheep cowering in dripping sheds.

'It's nice,' Catherine said.

She didn't stay away from home very often. She had pre-school children and had tried, very hard, not to allow herself to look at this single night away as a holiday.

'Hopefully it's watertight,' Rebecca said, pressing the button to lock her car even though there was nobody else anywhere near. 'Where's reception?'

'No staff. We have the place to ourselves. There's a

woman who'll come with the keys and let us in,' James said, checking the confirmation email on his phone.

They waited in the yard. The building looked tired rather than rustic; the render had been obviously patched and something springy and twiggy was growing from a crack on the side of the chimney stack. There was a 1960s extension at the back that had not been visible in the photographs James had sent to his older sisters when they'd agreed to come. He felt personally responsible for all of this. Not that he cared for himself: actually, he was happy to sleep anywhere and get the job done as quickly as possible. But, he was so often made fun of and distrusted that he'd hoped, just this once, to take the lead and impress.

'Leave it with me,' he'd said, once they'd decided to find somewhere in the countryside, 'I know a little hotel. It's not open to the public yet.' The estate agent he worked for had handled the last sale of the place: his connection to the new owners was tentative, but it had been enough.

Rebecca was peering through the windows with a look on her face that he knew well: she'd become used to better things.

'It's recently refurbished, you said?' she asked.

Their father had died earlier that year. The funeral, a barely attended affair at the local crematorium, was largely organised by the funeral directors. They had seen adult children like this before, damaged or ungrateful, and did not find their reluctance to take charge and make decisions about music and flowers remarkable.

A few days after the service, their father's ashes were ready: Catherine collected them and lived for some weeks with the tin on the top of her fridge, which is where she kept all the things she didn't want her children to get into. Their father sat up there with the attachments to the handheld vacuum cleaner and a Tupperware box full of Calpol, plasters and antihistamine tablets. Eventually, she convened her siblings on Zoom.

'We have to do something with them,' Catherine said. 'It's not fair they're left with me.'

Rebecca's nose twitched. *It's not fair.* The refrain of Catherine's entire childhood and at thirty she was still singing it. Always someone else to blame, always something she could whine about while awaiting rescue.

'What ideas do you have?' Rebecca asked sharply. 'Or do you just want us to sort it out?'

It was James, the charmer, the peacemaker, who suggested they do it on the moors. He knew of a house they could have. He talked the place up a bit: it was where their father had grown up, out in the east of the county.

'Fine. We could go around in circles talking about this for months and not get anywhere,' Rebecca said. 'Let's get it sorted. Give ourselves a fresh start.'

'We need to do it properly,' Catherine said. 'We'll feel better if it's done right.'

The other two agreed, without knowing exactly what, in this context, 'properly' might mean. But Catherine had articulated something they all secretly felt: that completing this final duty would release them from the heaviness that had settled on them, that sense of belonging to their father that they had not yet been able to shed.

Catherine had married young, divorced a year later, and kept the name of a man she hadn't seen in three years. In Rebecca's profession, women didn't change their last names – but she had, and pretended to the other doctors, who teased her a little, that her old-fashioned decision was a concession to her husband's family. James would remain a Stanley until he died, but he'd decided in his twenties there'd be no more Stanleys after him.

The three siblings arrived at Little Fell House with a sense of exhausted duty and a shared hope that relinquishing their father to the damp moors where his ancestors had toiled would provide them with some release not from their grief, but from the time they had spent on earth as Peter Stanley's children. Or in other words, that taking him home would finally allow them to leave it.

The woman whose job it was to let them in arrived on a muddy quad bike with a black-and-white dog with light-coloured eyes that followed at her heel as she strode across the yard, retrieving the keys from the pocket of a raincoat. Rebecca could smell her: animal sheds and sweat and manure and unwashed hair and cigarette smoke and, improbably, a thick musty perfume. Evidently not a housekeeper, and not likely to lay a fire for them or welcome them with a complimentary coffee or know anything about the best place to buy some local cheese.

'Welcome to witch country. Lock up at night or not, suit yourself,' the woman said, as she unlocked the door.

'My farm's over there,' she gestured vaguely towards the low fells at the neck of the valley the house squatted in. A neighbour, then. 'Wood for the fire is out back, in the store. Go through the door behind the bar.'

She let them in. The place looked exactly like the thing it was trying to be: a newly refurbished pub with aspirations. The carpets on the main staircase were new, the small kitchen had been redone in stainless steel and there was a bar with an empty till that had not been plugged in yet. The wallpaper was fancy: greenish and thick with birds and flowers. Someone had hung framed maps of the old county palatine on the walls and there was a coat rack made from deer antlers.

'Any more of you expected?' she asked.

Catherine wanted to be very friendly in case this woman thought they were above themselves. She introduced herself and her siblings and made it clear that none of them had come far.

'My father's family lived around here,' she said. 'His grandmother was a weaver.'

This could have been true, though the stories he'd told his children about his past were vague and often contradictory. Rebecca said that was the drinking: it had cleared out the places in his brain where his past had been kept.

Still, if he'd been right, the three of them belonged here, sort of.

'Was she now,' the woman said, without interest. 'You won't find any weavers around here anymore. They've put a call centre into the old mill up by.'

Catherine wasn't sure if she should tut at this, or praise the area for its ability to evolve, and compliment the forward-thinking attitude of the local property-owners. Instead, what she communicated was a kind of frantic, servile condescension. The woman waited for Catherine to stop babbling, before she introduced herself, putting out her hand.

'I'm Jennet,' she said, obviously amused.

Rebecca put Catherine out of her misery. 'There's just the three of us, thank you.'

'You know there's no staff? You'll be catering for yourselves? You'll probably have to make up your own beds, too. I've no idea how many rooms there are.'

Jennet might have been thirty or fifty; she was strong and unkempt, her face lined with age or by the weather.

'I brought a lasagne,' Catherine said, then blushed.

Rebecca, tired of this, held out her hand for the keys.

'Will we drop them off with you when we leave,' she said, 'to where you live? Over ... there?' she gestured, imitating Jennet in a way the woman clocked immediately. It did not offend her. She only bent to scratch the dog's head and smiled.

'You can leave them in the pot by the front door. When you're ready. I'll come and get them when *I'm* ready.'

'It will be tomorrow,' James said. He smiled, flashing his teeth and turning on the charm. It never failed: women eased in and out of his bed in response to that smile, and strangers bought whole houses they couldn't quite afford, just to please him. Jennet seemed immune and only sniffed.

'I'll let you get on then. Maps in the snug, if you're planning on walking. Don't get lost, eh?'

She left the front door open. James and Rebecca both rolled their eyes. Catherine couldn't bear this, her siblings' newfound snobbery.

Catherine left them and went to get their tea out of the boot of her car. She carried the still-warm casserole dish through the little bar and restaurant area – the new tables shiny and bare, everything smelling of plastic and polish – and into the kitchen. It was as clean as an operating theatre, had clearly never been cooked in, and there was a double oven with an electronic operating panel as complex as anything she'd seen. She'd brought the urn in with the lasagne and now she placed them both on the stainless-steel counter. She couldn't take it back home again. She had a vision of emptying its contents out onto a grassy verge, the three of them parked up in a layby, and before she could smile, bit her lip. He'd be furious. Rebecca fetched wood and laid the fire in the little snug room, telling them she had wood burners (plural) in her own house and knew what she was doing. James sniggered at this, then went to figure out the cooker and heat up the lasagne. There was a bookshelf in the snug, full of hardbacks on local history, with black-and-white plates featuring Bronze Age burial urns and bog bodies.

'You remember when we saw one of those,' Rebecca said, looking through the books. Catherine, knowing she was about to be made fun of, because she did remember, pretended not to hear while she looked for the maps. She'd only been a child, and had cried about the strange, desiccated thing kept behind glass in the museum. It had looked like a damp piece of clothing dropped in the garden on its way to the washing line and dried out stiff in the sun. But it had been a person. Or part of a person, cut in half and exposed as the peat was dug and now presented behind glass as a local artefact, its leathery flesh the colour of wet teabags.

'I just didn't know people could be so *horrible*,' Catherine said quietly.

Rebecca laughed at her, quite meanly. But it was good, really, that they'd had their father cremated. She knew about bodies, about what happened at the undertaker's before a burial. Once, she had been allowed to observe the post-mortem of a man who had been exhumed six weeks after he'd been buried when the police belatedly began to suspect his son had poisoned him. The pathologist had opened up the chest with a scalpel and the flesh had been brittle and yellowish, like salted cod. She'd been surprised at how intact the body had been, and how easy it was to find the traces of poison. Rebecca, not yet twenty, had vowed to make sure that when her time came she'd be cremated, and had later been relieved when her preference had turned out to be the cheapest and least fuss for her father too.

James came back from the kitchen with a tea towel over his shoulder. He took the map Catherine had found, shook it open and inspected it. 'We could drive down here,' he pointed, 'walk across this access land? And,' he tapped a spot on the map, 'there's a hill. Some stones on the top. Not far. It will be nice.'

Rebecca examined the map. 'Hanging Stones?'

'All the places round here have weird names,' James said.

Rebecca shrugged and turned again to the fire, and Catherine took herself away to find the sheets.

There were three small bedrooms upstairs, and three more, much larger, and a kind of function room in the 1960s extension. The refurb had not made it as far as the extension: the walls were painted magnolia, the ceilings swirled in Artex, the windows made of textured glass reinforced with wire, as if whoever had designed the place was expecting its guests to try hammering their way out. In the centre of the function room there were plastic chairs gathered in a circle and, against one wall, cardboard boxes full of fresh, unused bed linen.

Catherine opened some of the other boxes to find brand-new cutlery, stacks and stacks of white dinner plates and soup bowls, light bulbs, and wooden trays full of long, pale candles. She took a few candles and counted out sheets.

There were posters on the walls. Signs, really, that had been done up on someone's home printer. The slogans were either trite or nonsensical:

LET GO AND LET GOD.
THE SOLUTION IS NOT IN THE PROBLEM.
KEEP IT SIMPLE, STUPID

and, most curiously of all,

GO TO THE BARBER'S OFTEN ENOUGH AND YOU'LL END UP GETTING A HAIRCUT.

So, this had been a rehab, then. People would come, perhaps delivered unwillingly by their families, or ferried in patient-transport ambulances. She imagined them traipsing across the yard, trembling and sick, the worst of them already turning yellow, like walking bog bodies. Had James known what sort of house this used to be? Was it some kind of joke? She imagined their father being part of the circle and sitting in one of these chairs, clear-eyed and sorry, drinking tea harmlessly and quite transformed by whatever mysterious process forty days and forty nights in a clinic like this would involve. She wiped her eyes.

For a long time, she had tried to cheer her father up. Even when she was quite small, she'd gone to the dressing-up box when he was due home from work and made herself into a fairy princess to greet him. The other two had made fun of her for that. But she remembered spinning and twirling so that her hair flew out around her, the feel of the rustling skirts against her legs, and swiping the little plastic wand through the air as she waited for the sound of his key in the front door. It wasn't wrong to want to make someone happy, was it? Wasn't her fault, either, that it had never worked. He was always tired when he got home, easily irritated, and in need of his chair, and the telly, and the cans that even back then her mother would bring in from the kitchen for him. His life tired him out, their mother said. Catherine, young, had taken that to mean Rebecca and James, who'd been born first and fought a lot and always needed new shoes. They had tired him out and Catherine had never been able to cheer him up. Now all the chairs were empty and the men and women that had sat in them were long gone, returned either to their changed lives or their old habits. She went back to her task and wondered if taking the candles counted as stealing. Sheets were one thing – but the candles couldn't be returned to the box once they'd been lit.

They ate in the snug, the candles and sputtering fire making the place seem homelier than it was. The fridges were empty, but James stood behind the bar, gesturing towards the empty spaces, pantomiming.

'What will you be having this evening, ladies?' he asked, trying to gee them along with the box of wine and little cans of gin and tonic he'd brought. He carried the glasses over. The food was good. The girls were behaving. But Catherine wasn't eating, too busy telling Rebecca about some room she'd found out the back. In his mind he did an impression of her, fussing and squeaking. *What if the people who used to live here – who had been kept here – turned up again, in the night?* She was fretful and fussy, just like their mother. She should have moved away, like he and Rebecca had.

'You told us it was a farmhouse,' Catherine said.

'It was. But no farmer makes money around here. So, then it became a rehab,' he said. 'For about ten years. But that didn't make any money either, so the owners sold up and took their equity to Thailand and bought a big hotel there. Right on the beach. They're setting it up as some kind of wellness retreat. Spas and yoga and green smoothies in the morning. That sort of thing.'

This was the kind of enterprising behaviour James approved of. Everything was an opportunity. Another few years, he thought, admiring the newly plastered ceiling in the snug, and he'd be buying into a little business like this himself. Something local. Just to start off. He liked the taste of the word *equity* in his mouth.

'A funny place for a rehab,' Catherine said. The dark had come and pressed itself against the little windows as they ate.

'All this fresh air and rolling green pastureland?' James said. 'It'd cure anyone.'

'It's good there's nowhere to go,' Rebecca said. 'Nobody running to the off-licence in the middle of the night. You're well away from temptation in a place like this.'

'They could go out on walks,' James said. 'It wasn't run like a prison. There were a couple of horses for them to look after and take out on rides, if they wanted.'

'That sounds nice,' Catherine said, in her choked little voice.

James topped up his glass. That was the sort of thing she always said. Things were either *nice* or *horrible*, and if they were *horrible*, they weren't worth mentioning. This meant it was impossible to know what Catherine really thought about anything, which in the end, made her a lot more irritating than Rebecca, who always assumed you needed to know precisely what she thought, and would be greatly improved by hearing it.

'A lot of the people here came on local authority funding and when that dried up . . .' he shrugged. No point explaining business to her. He glanced at Rebecca hoping for some support. She looked better than she had earlier, her face less pinched, her demeanour less harassed. She'd changed from the officey clothes she wore to see her patients to jeans and a jumper and looked rosy in the firelight. The gin suited her.

'We should talk about how we're going to handle things tomorrow,' she said.

'Raincoats on. Drive into the village. Bit of a walk. Then,' James mimed shaking a salt cellar. 'No messing about. Job done.'

'Isn't somebody going to say something?' Rebecca said. 'We can't just tip him out onto a cow field.'

'We've had the funeral already,' James said. 'I'm not doing another eulogy.'

'I'd hardly call *that* a eulogy,' Rebecca said, but he didn't bite.

'Maybe I could read a poem?' Catherine said, desperately. She looked towards the little bookshelf. 'There's bound to be a book of poems somewhere.'

'You could *write* something,' James said. 'That would be *nice*, wouldn't it?'

'James,' Rebecca warned. It was so easy to take it too far with Catherine. And when they were in high spirits together, they liked to take it in turns; one to make her cry, and the other to stop it. Now it was her turn to be big sister. 'It was a good idea.'

'I'm just saying we should plan,' Catherine said. 'It'll be dark by late afternoon, and we want to be away before that Jennet woman comes back for the keys.'

They cleared the table and shook out the map again. James got out his phone to double-check the directions and discovered that these Hanging Stones – according to some – were nothing more sinister than old geology marking the dead centre of the old kingdom. Nothing had been hung from or on them other than the spinning axis of the country itself, in the imaginations of the folk who had populated these moors and valleys. He shared this fact with his sisters, pleased with himself.

'The perfect place. Dad did always think the entire world revolved around him,' James said.

'He was sick, James,' Rebecca said sharply. 'It's a disease.'

'Shh,' Catherine said. She'd only had two drinks, but she pulled that baby-girl face that got her what she wanted, and reliably enraged James.

'Remember that time he went into Manchester to get Christmas presents for us all and came back with a supermarket trolley with three bikes in it?' Catherine said.

James didn't answer but leaned into the fire and attacked it furiously with the poker. The glowing logs fell apart into cinders and he threw on fresh wood, trying to get it going again.

'You'll put it out,' Rebecca said calmly.

'I know what I'm doing,' James replied. 'I might not have a wood burner in the house but . . .' he paused as he realised he'd smothered the fire. Smoke unfurled into the room. James wafted at it and knocked over a glass, which smashed on the stone-flagged floor. He looked up from the fragments to see Catherine and Rebecca had gone pale, both of them frozen.

Their father dead for six months and all of them adults, own houses, own cars, proper jobs, and *still* the memory of him whirling through the back kitchen like a poltergeist haunted them, every dish in the place a victim-in-waiting to his rage. Something had got hold of their father in the eighties – some old injustice to do with a job he'd done where he'd not been paid properly, taken for a ride, humiliated, really, and he'd never been able to get past it. It would come out at night, and because the men who'd got one over on him were long gone he'd throw dishes instead, then pass out on the sofa, a cigarette burning between two fingers, smouldering. The sofa cushions were speckled with burn marks; their mother would buy throws to cover them, sometimes even entirely new covers, telling him when he complained about the cost that it was nice to change the colours in the living room now and again, draping the fleecy material over everything, so he'd never need to look at what he'd done. Then their mother died, and Catherine took charge of buying the throws.

'It's fine, it's fine. It's just a glass. They won't charge us,' James said.

He knelt and started picking up the glass while, trembling, Rebecca went outside.

There was an automatic light near the front door that switched on and illuminated the wet yard. She stepped out of the reach of its sensor and let it switch itself back off. She'd taken James's coat from the rack in the hall without thinking and turned up a packet of cigarettes in one of the pockets. She shook it open, lit one, inhaled.

It had been years. Not once during those last days driving up and down the M6 after work every day to see her father in the hospice and translating what the nurses were gently telling her siblings into something harder, more direct, something that neither Catherine nor James could bat away or ignore. *Of course* he wasn't going to come home and have one last Christmas with them all. Of course not. He was *dying*. They'd listened to her because she was a doctor, though not her father's doctor. She had not smoked then, and not at the funeral, because of course Catherine's rugrats were there and what kind of example would that set. But she did now and blew out great plumes into the chilly, mothless dark. She could see through the little window into the snug, where Catherine was remonstrating with James about something. Catherine kept wiping her eyes, as if to draw attention to the fact that she was crying, but there were no tears.

James took a sudden step towards her, but the low table was between them and it wasn't Catherine he was heading towards, but the map. He flattened it out with both hands and, exasperated, pointed at some spot. This was why they avoided each other. It never took long before they started bickering, each of them as bad as the other. Rebecca didn't like the version of herself she was when she was with her family: brittle and supercilious, nothing ever quite good enough, everyone just a shade less than acceptable – as if some great injustice had been done to her, and her life, more charmed than either of her siblings', was a great injury to her.

She threw her cigarette, which was making her feel sick, into the hawthorn hedge and went through a side door into the function room that Catherine had discovered in the annex. It was Catherine who'd gone into their father's flat to sort out the sick room once he had left for the hospice, and it was Catherine that had phoned Rebecca to tell her she'd found the slim little glass bottles tucked down the side of the bed. He must have been hobbling out to buy it, right up until the end, when he died out of his mind on morphine and withdrawal, convinced his mother was calling him in from the moor.

Rebecca switched on the overhead strip light in the function room and surveyed what she saw. Counted a coven's worth of chairs, then slowly, without anger, took all the signs down off the walls. They'd been stuck up there so long that the paint came off with the Blu-tack, and when she was done the wall was speckled with marks. She pushed the posters behind the box that had the bed linen in it.

They went to bed, leaving the dishes for the morning. James lay on his back, flipping through photos on his phone without seeing them. He should make notes because Catherine and Rebecca were going to ask him to say something tomorrow, he could tell. He tried to remember the name of the village his father said his people had come from. Had his grandmother worked at the loom? Perhaps not his mother, but aunts or cousins. Someone who'd lost a hand in the machine, someone else who coughed herself to death after the fibres chewed up her lungs, most of them losing their eyesight before they were fifty.

James had told this truncated, possibly made-up part of his father's life at the real funeral to the disinterested audience of his sisters and the Co-op pallbearers. It was a cover story, sung first by those weaver, witch-country women who had urged the strong, blond-haired boy they'd all been so proud of to move away and do something else, because even back in the sixties they could see the mills were on their way out. Peter Stanley had gone to Preston and cleaned trains, portered in hospitals and hotel kitchens, spent a decade doing nights in a sandwich factory, saved a couple of thousand to go in on a smallholding, a dairy farm, something like that. He had imagined this little investment in someone else's bit of land would get him outside again, back in sight of the moors. He'd worked clearing rubble from old buildings he thought he part-owned. Was under the impression he was helping to renovate his own milking sheds. Rebecca had raised an eyebrow from the front row, and James had stopped. Left it there.

He'd had to go back to cleaning the trains at night, stopping off at Wetherspoons in the morning and bringing home the odd umbrella or handbag or lightly used lipstick he'd found on the train for his wife, who didn't often get things like that. Tomorrow, when it was just the three of them, perhaps James could tell the other part of the story. About the humiliations that had bookended his father's life: first, being told to leave the moor for better things and making it no further than Preston, then unable to get back home, swindled by idiots. If he could work it out, James could make sure the three of them were facing the right direction as they scattered their father. Was it Barley or Sabden where his mother had raised him? As far out as Read?

He got up and went into the kitchen for a glass of water, saw the urn, popped the lid and had a look. Grey sawdust and cat litter. Nothing special. He took his glass and wandered through to the function room. The heating wasn't working there, and he shivered in his T-shirt and boxers as he surveyed the place where the poor wrecks had gathered. There was no way to understand how they got better; this transformation that occurred as they confessed the worst things they'd ever done to each other and – what – released their demons into the bracken?

James had no memories of his childhood. He laughed along when his sisters remembered theirs and pretended to enjoy hearing Catherine's tall tales of shopping trolleys full of bicycles arriving just in time on Christmas Eve. But even if it wasn't wishful thinking that made Catherine concoct her happy little tales and those things had really happened, the truth was, his own very earliest recollection was of Rebecca leaving for university when he was twelve. She'd been wearing a blue velvet scrunchie in her hair, stiff and pale and waiting for the pat on the head from her father that would never come. The rest of his childhood was an empty spot behind his left shoulder, or something hunched that flickered at the corner of his eye now and again. He knew that couldn't be right. Knew it wasn't normal. But there it was. He tried to imagine what it might have been like if his father had been able to come to a place like this, lay hands on what had possessed him and cast it out onto the moorland. He was still a little drunk, knew he'd be hungover in the morning and went back to the kitchen to refill his glass.

Rebecca's car was the biggest, but James's was the flashiest and the next morning he insisted on taking the wheel and driving them to the village, where there was a little shop selling walking books and ice-cream and souvenirs. The shop had a dummy dressed up like a witch with a pointy hat standing outside, its nylon hair sticky with rainwater, a sign saying it was alright to have your photograph taken with it, but not to touch it.

    Rebecca flicked through the postcards and bought a box of fudge in the shape of a black cat because supporting a local business was a decent thing to do. James stood next to the dummy, putting one arm around her shoulders, dangling his hand over the place where her breast would be. He called her Granny and made Catherine take a picture of him. Catherine, entertained, took the picture and they were laughing like teenagers when Rebecca emerged, fudge in a paper bag.

They walked.

'It was funny what that woman called it,' Catherine said, 'do you remember? Witch country?' She had on a cheap anorak, and she shivered.

'They shouldn't call them that,' Rebecca said, because Catherine, who once had an aromatherapy phase, was credulous. 'They were women who got strung up because nobody knew any better. And now they use it to attract the tourists.'

She was suddenly angry, bored by the walk, which led softly through a rickety gate, the wood wet and spongy under her hands, and followed a path up a gentle hill through the long grass and bracken. She went on: there was no peculiar haunting clinging to the outbuildings and nothing hunching in the gorse except damp. The land was barely fertile, almost sick, the villages hardly populated, the weather relentless. What animals there were rotted while they lived, devoured by fly strike. The children coughed, scratched, got fevers and went soft-headed. What little there was, the farming folk fought over, and as they fought, they turned on the women who, short of any other way to make a living, tried to con them out of beer and eggs by pretending that the devil had taught them how to make the cow give milk and clear up the impetigo on the baby.

'Sick places need sick stories,' Rebecca said. Now there was such a thing as penicillin and minimum wage and the internet, so no need for spells and curses. That's all there was to it, and anything else was exaggeration because there was no such thing as the devil. It was quite a speech. James pulled a face.

'Thanks for that, sis,' he said. 'I think it's up this way.'

In a few weeks, the frost would harden up the rain-sodden fields, kill the scum growing in the ditches and water troughs and cover the place in a glittering white that would make it almost attractive. It would never look like a Christmas card around here, not even in deep snow, but December would improve the place. Now though, the ground was wet and boggy, the standing water in the tractor ruts clotted with green foam that looked like phlegm, the ground's lungs infected.

They slowly crossed the access land. James wore expensive trainers and every few steps looked down at the state of them and tried to wipe their edges on the grass. After an hour, they reached the top of the hill and found the place where the Hanging Stones were: smooth protuberances from the ground, squat, and almost liquid-looking – as if someone had dropped something heavy and grey and viscous into the hill and watched as it set.

James pulled out the urn from his rucksack. If he was going to say something, as the only son, now would be the time, but instead the three of them looked at what was around them: moorland and fields, mainly given over to grouse now. Their gazing was a request, and the valleys sent them away empty-handed, and they shivered, not getting what they and countless others had asked of this place: refuge or nourishment or some kind of healing, or even the answer to the riddle of who they were and why they did what they did. They could jettison their father here and release him back into the moors. Then they could go, inheriting nothing but a vague connection to a place that was indifferent to them, as indifferent as their own father had been. James looked at his sisters. Catherine pulled herself up straight, tucked her hands into her pockets. Rebecca wouldn't look at him. Had they all spent too long in the barber's chair and ended up getting their hair cut? He laughed at this and pulled off the lid and tipped the contents onto the ground near his feet. Perhaps the three of them had expected a breeze to blow it all away, but the sediment was rough and heavy and the air still and sticky with a gathering mist.

'It's hardly something to laugh about,' Rebecca said. Always criticising.

'Let's not fight,' Catherine simpered, after a moment of silence. 'It's getting colder.'

The path they had come up had melted into the fog, and they circled the rough ground, looking for it. Even the place where they'd emptied the urn, where the ash had been clumped on the bracken, had disappeared.

'We're a couple of miles from the village. We should be able to see it. This is fucking ridiculous,' he said. Both of his sisters flinched; he was being too loud, he knew, but they were going to blame him. It had been his idea to come here. He'd pointed out the place on the map. And now – the phrase that came to him was old, or very young, depending on your perspective – now he was going to *be in trouble*.

Catherine patted at his arm. 'Shh,' she said, 'getting angry won't help.' Now she was handling him, like she'd handled their father, like she handled Rebecca sometimes too.

But Catherine was remembering the Jennet woman, who had laughed at them and told them not to get lost, and a sudden paranoid thought consumed her – that this woman had wanted them to get lost, had, in some way she was suddenly certain of but could not describe, *made* them get lost. She thought of the dummy in the silly pointy hat. She was about to voice some of this to James, who, shouting again, furious with panic at the mist that had descended, turned and slapped her. She didn't feel the blow, not until she was lying in the wet grass, holding a hand to her face and tasting blood on her teeth.

'James! What the fuck are you playing at?'

That was Rebecca, who seemed to think her schoolteacher voice would take charge of the situation. She'd carried on walking around the stones looking for the start of the path and somehow, though she had not overtaken them, met her siblings face on, as if approaching them from a long way off. It shouldn't have been possible. This silly weather was disorienting them. Catherine was wailing and James was looking at his hand, as if it didn't belong to him. This was a familiar tableau, and Rebecca started laughing, or rather, the laugh took hold of her body and wouldn't let go, and she heard herself, retching and cackling into the quietness of the afternoon.

'Do you like what that feels like?' she said, rounding on James and grabbing a handful of his hair. She pulled it back and forth, shaking him like a doll. It was a question for herself too. To let her body know this – to become her father in this last, most important way. *Did she like what it felt like?* Her brother was taller and bigger, but still, he did not resist her, and in a moment was on his knees as she stood over him. Whatever had gripped her ebbed away and she let go of him, only to turn and see Catherine, her eyes as round as moons, shaking violently as she watched them. The planet they all orbited was gone now.

There was nothing else for it but to wait for the fog to lift, then they'd be able to see their way back to the car. It was stupid to blunder around. Someone might break an ankle. They waited, surveying the misty view. This was the last time they'd all be together, and they would never speak about it again. James would end his days in less than a year, felled outside a Manchester nightclub by one unlucky punch from a friend whose wife he'd been sleeping with. Rebecca would take up drinking, in secret, and eighteen years from now would lose control of her car on the way home from work and smash it and herself into a tree on a tight bend. Her husband would never tell her sons she'd been drunk behind the wheel. Catherine

The Hanging Stones

would last the longest, living until the time when the valleys around the Hanging Stones would be entirely underwater, and die quietly, her daughter holding her hand, in one of the new brownfield care homes that had not been built yet.

The Keepers

NATASHA CARTHEW

Natasha Carthew is a Cornish working-class writer. She is published by Hodder, Bloomsbury, Quercus and the National Trust. Her latest book with Hodder, *Undercurrent: A Cornish Memoir of Poverty, Nature and Resilience*, was shortlisted for the Nero Book Awards 2023.

She is known for writing on socioeconomic issues in publishing for several publications, podcasts and programmes, including ITV, the Society of Authors journal, BBC Radio 3 and 4, the *Bookseller*, *Guardian*, *Observer*, *Mslexia*, *Writers' & Artists' Yearbook*, ALCS, the *Big Issue* and the *Economist*.

Natasha is founder/director of the Working Class Writers Festival and has collaborated with many organisations including the Booker Prize and the Women's Prize, and guest edited the first working-class edition of the *Bookseller* in 2022.

Braced within the bow of the small fishing boat the young woman rubbed her head to try to relieve the hangover she had yet to shed and she wrapped her arms around her shoulders and told herself to forget about the treacherous ocean, keep her eyes on the darkening horizon instead. Out there somewhere, yet to filter its brilliance through the cold mizzle rain was the lighthouse, a building that despite its small stature, had towered like a thunderous storm cloud throughout her childhood.

Back at the dingy harbourside B&B all she'd had for company was the wretched ocean. For five damn days straight she'd had to endure the constant beat of it, blue in the morning, black in the evening, and every bad breath of it observed from her bedroom window. Meanwhile downstairs in the bar the local fishermen, what was left of them anyway, drank the afternoons down to a bar-punching puddle. The background cacophony had suited Ruvanes, both the raucous laughter and the troubled silences that fell between filled the four walls of her tiny room perfectly as she sat and drank alone. She knew the cause of the men's misery of course she did, fish stocks were at an all-time low, whilst the relentless winter storm had hammered the ultimate nail into the coffin of their trade. Everyone in Cornwall knew that the main culprit was the stern trawlers, the floating factories that had pretty much wiped the sea clean of its stock, Ru had even written an article about it in the national newspaper, the one she was close to being sacked from because of her hedonistic meandering.

The thought of work and city life transferred to this place made her feel uneasy, it was a strange sensation that merged with the image of Keepers Island and its beacon, out there somewhere, silently watching. The lighthouse was a childhood monster, a beast only glanced at the corner of your eye, it was a pillar never quite noticed except for the storms it conjured, pulling at nature's softest edges and turning them into tempests that came in fast and took things from their mainland village. There were many times when the storms arrived seemingly from nowhere in order to steal a boat from off the beach, and Ru recalled one time when a hurricane had taken a huge bite out of the coastal path. If she closed her eyes she could still remember the teeth marks, the way they dragged in vertical lines down deep into the sea, earth eaten. Local fishermen swore that the lighthouse and Keepers Island was under some kind of possession, an ancient curse that eddied at its watery roots and made it emanate evil, they even sang a shanty about it:

The Keepers

calm sou'west
always best
keep the island to your right side
cus on the left
is where the storm builds fast
and fore you bout turn
Bucca's storm will pull you down

Even now at the age of thirty-three the bullying beacon of Bucca's lighthouse pushed its way into her dreams, it voided her of voice or clear thought and twisted them into nightmares, but despite this, Ru had had to return, she had to write this one last story that she hoped would save her career by gaining access to the island and the secretive community that lived there.

Throughout her childhood the lighthouse and the ocean had made her fear for her life, the sea had even tried to drown her once. Growing up the villagers used to say that you only got to see the lighthouse when you weren't looking for it, like somehow it worked in strange opposition to what it was meant, but as a kid Ru always noticed at least some part of it, the spiralling white-washed bricks or the glare of the lantern on a summer's day, even when the light was switched off. It was the same for her mother Ro, the warm days when they'd be down on the beach playing in the soft silver sand, or splashing way out in the rockpools when suddenly they'd see it, their shared secret thing.

You remember, my beautiful daughter

That was how it was that late summer afternoon when

they had gone for a swim that meant her mother was taken for good, the flat-calm ocean that without warning built a sandbar across the bay and filled the basin with rising bubble-bath currents, the distant lighthouse flashing sudden filament fire through the dazzling daylight, almost as if it was laughing, storm warning.

You remember me?

Ru shook her head and looked down at her hands in order to rinse the mizzle from her woollen gloves. By returning to the furthest south-western peninsula of Cornwall she knew she was stepping towards a path that would hopefully lead to the truth in regards to what happened to her mother, a visit only made possible because of the invite she received from the notoriously secretive inhabitants of the island.

Ru still didn't quite know why they had written to her, perhaps it was just that she was a girl who had grown up there, a girl who wrote articles for a living, articles that strived to tell the truth, nobody had ever been allowed access to the island and the privilege both scared and excited her.

This was her first homecoming in many years, spurred on because the invite didn't just mean she might be able to save her career with a brilliant article, but gifted her the chance to step onto the beach where rumour had it her mum's body would have likely washed up. Truth was nobody knew for sure what had happened to her, there was no body to carry home and there was a part of Ru that dreamed perhaps her mother was still alive, living beneath the shadow of the lighthouse on Keepers Island.

She looked back at the fisherman who had agreed to bring her as far as the jetty rocks and smiled, grateful that he wasn't one for grilling, just concern.

'Not long now my love,' he shouted when she caught his eye, 'just if you're wonderin'.'

She wasn't and she returned to looking out to sea. Despite the icy rain it was a good flat night. The air tasted sweet like gorse honey and the temperature balanced precariously between cold and freezing, the kind of winter's night that laid itself bare of wonder, no stars or moon to distract, just infinite black, dangerous perhaps, but to Ru it was perfect.

'You won't see it until we're upon it,' the fisherman continued, 'it'll probably just jump out on us.'

'I'll see it,' Ru shouted, pulling out a cigarette, and she added that she was from here, that she knew the lighthouse and all its tricks.

The fisherman nodded, his name was Jowan and she remembered him from childhood, how he used to hang round the harbour wall with some of the other men, drinking Newquay Steam and shouting at the tourists. She was glad he didn't recognise her, if he had he would have started with the questions about her mum's drowning.

Bucca

'If you're from roundabouts you'll know the story,' he said to Ru, 'the legend and all that.'

Ru nodded and wondered if he'd read her mind, of course she knew.

'That lighthouse int nothin' but trouble,' he continued. 'I reckon it sinks more ships than saves 'em, and now some rumour's goin' round that the island's gonna be developed into a rich holiday resort or somethin', good luck to 'em.'

Ru kept her mouth shut.

'You hear about that? All signed and sealed as far as I heard, although I don't know how they managed it cus 'em keepers don't mix do 'em.'

She shook her head, despite it being the reason she'd swapped her life in London a week ago for this jolt into her past. Truth was if she hadn't thought to write this piece it wouldn't be long until she lost her job, then the lease on her flat.

'Tell you what,' he continued, ''em keepers int gonna be happy, you ask 'em when you're over there.'

'I will.'

'So they know you're comin'?'

'They know, they invited me.'

'The keepers invited you?'

Ru nodded.

'Bloody keepers,' he laughed, 'they got lucky is all.'

'How's that?' asked Ru.

'Descendants of the original keepers they is, the only lighthouse in Cornwall to still be worked manually, won't let anyone argue otherwise.'

Ru moved closer, 'So do they own the island or not?'

The Keepers

The fisherman shrugged, 'Maybe, maybe not.'

'I was told it was owned by Duchy.'

'Duchy,' he started to laugh, ''em lot think they own the whole of Kernow, but legend has it the keepers were gifted it, by 'em pirates or descendants of, they're the keepers of ancient spirits, but who really knows the truth?'

Bucca Boo does

Ru ignored the hairs that had started to scratch at the back of her neck and she reached into her backpack until she found what she was looking for, the small pewter hipflask that she carried everywhere. Carefully she twisted off the tiny cap so as not to spill a drop, taking a quick swig to soften the edges, before slipping it back into the pocket next to her laptop and notebooks. She checked her phone to see if there were any messages from Thomas, the bloke at Duchy Coastal Properties she had contacted and arranged to join her on the island tomorrow so she could get a balanced story alongside the keepers'. There was just one problem, because of the continued storm, time had moved on, she was meant to visit the island a week ago, before the forced purchase went through, but now she had been told that the inhabitants' eviction was imminent.

'You know you won't get no signal over there don't you?' said Jowan, looking over her shoulder.

Ru was quick to put the phone back into her bag, 'I'm not stupid,' she said. Truth was the comforting light made her feel like she was back in the real world, not floating out on the eerie, infinite signal-less ocean.

'No electricity either,' he continued and Ru could only smile at the silly city girl that she had become. She returned her gaze towards the horizon too, her eyes sunk deep into darkness whilst her ears filled with the colourful lapping of the tide against the hull of the boat.

'You dint believe in 'em then, growin' up?' asked Jowen suddenly, 'Bucca Boo I mean.'

'No,' said Ru flatly, it was the truth.

'Bucca Boo gonna get YOU!'

'No,' said Ru, 'never.'

'Sea creature, water spirit, whatever they wanna call 'em,' he started to laugh, 'me neither, but you int gonna get me visitin' that island just in case.'

When her mother first went missing at sea every kid in their tiny village said it was at the hand of Bucca Boo, and there were many times growing up that Ru had heard her foster parents talk about it with others on their council estate. To the young Ruvanes Bucca was a stupid story about a vengeful merman made up in order to scare disobedient children into doing what they were told, but she never believed it. Ru was all about the truth, it was why she had become a journalist, why she wanted, needed to tell the truth. Her friends and colleagues often joked that she'd run after a story no matter the cost, but this one was different, she was supposedly home after all. Fact was after her mother disappeared the coastal village never felt like home. Ro had been an orphan too, and Ru had never met her father, probably just a passing shag at some lonely New Year's Eve party, she was born early autumn after all. At eight years old her foster family didn't feel like kin either, they were just strangers that fed her, looked after her, but they never talked to her, never asked what it was like to lose the only person that meant anything to her in the entire world. Things were made worse because Ru Carne's mother didn't die in the same way folk did on the TV; like in *EastEnders* and *Corrie*, the shows that always seemed to be on in the corner of the front room, or *The Archers* that blasted from the kitchen radio – there was no funeral to remember her by or a gravestone for the young Ru to visit, and there were times when she wondered if she had died at all. Reminiscence appeared purely as words caught and lost on the wayward wind or in the lapping waves that slid into consciousness, it was a beautiful trusted thing that sounded like her mother's voice, breathing in, then fading away.

Ru's grief was always the most deafening at the coast, but in recent years she knew she would never be able to find the answers she needed by staying away, or by numbing her pain with alcohol and cheap recreational drugs.

Looking back Ru realised her foster parents had tried to do their best, early on in her career she'd even written about the trials and tribulations of growing up in poverty, about being a charge of the care system whilst daring to dream of a better life, the article had won an award and everything. Not that her profession was about glory, far from it, she was just interested in validity, including everything there was to know about Keepers Island and why the ink of it still scratched and scarred beneath her skin like a poisoning. When the letter from the keepers arrived out of the blue two months ago inviting her to write about how the development would destroy both their cultural identity and the ecology of the area, Ruvanes Carne was ready for it – no sentiment, no distraction, just fact. The article wouldn't bring back her mother, but by experiencing the island from the inside, perhaps she would be able to face her personal fears whilst giving the island community a voice.

Until Ru discovered more about the place where it was rumoured her mother's body had washed up, the memory of them together would always be out there in the ocean, sometimes swimming, occasionally floating, but mostly drowning.

Instinctively her hand returned to the secret pocket in her bag in order to find the flask which would calm her nerves, but when she looked up she saw it, smack-bang face on.

From a distance the lighthouse looked like an angry young man, the brow of his forehead scrunched tight and the neck of him, the light part, shining like gleaming brass, beaming proud and bright. But up close it looked more like an old man that had been stripped of his clothes, the way his thin hoary spine buckled and bent against the rock, the bold lantern hanging like a head too heavy to hold all the secrets that plagued him.

'I'll drop you off on the slipway over there,' shouted Jowan suddenly, 'and I'll be back with the other bloke tomorrow, just get ready to jump.'

Ru strapped her bag tight onto her back and sat forward on the wooden bench.

'When I shout ready you get ready.'

'I'm ready.' Despite her legs shaking and her mouth filling with the memory of sand and seaweed, there was no turning back.

'I'll count down from five, cus I int stoppin'.'

'Fucksake just shout jump,' she yelled.

'Five, four, three . . .'

Ru jumped from the boat and skidded onto the causeway, her hands and knees slipping in the water as she tried to stand straight, her eyes squinting through the flinty rain until finally she saw a light making its way towards her.

Welcome

As quickly as she could Ru stumbled to her feet and she bent to brush the wet sand from off her knees, glancing at the seawater that lapped against the sides of the raised path and suddenly remembering her mother's reflection, her inquisitive eyes her own.

'Mum,' she whispered, 'you were here, you must have been,' she scratched her head, 'right here.'

'Bucca callin'.'

Ru looked up and into the bright light of an oil lantern and shook her head, 'I don't believe in . . .'

'The wind,' laughed the young woman, 'when it's a strong north-easterly it's Bucca's voice, carried on the wind.'

Ru started to laugh too, relieved to not be alone, 'Like a warnin'?' she asked.

'Maybe,' the woman smiled, 'maybe you'll get to meet him.'

'Or maybe I'll get to find out he's not real, maybe just made up to keep folk off the island.'

'Maybe.'

The woman held out her hand and waited for Ru to take it, guiding her carefully from the rocks and towards the safety of a mainland-facing beach, their first and perhaps most important watch.

When they reached a bench made of driftwood the girl set her lamp in the sand and sat down.

'Where is everybody?' asked Ru.

'Watchin'.' The girl patted the seat beside her.

'Watchin' what, the sea?'

'You.'

Ru looked around. She wanted to laugh, wanted to ask if they believed their own rumours, that they were not actually lighthouse keepers but a dangerous cult descended from pirates. Looking at the pretty dark-eyed woman it was hard to believe. She thought about the flask of whiskey in her bag, how if there was ever a time for a quick galvanising sip, then this was it. She watched the lamplight dance in the other's eyes, like an idea or a question was forming, taking shape.

'We wanted to thank you,' the woman said at last, 'wanted to thank you for comin'.'

Ru looked around at her surroundings, she had never visited the island, nobody in living memory ever had, but still it felt familiar, welcoming even.

'It took them a while to track you down,' the woman pointed towards the cliffs, 'thought you might never visit, but here you are.'

'I'm grateful for,' Ru searched for the right words, 'being allowed access, to the island, the community.' She smiled and looked towards the dark meandering line of pine trees that banked onto the sand, noticing suddenly that the lighthouse had begun to shine brilliant and bright, its beams fingering apart the canopy and pushing through from the other side of the island.

'In your honour,' the young woman smiled.

'As a kid the lighthouse used to scare me,' said Ru, 'I always thought it was looking at me, waiting for me to do something, god knows what,' she looked at the other woman and asked her what her name was.

'Steren; it means star, in Cornish.' The woman stood before Ru could ask any further questions. 'Anyway, time to meet the others.' She turned and started to walk a pathway that twisted through the trees and Ru followed obediently.

All around them the night pulled in tight, the canopy above their heads gently swaying in the breeze and the pine needles beneath their feet releasing a dizzying scent of decay as they approached an outcrop of rock that hid behind the tree line.

'Not far,' said Steren, 'follow my lamplight and you'll be alright.'

Inside the cave Ru was far from fine, it smelt of rotten fish and seemed to take forever to adjust her eyes to the muted light, catching only glimpses of the other woman as she moved through the cavern, until finally she pushed through a narrow fissure of rock and Ru did the same.

Outside, tangled within the circular clearing dead centre of the island Ru could see an array of makeshift wood and corrugated buildings, each of them carefully connected to the next with walkways that straddled streams and rills, everything made from what was salvaged from the sea over many years, it had her think of the miniature villages her mother used to build for her out of Lego.

'Ruvanes, over here.'

She followed the woman towards where thirty or so men and women were sitting and talking by a fire, stopping only briefly to look at the two of them.

'Let's walk,' said Steren.

At the far side of the flaming pyre Ru could just make out several wooden cargo crates of different sizes stacked in the sand, and through the firelight the sight of a motorbike displayed on the lid of one of them made her laugh.

'Our latest haul.'

Ru narrowed her eyes. 'You pulled all this from the sea?'

The Keepers

'Of course.'

'How did you move it here, to the centre of the island?'

'There's a secret track at the rear of the isle.'

'And you towed it up by hand?'

'Don't be daft, we have a boat winch.'

'And all this?' Ruvanes looked around her at the various-sized boxes, 'do you keep it all?'

The girl laughed, 'We're keepers but not how outsiders think.'

'Sounds like finders keepers,' she thought about what the fisherman had said, about them being descendants of pirates.

'Nah, we just keep it until the elders decide who along the coast could use stuff, to sell or whatever.'

'Even motorbikes?'

'Course, whatever washes up.'

Ru wondered how they managed to cart crates out of the sea. She remembered from history that at the mouth of certain rivers up and down the coast swashbuckling buccaneers used to rig wire cables from end to end in order to drag freight from off the top of cargo ships, but she knew nobody would be able to get away with it these days. She closed her eyes to try and digest this new version of piracy and raised her eyes towards the night sky, turning her face into the increasing icy wind. She couldn't help but smile, there were many rumours that circulated around the keepers, including their bootlegging history, but gifting to the impoverished, of which there were many in Cornwall, had never been one of them.

'Let's sit over here,' said Steren.

Together they found an old couch situated a little way back from the fire and sat down, whilst from across the circular cliff-locked shale beach the wind moved closer, stroking Ru's hair back from her face.

Daughter

'You have everythin' you need on the island?' asked Ru.

'Of course, we're a community that's lived here for hundreds of years, got everythin' we need right beneath our feet.'

When Ru was offered a jam jar of homemade cordial by one of the elders, she offered up her flask of whiskey in return.

'Survival,' she nodded to herself.

'We're poor but make use of everythin'.'

Ru took a sip of her drink, it tasted of late summer blackberries and early autumn blackthorn sloes, the best part of childhood.

'This is great,' said Ru, taking another sip, 'the background to your livelihood means we get a balanced story,' she opened her rucksack and pulled out her notepad and pen, 'do you mind if I take notes?'

The girl looked around at the others who were starting to move closer.

'I'll interview everyone,' she said, 'if it helps?'

The innate silence that surrounded them made Ru think again of the Bucca stories, how the unpredictable presence of him growing up made her fear things that she could not understand, except maybe now.

'I'll write the truth, I promise.'

'There'll be no need for writing notes,' said one of the older women who had started to come closer, her name was Kerenza, 'we don't need to record nothin' here, we believe in the oral tradition, droll tellin', just talkin'.' She snatched the notebook from her and Ru swallowed her anger and thought about pressing the record button on her phone instead. There was nothing in the letter they'd sent to her that suggested she couldn't record them, nothing to suggest that she wasn't allowed to do her job properly.

'So,' said the old woman, 'Ruvanes.'

Too late, she had already made herself comfortable beside her.

Ru smiled politely, she didn't like familiarity, and the way the woman said her name made her skin needle with apprehension. Why the hell had she come? Why had she thought returning to Cornwall after fifteen years of absence would somehow cure her of her loneliness, her anger, her misery? Back in London this one last story was all she could think about, one final pitch towards saving herself.

'This story you're writin', for the papers.'

Ru nodded, 'Yes.'

'The truth is what you're after,' the woman scratched at her curly grey hair, 'correct?'

Ru nodded again. Correct, kind of.

'Good.'

'So can I interview you?'

The woman gave a little smile, 'Maybe, but first you need to observe.'

'Observe what?'

'You'll see, now drink up, tomorrow's our big day.'

'But I need to interview the community, get your side of the story.'

'You will tomorrow, it's late.'

When the old woman got up and started to walk away Ru did what she was told and followed. Together they made their way up the steep incline towards a hut that was built into the internal cliff.

'Only our very special guests stay here.'

'I'm nothing special.'

'Is that right?'

'I promise you.'

'Up you go, just a couple of steps,' the old woman smiled, 'door's unlocked.'

Ru thanked her.

'Everythin' you need is inside.'

'And we can talk tomorrow?'

Kerenza turned and looked at her. 'Whatever you want.'

'So you'll do an interview?' asked Ru.

'There'll be no need for that,' the old woman laughed.

'But the developers—'

'Ah yes, our new visitor.'

'His name's Thomas,' when the woman didn't speak

Ru continued, 'he's responsible for mediation, to make sure everything goes smoothly between you and . . .'

'Duchy developers, I know,' she stepped forward and looked Ru in the eye, 'You know anythin' about 'em, who owns the company that plans to sell our island even though it int theirs to sell?'

Ru shrugged, 'Some old bloke called Charles, apparently his company owns a lot of Cornwall.'

The old woman shook her head, then sighed. 'We've been lighthouse keepers here a long time, you know that? Hundreds and hundreds of years, got the paperwork and everythin', not that them regal lot recognise it.'

Ru nodded, 'We had a history teacher at school for a while who used to talk about local history, you guys and our Celtic heritage.'

'What happened to him?'

'Got the sack, he was meant to be teaching us about British history, kings and queens and all that.'

The woman laughed, 'That'll be right.'

'Anyway, Thomas sounds okay, willing to listen to your side of things to try and find a way forward.'

'A way forward?'

'Maybe,' Ru shrugged, 'maybe he can mediate between you and the developers.'

'Girl you got a lot to learn.' The old woman continued towards the cabin, then looked back at her, 'You're not here to talk Ruvanes.'

'I am, I'm here to ask questions, for the article, for the paper.'

Kerenza started to laugh and pointed past her, 'You'll be sleepin' up in here tonight, and sleep you must cus tomorrow's a big day.'

'But I've got questions.'

'Tomorrow.'

'But . . .'

'Tomorrow Ruvanes,' through the light of her lamp the old woman started to smile, 'means "queen" in Cornish, did you know that?'

'What does?'

'Your name, Ruvanes,' she opened the door and allowed her to push past.

'It does?'

'You didn't know?'

Ru shook her head, 'Nobody ever told me, my mother disappeared when I was eight.'

The old woman ignored her, turning her back and removing the lamplight and leaving Ru to adjust her eyes to the dim burn of one single candle that had been placed beside a low pallet bed.

Outside the dingy room the sound of the waves as they struck out against the bedrock of the island echoed all around, the surge of sea spray and salty surf was like music from childhood, the opposite of a lullaby it was hard-hitting, hostile. She sat down, 'Now what?'

Ru watched the candle dance for attention, it demanded that she kick off her boots despite every part of her body screaming to run, somewhere, anywhere but here. She pulled the woollen blanket that had been provided around her shoulders and told herself to close her eyes to the uncertainty that was out there, observing everything.

Tomorrow she would talk to some of the keepers and discuss the developers' plans with Thomas, determined to be back on the mainland before nightfall. There was nothing to fear, nothing to worry about, and she told herself the worst things in her life had happened already.

At some point in the night Ru must have fallen asleep, because when she woke the night had been tucked neatly behind her and dawn had started to appear messily through the crack in the door. There was another light too, a soft amber radiance that seeped through the rockface wall of the cliff; it had her think of her mother, the way her hair used to catch the last embers of sunlight as Ru scrambled into her lap; her mum always liked to watch the tide, forever waiting for something to happen, some gift to appear in the shallow flotsam flow, a precious keepsake to pocket for herself.

Ru sat up slowly and rubbed her eyes so she could better focus on the transient light, and she pulled on her boots all the while keeping her eyes on the rocky alcove that burrowed into the cliff.

Aureate
Ruvanes
beautiful

She stood in the semi-darkness and narrowed her eyes towards where she thought the voice was coming from, but it was all around her. It was moments like these that she'd look at whatever drink was inevitably close at hand, but annoyingly she'd given her flask away.

'Hello?' Ru asked tentatively. She pushed further into the cave, her hands brushing against the barnacles that covered both sides of the rockface and her feet kicking blindly at the narrow path until suddenly she bumped into a shopping trolley full of gold ornaments and in the middle of it all, a crown. She put a hand out towards where she saw her name inscribed and lifted the intricate gold garland until it rested right in her hands.

You found me I found you

Majesty

Ru dropped the artefact and ran outside into the centre of the island. She had to get away from the suffocating circular chamber, and when she spied the gap in the cliff that she'd passed through with the young woman last night, she went to it.

Emerging onto the main beach she looked out towards the ocean, it looked different in daylight, different to their village cove too, somehow the water looked bluer, deeper, its secrets infinite.

'Hey,' she jumped into the path of a group of children who were running across the beach, their arms loaded with planks of driftwood and tangles of fir.

'Ruvanes,' they shouted as one.

'What's going on?' she asked.

'It's today,' shouted the youngest kid, 'the ceremony, up on the hill.'

Ru looked in the direction he was pointing to see that some of the adults were carrying larger pieces of wood towards a path that snaked its way along the edge of the cliff. She noticed too that it had become colder, and she pulled up her collar and grabbed a hat from her bag.

'What's today?' she asked.

'The alignment.'

'The what?'

'The alignment, that's why you're here.'

In the caves behind her Ru could hear that the voices were becoming rowdier, and she tried to listen but the words seemed caught in a tangle of shanty.

'They're wakin',' said one of the others, ''em wakin for real.'

'Who?'

'Bucca and 'em lot.'

As they ran towards the cliffs Ru shouted after them, catching the arm of the youngest, 'Who's them lot?'

'The pirate spirits, ancestors.'

'Whose ancestors?'

'Yours dafty!'

She let go. Above her head she saw that the rain of yesterday was starting to fall in as paring sleet, and she watched as the tiny shards of ice fell hard and made pock marks in the silver sand.

What ancestors? She didn't have any.

Ru looked out towards the mainland and wondered

if Thomas, the developers' go-between, was on his way. She took her phone out of her jeans pocket to see if there were any messages despite knowing there was no signal on the island. 'Fuck them,' she switched on the microphone, if she couldn't have her notebook then she would record this way, even if it was just the sound of spluttering waves and the cawing gulls that occasionally came close and got caught on the wind.

High up on the clifftop she could see the flames of a bonfire burning bright through the cold damp air and instinctively went to it. The path she noticed had already begun to ice over, and she took her time to step carefully onto the wooden slats of a rope ladder until she reached the top.

'Ruvanes,' said Steren.

'The fire's something else,' Ru pointed towards the flaming pyre that was starting to lift high above the island, the golden hue that radiated warmth in contrast to the white of the lighthouse made her think of the shopping trolley full of gold artefacts, the spattering of colour reminding her of fireworks and bonfire night, then suddenly sacrifices and ritualistic murders, but that thought she was quick to keep to herself.

'The cave I slept in last night,' she began, 'I found . . .'

'The island is the spiritual epicentre of the ocean,' said the girl suddenly, 'did you know that?'

'I didn't,' laughed Ru.

'It's no joke, we've been waitin' for this moment a long time.'

'And what is this moment exactly?'

'The changing of times, how the death of something brings new hope.'

Ru shrugged, 'Dunno about that, but it's beautiful anyway.' Something about the cold air and the blazing warmth made her feel settled, content, when for so many years she had felt at odds with the world, like she was living somebody else's life. For some unknown reason it had her think of her mother, not quite a recollection but something unexplainable that sat just beyond the periphery of her memory. It made her sad, confused and sad.

'This,' she said to herself, 'this moment,' she looked at the other woman when she realised she was speaking.

'Anyway we've been plannin' this day for a while.'

'Planning what?'

'The day we get to reclaim our land.'

'The island? But you have to leave it, it belongs to Duchy,' Ru didn't like where this was going, it sent a strange jolt of terror through her veins, the hairs on the back of her neck prickling with sweat despite the freezing-cold air.

Steren pointed beyond the fire towards where the others had begun to gather, and together they watched them lift gardening tools from off the back of a trailer, whilst all the while chainsaws could be heard gunning in the distance.

Ru stepped forward, 'What are they doing?'

'Preparin'.' Steren took Ru by the hand and led her towards the fire and the others.

'Preparing for what?' Her words came out calmly to

attest to the curious journalist she had become, whilst inside all she could think was *fuck fuck fuck*.

'Ruvanes,' said Kerenza when she saw her approaching, 'you must be wonderin' what's goin' on.'

'A little, I thought I was here to interview some of you, I don't want to get caught up in a fight.'

'I knew your mother,' the old woman smiled, 'did I tell you that?'

Ru shook her head, 'Must have been a long time ago.'

'Not at all, just a month since she passed.'

Ru felt the earth beneath her feet shift and she waited for the sudden loss of time to catch up and she crouched to the ground and put the palms of her hands against the frozen earth.

'Mum?' Ru imagined her walking towards her, perhaps dancing out on that exact same scuff of earth – she so loved to dance – and she closed her eyes, imagined her always and every day close.

'This must come as a surprise to you I know,' said Kerenza.

Ru stood up and shook her head, and when the woman tried to put an arm around her shoulder she pulled away.

'A surprise, is that all you have?'

'As a direct descendant of the keepers it was important that you didn't know until now.'

'Know what? That my fucking mother left me to live on an island for twenty-five years?'

'Ruvanes, dear.' She took her hand and it was a surprise to the younger woman that she let her.

The Keepers

'And it's not Ruvanes it's Ru,' she shouted.

'It's a lot to take in I know.'

Ru started to laugh in disbelief.

'It's your destiny Ruvanes, as it was your mother's and her mother's before that.'

'So let me get this straight, I'm from a long line of keepers, and my destiny is to,' Ru scratched her head, 'what exactly?'

'Protect the island.'

'From who, blow-ins?' She started to laugh.

'Everyone.'

'But why?' Ru remembered a story that her mother used to tell her about the island to help get her to sleep, that it was a very special, magical place, but growing up she thought that perhaps she just meant it was an environmental distinctiveness that set it apart from the rest of Cornwall.

Kerenza stepped forward and lightly touched her shoulders, 'You're from a long line of keepers.'

'Like fuck I am!'

'Bucca queens, same as your mother, Bucca will only let us live here if a true blood leads, it's what's meant.'

Ru pulled away, 'What if I don't stay?'

'Bucca will come in as the worst storm anyone has ever known, he'll destroy the island and a great part of the coast, all our community and everything we've done to support the poorest coastal families.'

'And this is why you took away my mother, kept her captive for so many years?'

The old woman turned away.

'Well is it?'

Ru could hear her voice start to break with anger, a few tears escaping and making tracks down her face, 'For fucksake,' she shouted. She closed her eyes and tried to imagine her mother in this place, wondered if she had ever tried to escape.

'Mum, where are you?' She put her head in her hands, wondering for the first time about what her life would have been like without the endless parties, the drugs and drink, she wondered about her own fate if she'd never known grief. There was so much more she wanted to ask the old woman, but when she opened her eyes Kerenza had already gone.

Out to sea the faint feathered light of a fishing trawler was approaching the island, but Ru noticed it wasn't the boat she'd arrived on yesterday, but a much bigger vessel.

'Shit.' She didn't have a good feeling about this and instinct told her to run towards the precipice of the cliff before it was too late, but the rope ladder had already been removed. Ru's head filled with questions and her heart burst with the pain that ached for her mother, she had been stepping-stone close after all. She looked towards where the mainland was supposed to be, and despite the blasting blizzard snow, imagined her mother standing in that exact same spot. Perhaps at times, regardless of the distance, their eyes had met, maybe there were even moments when her mum got to watch over her, maybe she'd been guiding her this whole time.

Ru noticed as the boat got closer, that five maybe six people were aboard it and she knew this didn't bode well. She looked towards the circle of trees that crowned the pinnacle of the island behind her and ran towards them, surely somewhere on that far side of the isle was another way down onto the beach, it was where they hauled the cargo after all.

She sprinted past the fire that without supervision had suddenly become a beacon of fury, and across the stony plain until she entered the cluster of trees, all the while she could hear calls of ahoy resounding from all over the island.

Inside the tiny forest Ru took a moment to catch her breath and she adjusted her eyes to the sudden darkness. Beyond the canopy of trees she could hear raised voices, no longer calling but shouting. She looked around her and down at the circle of pine needles at her feet and every path that pointed starward.

'I don't know which way to go,' she whispered to herself. She spun around and chose a path and ran, only stopping when she reached the crest of yet another cliff. Way down below she could see people jumping from the boat and splashing into the surf. She could see Thomas the mediator dressed in an inappropriate suit and another man holding up a ream of paper and Ru guessed he was a solicitor. She knew by the tone of their voices that they were trying to speak with authority, but the keepers, now standing hand in hand in the surf, were having none of it. There were others too, several heavies dressed in black who were no doubt brought in to protect the developers, or fight, whichever came first.

Battle ready

'Stop it!' she shouted as loud as she could, 'we can talk this out,' she turned her back and struggled to climb down the cliff. If she was meant for anything it was to stop the fight that was ensuing. What if she really was meant to save the island from expansion? What if she was meant to rescue it from Bucca's wrath? Ru didn't believe in superstition but there must have been a reason why after their near drowning her mother couldn't get back to her.

She needed to tell Thomas and the developers that the keepers needed more time, and she struggled to get her words straight in her head, but when she lost her footing in the shaly rock and fell, every truth she knew about her life turned to confusion, then nothing.

Ru lay on the beach until her eyes filled with snowflakes and she sat up and rubbed them clear, then felt around on her head until she found the bump where she must have hit it. She didn't know how long she had been unconscious, but everywhere she looked the blood of combat flashed bold against the white of the snow. Where was everybody? She held out her hands and waited for them to stop shaking, instinctively reaching into her pocket for her phone, perhaps she would be able to make an emergency call.

'Shit,' the battery was critically low, made worse because stupidly she had forgotten to switch the record button off.

She pressed restart and listened:
The fire's something else
It's to welcome you home
It's beautiful, perfect . . . just this, out in the open
With your community

Ru pressed pause and stood up quickly, 'What the fuck!' It was the conversation by the fire from earlier, only somehow different, and she looked around to see if anyone was messing with her.

'Okay,' she said to herself, 'it's just a recording, press play.'

We've been plannin' for this day a long time
'Who's that?' Ru pressed pause, then continued:
My girl, golden
'Mum?'
Ruvanes means queen, did they tell you that?

Ru nodded. Despite her anger and all the questions she wanted to ask her mother, she nestled the phone close to her cheek instead, 'I miss you Mum,' she whispered.

My girl
'I miss you more than anything.'
But you're here with me now aren't you?

'I'm lonely,' Ru started to cry.

Don't be, you're with your people now

'But I don't understand, why couldn't you bring me?'

I tried but the current was too strong, it pulled you away from me

'I miss you.'

I'm all around you, have always been

'Bucca?'

Bucca calling, he lets me speak to you on the wind, always, you just needed to believe in me

'Sometimes I heard you, growing up, I swear I did.'

When the phone went dead Ru accepted it, the same way she would accept her fate, the things that were written in the stars and in the freckles on her arms were inevitable, perhaps this was where resilience was allowed to build, in every eventuality.

She could feel her mother all around her now, fully, not like the brief moments of transient sound that she used to hear as a kid. She no longer had to live with ghost sounds, trying to decipher the fizzy, frothy static of childhood.

She carried the phone to the water's edge and placed it into the surf, her old life over, making new-root space for where her destiny could start to bud and grow again. The thought of staying scared her, but perhaps the thought of leaving frightened her more. If her future was to lead the island, she would make sure that there was no more violence, no more incarceration and no more mistakes. Somehow they would have to fabricate a story around Thomas and the property developers' deaths that involved a sinking ship, and maybe in time Ru would learn to be less selfish – gifting to the poor, there was something head-high gallant in that.

She sat in the damp sand and let the surf curl around her ankles as she looked up at the cliffs and noticed that the fire was still burning bright. Maybe this was what they meant by alignment, the positioning of everything; Bucca, herself and her mother, each of them were made up of the elements: wind, earth, fire and water. Perhaps her own near-drowning and her mother's disappearance twenty-five years ago had led to this singular moment, the positioning of karma against chaos to ensure a fairer future.

She watched the tide draw up around her and when she saw something glimmering in the spume Ru reached out to pick it up, it was her crown, the one with her name inscribed in gold, Ruvanes, Queen, maybe, just maybe she was someone after all.

I Am Hagstone

SALENA GODDEN

Salena Godden FRSL is an award-winning author, poet and broadcaster of mixed Jamaican-Irish heritage. Her debut novel, *Mrs Death Misses Death*, won the Indie Book Award for Fiction and the People's Book Prize, and was shortlisted for the British Book Awards and the Gordon Burn Prize. Her most recent books include the literary childhood memoir *Springfield Road* and poetry collections *With Love, Grief and Fury* and *Pessimism is for Lightweights: 30 Pieces of Courage and Resistance*. Her work has been shortlisted for the 4thWrite Short Story Prize, the Ted Hughes Award, Jerwood Compton Foundation, Bridport Poetry Prize and highly commended by the Forward Prize. She is a fellow of the Royal Society of Literature, a patron of Hastings Book Festival and an honorary fellow of West Dean, Sussex.

1.

Who do you think I am? Who do you think you are speaking to? Do you know who you are summoning? Who do you believe you conjure?

I am held in your warm hand for the first time. I take a deep breath. It is good to be on dry land again. You hold me up to the light, the crisp blue sky above us, wintry sunlight pouring through my hole. With your breath I am awakened, I am alive again. You peer inside me, up and through me to see the pebbled beach and the sea, see where land meets water, the line of the horizon. You look at me, this way and then that.

Look what I've found, you say, and you show me to your friends, Yasmina, Catherine and Ramona, this is a Hagstone, it's magic. Then you kiss me and squeeze me, hold me in your soft hand and put me in your coat pocket. You rub me with your thumb as you walk. It is dark and warm inside your hand. I hear your boot heels crunch on the pebbles and shingle, then tip-tap onto the pavement. I hear you chatting and laughing with your friends, I hear the world pass by us, the sounds of engines, perhaps a train.

I'm so happy to be warm and dry and back in the land of the living. Delightful.

By the time we get to your home, I am tethered to you, but I'm unsure of your year. It takes me a while to get the compass to work, to ascertain who my new mistress is, which language, which country, which century – please do excuse me, I have been under the sea for a very long time.

You take me out and hold me, you examine me again. Then you sit at your kitchen table and gently thread a red silk ribbon through me, into me, then you tie it neatly to wear me around your neck. You look in the mirror and like what you see. I can see you looking at me and at yourself. Can you feel me then? Do you know I also look at our reflection?

How pretty you are, Miss Everleigh. My new home is you, Miss Everleigh Davies, what a delicious creature you are. What a modern wonder you are, and your soul, so open and quick to latch on, I feel you pouring into me, like a sweet wine, thick as blood, warm as candle wax.

I can see your face in the mirror, how it is a kind face, brown and freckled. You have curious dark eyes, dramatic black eyeliner and bold eyelashes. You remind me of your grandmother's mother. Your hair is ink-black and bobbed. You paint your lips red, you have a beautiful mouth, your lips are pillowy; a perfect cupid's bow. How I would kiss those lips if I could, gently at first. Now you put on a tight scarlet velvet mini-dress with a low and scooped neckline. It has dramatic bell sleeves. Your neck is long and elegant. Touch it. You do so and stay gazing in the mirror for a while, looking at me around your neck, holding me. You smile, I smile with you. I grin at you. Do you see me grinning? I'm right here, I am behind you in the mirror, a black shape, growing bolder. If you looked past yourself, over your shoulder, you might see me, a faint outline, a shadow in the background of your image . . . Can you feel me with you yet?

I am Hagstone.

You found me. This is what you tell everyone you found me on the beach in Hastings, and as you say this you touch me, and feel me in your gentle fingers. I am worn as a talisman and lucky thing. I am not *a* hagstone, I am Hagstone. There is only one of me. You did not find me, I found you on purpose, dear, and every day forever now I'm with you, nestled at your warm breast. You wear me as a pretty keepsake, you wear me for protection and I wear you. I'm kept close, the ribbon tight about your throat. I breathe with you; I feel your pulse and life. I listen to your thoughts and your strong beating heart. I soon learn what excites or frightens or repels you. I soon know what you live for, what you would die for.

2.

We are outside. We walk from your home down the busy Kentish Town high street towards Camden. From under your scarf I hear the activities of the world, slightly muffled; I hear high street noises, the engines of double-decker buses, the chatter of passing voices, maybe a baby mewling and crying, then some disgusting carol singers and jarring church bells. Oh, so I now know it is December and soon to be Yuletide. I'm still unsure of your year. I haven't been here before; there is so much noise, music and motor traffic. How the city of London has changed since I was last here. I cannot smell or hear any horses.

Things get exciting when we stop at O'Reilly's butcher's shop, wafts of raw meat, flesh and blood. Exciting for you too it seems, Everleigh. I can feel your heart race, your pulse quicken as you look in the window, see the fresh kills, dead turkeys and chickens, pheasants and pigs hanging from hooks in a row; there are chains of sausages, slabs of beef steak and legs of ham. I would salivate if I could, if I were more than stone. I live vicariously through you, my Miss Everleigh. I can see myself there, look, see my blurry reflection in the bloody butcher's shop window, my shadow looming behind you beneath the red-and-white-striped awning. You do not see me yet; you gaze past the meat display at a blonde boy working inside.

Then quite suddenly the butcher's dog sees me, or perhaps at least senses me, and he barks and snarls and

I Am Hagstone

charges towards us, he growls and leaps up. He surprises us both, damned mutt. Your heart bangs like a drum, clanging in your chest. You crouch down to restrain the beast, you calm and pet the bulldog. You call him by his name: you say, hello, Crowley, as you stroke his black and white fur; you say, hey good boy, good dog, Crowley, as you scratch behind his pink ears, good boy, Crowley.

Crowley, Crowley, Crowley.

The butcher's son calls out to the dog and then appears at the doorway; he beckons you to come in. Actually, he does much more than that, he winks at you and then as you pass he pats your bottom. You like that, you blush, you jiggle, you get hot about the chest and neck. I can hear your heart sing.

Do you love him, Everleigh? Oh, I feel that you do. Yes, yes, yes, you do.

Inside the butcher's shop, we are met with the divine smell of death, blood and flesh. You take your leather gloves off and loosen your scarf and unbutton your faux-leopard fur coat. I look at some globules of kidneys pooling in dark red blood. It has been so long since I feasted, so long since I was made flesh and walked among the living.

On the counter top there are free samples: chunks of cheese, slivers of ham and pickles on toothpicks. I listen as you laugh, pick one and chew slowly, the cheese, the ham, the creamy salty saliva in your happy mouth. You joke and pretend to make an order for a delivery to keep the boy's attention. You point to the goods displayed and say, write this down, you say, I require a large turkey, two pheasants, four pork pies, two dozen sausage rolls, a chain of sausages, two dozen of your finest eggs, a pound of bacon, a jar of that goose fat, a pound of salted butter, a family cheese box and four pints of the good milk, the gold top milk, all to be delivered to the manor. You are laughing as you give your address. The handsome butcher's son is called Charlie; he grins and plays along and says he thinks he knows your address alright, and then he laughs and calls you *m'lady* as he scribbles in his notebook. I am guessing he's your beau? He's good-looking, sandy-haired and tall. He's charming, alright; he has a flushed face and bright green eyes, and he cannot stop smiling at you, Miss Everleigh.

See how he took the pencil from behind his ear, see how he licked the lead as he wrote your name and drew a heart. You stand on tiptoes to look over the counter, and watch him keenly. You look at his big capable hands, notice the fair hair on his strong forearms; you like the way he licks the tip of the pencil and draws a heart.

Oh, Miss Everleigh, how you love to flirt with the butcher's son; you laugh girlishly, your skin is warm, your heart is skipping, beating a happy tune. You take another cube of cheese and bite it thoughtfully and lean on the counter as you point and say, I'd better buy some nice sausages for tea tonight. Charlie wraps the sausages and then tells you he slipped in a couple of free rashers of bacon for when you let him make you breakfast. As he says this his eyes twinkle; as he laughs and you laugh, he looks up at you through his long pale eyelashes, then he says, what are you wearing under that fur coat then, he says, you know what they say, fur coat and no knickers. You blush and reply, the red dress, the one I told you about, you open your coat and give him a flash of your lovely figure in red velvet. He says he loves you in that red dress, he'd like to see what that dress would look like on his bedroom floor. You laugh and say, oh, Charlie, stop it, you're so naughty. He says, I could be really very naughty if you'd only let me, Everleigh.

Charlie! You say his name again, thank you, for the bacon, I mean, thank you, you both laugh. You're welcome, Everleigh, hey, there's plenty more where that came from. Thank you, Charlie, you say his name again, as you button your coat and tie your scarf and begin putting your gloves back on. Merry Christmas, Everleigh. Happy Christmas, Charlie, you reply, and thanks again.

I watch all of this, this song and dance, this flirtation and, well, frankly I'm not so sure about this Charlie fellow, Everleigh. I'm not sure about him at all. To be frank, I'm not sure what I dislike more; first it was his grimy immaturity, then his breath and the smell of stale sweat, the salt of sex on his unwashed skin, his bitten nails, the secretions and bacteria in his chin bristles, the smear of other women all over him. If only you could see what I can see, smell what I smell, Everleigh, if only you could know what I know.

Just then, his father arrives from the back room – I am guessing you hope this might be your future father-in-law? The grumpy yellow-bearded butcher appears behind the counter and grunts and nods in your direction. He's terrible; I smell it, sense it, I know it right away. I know his past and this bloodline well, I know these men from time before times. These are not kind people, Everleigh; these are the sons of the sons who'll only wish us harm, to hurt us, hunt us, burn us.

Hello, Mr O'Reilly, you say, bright and as politely as you can. You are sure that Mr O'Reilly does not like you, Everleigh, and that is because he doesn't, Everleigh, he never will, nor anyone like us. Trust your gut, Miss Everleigh, you must learn to trust your instinct. Ronald O'Reilly sniffs with disapproval and looks away to serve another customer, an elderly priest, who stands behind you. We didn't see the fat priest come in. Oh, the stench of it. Oh the heady sweet sickness in the air. Ronald O'Reilly says, good morning Father Johnson, sorry for the wait, what can I do you for? The vile priest moves towards the counter and takes a cheese cube with his pink fingers and throws it into his slack mouth, chewing the hard cheese with stained and dirty teeth. His dirty tongue now creamy, masticating, the cheese mixing with this morning's stale pipe tobacco and whisky-coffee. He points at the tray of congealed livers and kidneys, and as he does this, he glances over to shoot you a judgemental look.

Everleigh, I feel you shrink, I sense you feel small. Father Johnson wants this, you give him what he likes; he wants you to feel belittled, he wants you to feel like a harlot for having a flirt and getting free bacon from Charlie the butcher's boy. I feel my temper rise with every second of your rising shame. No, this is unacceptable. Now, Father Johnson's body jerks with coughs and splutters. The priest begins to choke, haha, the cheese is stuck in his windpipe; he keels over, red in the face, his eyes bulge. The priest is breathless, gurgling, panicking. I laugh and laugh. Then Ronald dashes over and smacks Father Johnson on the back, once, twice, three times; the cheese dislodges, and he projectile vomits all over himself and his leather boots and the black-and-white-tiled floor. You leave and look back through the butcher's window; Charlie looks down at the floor and is told to get a mop to clean up Father Johnson's mess.

3.

I am Hagstone.

Some might call me other names: Odin Stone. Witch Stone. Magick Stone. Fae Stone. Over the years I've been treasured by so many – witches and wizards, dreamers and poets, magicians and moon dancers. I have been hung by silk, silver, leather and string. I remember my last time here: a wise medicine woman plaited me into place on a strand of her twisted grey dreadlocks. When she died, she was buried at sea; she sank to the depths, her blue flesh eaten by sharks and bottom-feeders and I was left to join the shingle. I'm small and neat; time's own spit, sea salt and loving fingers have rubbed my edges smooth. Over the centuries, I've been worn in secret, or surrounded by candles and placed on sacred altars. I have been given power by everyone that believes in me. I have been kept inside matchboxes and hidden in shoes. I have been dangled in windows, hung above fireplaces and on copper bedsteads to *keep the devil away*. I have been thrown off bridges and over the cliff edge and told to go back *to the watery grave from whence I came*, their words not mine, more times than I dare recall – but someone, some soul, some believer, somebody comes, finds me, feeds me with belief, or rather perhaps I fill them with belief.

And you? Who are you exactly?

You are all mine, Miss Everleigh Davies.

You don't know it, but you're a daughter of resistance and rebellion; there is an ancient courage embedded in you. You'll know it when you watch a full moon rise, you'll feel it when you walk barefoot in the forest and touch thick green moss, you'll taste it when you burn your tongue on good rum, you'll smell it in sea mist. I remember everything about you, Everleigh, I am yours and you are mine; if you keep me about you, you won't be alone ever again and nor will I. With your belief I grow bolder, stronger, the longer I'm tied about your throat. Touch me. Feel me in your light fingers, hold me close. Love me, love me, Miss Everleigh, love me.

As you sleep, I watch you. I listen to your breath, I lie with you, watching the fall and rise of your chest. I listen to your dreams and nightmares. I show you who you are, I whisper in your ear. I show you to your ancestors, I show up in your visions and dreams. When you wake up,

I Am Hagstone

I watch your eyes open, I feel the world of your memories and dreams fade, the world of your now and here come into focus. I hear your desires, your hopes, your dreads and fears, all of you, your loves and hates. All day and night I am growing, listening. I am faint in the condensation at the window. I am in the fog in your mirror when you are soaking in a hot bubble bath. I stand by you, by the kettle as you wait for it to boil, I curl in the steam. I am with you on the sofa when you read your books, I am crackling in the fire. You tied me around your own throat intentionally; I am around your neck, feeling your pulse, waiting, waiting, waiting. I am so happy to wait here to serve you, so happy to feel you, to learn you, to own your sweet and tender soul.

Now feel me banging against your warm bosom as Charlie kisses your neck and makes reckless promises to you. We are on the back row of a theatre. Your heart leaps with every touch. You are so sure he means to propose to you. You are so sure you are meant to be with him. He tries so hard to coerce you; he kisses your fingers and your face, he tries to melt you with sly words. He whispers persistently and says he wants you, desires you. You go so far ... but then you push his hand away and say no, stop it, Charlie. You've told him you aren't like that. Then he accuses you, he says that you are teasing him, that you make him feel bad, that you aren't the fun girl he thought you were. He calls you a cock tease. He leaves you standing outside the cinema and zooms off on his motorbike; he leaves you there, because you wouldn't let him have you in the back row of the theatre. You walk all the way home and once there, I wish you'd stayed home that night.

This is not acceptable, Everleigh.

You're a good girl from a good family. You're down-to-earth and kind – these are things people say about you. That you're a friendly face, a good laugh behind the bar at the pub. I want to know you better, to show you the powers of your grandmother's mothers. It is why we are drawn together, why we are so strong together; it is what draws you to me, what draws me to you.

Oh my Everleigh, this is an old love, you and me – I am your Hagstone.

When you are alone, you talk to me through divination. The first time this happens you come back from your shift in the pub and you are on your own in your room. It is something you know, something you do instinctively; a ritual, the moon rising, the burning of your intentions on paper, the yearning for guidance from your tarot and crystals. When you hold me, when you speak to me, I wonder if you know it is me yet; I wonder if you know who you're invoking. I wonder if you know I am listening and that it is me, Hagstone, it is me that you summon and speak to. Can you feel me shadowing you? I hear you, I'm here for you, with you.

Up until recently you lived at home with your mum and dad and helped in the family-run fish and chip shop, with your two younger sisters and grandmother. Nan's batter is the best in the country, you'd tell all the customers. Oi oi saveloy, you'd laugh, you'll not find a better battered sausage in the whole wide world. You loved it and loathed it at once. You felt both obliged and burdened by the shop. You watched your grandparents and then your parents live and work there, day in and day out and all year round, with the hectic summer season, and the dead depressing winters overlooking the grey sea. So many of the amusements, like the penny arcades and the clubs, may have changed name or closed down, but not *Chippie's*.

As you grew up it became suffocating. You took turns to do shifts after school with your siblings; the smell of salt and vinegar, the grease of the chip fryer, it was forever in your skin and hair. When you were a girl you blew bubbles; you had a gob full of strawberry bubblegum on the go constantly to get the smell of grease out from the back of your nostrils. How you were longing to leave home and be truly free. You longed for the bright lights of London. Well, look at you now, Everleigh, you're on your way: your own room, your own food in the cupboards, actual fruit in a fruit bowl, like an adult. You have your own bills and rent to pay, your own key to a house you share with your girlfriends, Yasmina, Catherine and Ramona; you all go to Central Saint Martins together, you're sharing your love of fashion and bottles of cheap red wine. It's a shame how things turn out, but, Everleigh, you do go to the funeral. You see how everyone will weep and call it a tragedy and wear black. Of course, you won't be able to look each other in the eye.

4.

I am Hagstone.

I am all yours, you can ask me anything, you do know that? Do you know that? Do you know I am here for you, Miss Everleigh? For centuries now I have roamed the layer between dreams and nightmare, the space between birth and death, your world and Netherworld. I am forever vibrating in the hole, which is an open door from my world to you. This is who speaks to you, Everleigh, this is who you have awakened. Think of me perhaps as a spirit sent from your own past self to your future self. Remember me? Call to me, speak to me, sing to me, feel our love growing stronger.

I am Hagstone.

My ancient name was erased. I have known all hell's weather. I have been banished, thrown away, discarded, abandoned, lobbed back into the ocean, time and time again, thrown back into the abyss for my misdeeds and mischief. I have been sunk and washed out to sea, but nothing can break the cycle, I cannot be destroyed. Time passes. Centuries pass. I loop back again. I am found time and time again; see how I go from hand to hand, heart to heart, soul to soul to find you. Sense it. Touch me. Feel how I grow more powerful and more knowing.

You are in drunk and jolly company. You are all quite merry, four laughing mouths: Everleigh, Catherine, Yasmina and Ramona, four beautiful young women. I see you light candles. The flame is winking, dancing with me.

I Am Hagstone

It is a full moon. Flame and stone, sea salt and rum. You stare down at me, eyes twinkling with flickering light. You each wear colourful paper crowns, Christmas party hats; you are rosy-cheeked and loud and boisterous. I smell the rum punch, and a sweet hashish smoke hangs blue and heavy above me.

Look, like this, watch this . . .

I am in your hand. Are you sure of this? Do you want to share me? Do you want to show me to your friends? Be gentle now, Everleigh. Can you feel me, feel how I come alive for you. You clever thing, I'm here drinking in your belief. You've taken me from around your neck and choose to share me; you use me like a party trick, Hagstone as a pendulum.

Show me yes.

I respond.

Show me yes.

Yes, yes, yes, I know how to play this game. Now see me move: I am swinging up and down, away and to and forwards and backwards and . . .

Show me no.

I stop dead still. Then begin shaking my head, side to side, no, no, no, I go, left to right . . .

Stop.

I stop swinging. Oh so obedient. Look how subservient I can pretend to be. I am so generous in this. Can you see my yes and my no? See my giving of answers to your questions so deeply rooted in your wants and desires? Oh I'm here for this. Hagstone as entertainment. Thank you for inviting me into your circle. I wait. I listen. I stop. Dead. Still. Ever so slightly fizzing, vibrating, pulsating. The candlelight flickering, how ancient is fire and this devils game. I dangle like a hangman, kicking, wavering, waiting for the big questions on the tip of four red tongues. The ribbon woven through the hole, the loop, the knot, your fingers. I feel it tremble; you hold the ribbon loose and easy. Easy does it, dear Everleigh, easy does it.

See, Ramona? It's moving on its own, look!
This is rubbish, Everleigh, I don't believe it.
Shush, Ramona, concentrate.
You must believe in it and be specific . . .
It's a yes or no question.
Ask it a question now.
Catherine, do you want a go?
Just ask it a straight yes or no question.
What shall I ask? Yasmina? Ramona? What shall I say, Everleigh?
Shall we ask it about the dickhead?
Which one? Charlie?
How many dickheads do we know?
If you are sure . . .
Ok. Sure, why not.
Ready?
Ready. I call upon a higher self, I call upon the spirit of Hagstone, Hagstone, Hagstone . . . Are you there? Yes? Ok. Is Charlie O'Reilly going to marry Everleigh Davies?

I swing hard left and right, left and right: no no no he is not.

I Am Hagstone

No! Hagstone says no – is it telling us no? It is a no! Look! I knew it! That Charlie, he's such a dickhead!

I mean, if it's telling the truth, he's a dickhead and also I'm so sorry, Everleigh!

Thank you, Yasmina, appreciate it.

Yeah, I'm sorry too, but also not surprised.

Let's do another shot now!

Oh, come on, everyone, do you all seriously believe a rock dangling on a ribbon?

I mean, maybe, Ramona – look, it's a definite no.

Come on, Cath, Yas – you two don't believe Everleigh's witchy crap do you?

Ramona, why are you so quick to dismiss it?

Yeah, Ramona, why don't you want to believe in it?

Shall we double-check, ask Hagstone again?

Hagstone, Hagstone, Hagstone: is Charlie unfaithful right now? Right now? Charlie? Unfaithful? Is Charlie O'Reilly unfaithful right now?

Oh, see me go: I swing hard yes yes yes. He is unfaithful. Mentally and spiritually and with his intention, yes he is unfaithful. Is he unfaithful? Right now? Yes. Was he unfaithful? Yes. Did his mind wander and did his feet follow? Yes. Did his mouth find another mouth? YES. Did his tongue dance with lies and other fancies? Yes. And did his hands reach for another's body other than yours, Everleigh? Yes. Did they fuck in the pub toilets? Yes. Ask me about who! Please ask me who! I wish you'd ask the big question: is Charlie sleeping with your friend Ramona behind your back? The truth? The truth! Yes, that is a truth!

Ooh he's unfaithful . . . Look, it is a big yes!

He is . . . it's a yes?

IS CHARLIE A DICKHEAD! Yes yes yes!

Look! It's going so fast now, it's going like the clappers, look!

What does it mean? It's doing wild shapes . . . We need another shot of rum!

I don't trust it, you're making it do that with your wrist, Everleigh.

Ramona, I'm not! I promise it is Hagstone, Hagstone knows everything . . .

It gives me the creeps. You're a witch, Everleigh, you're an actual witch; you should burn.

Whoever is shagging Charlie is a witch and should burn!

Hagstone can you make Charlie burn, can you burn Charlie to ash!

Yeah, burn burn, burn the bastard, burn bitch burn!

Death to the butcher's boy, burn Charlie burn, burn Charlie burn!

Death to the bitch, death to the butcher's boy!

You're a witch, Everleigh!

Louder and drunker and louder and drunker, I hear you chant the magic words, music to my ears, my favourite sing-song, death death death, burn burn burn. How you laugh, and do cheers and shots of rum. How I laugh with you and dance on your silk ribbon. I swing hard left and right. No no no, yes yes yes. I am dancing inside the stone. So happy you want Charlie dead. You ask for his death, delicious, death. I am lurching forwards and backwards. Yes, yes yes, left and right. Witch witch witch, bitch bitch bitch, yes yes yes, death, death death, then a happy zig-zagging anti-clockwise circle, jerking at the end of the ribbon.

You're a witch, Everleigh!

How very sudden is the unmistakable stench of burnt hair. Ramona starts screaming and slapping her own face and head: it seems her green paper hat caught fire; her bleach-blonde hair is smoking. Ramona's fake white hair in flames, she is shrieking as she runs to dunk her head in the bath, squealing like a sizzling pork sausage.

It must have been a candle, Everleigh keeps saying, are you ok? You must have leaned in too close.

The next morning, at first light, I notice Ramona in the kitchen, leaving without a word. She writes a note and puts it by the fruit bowl on the kitchen table: she writes to say she has to go home to Liverpool for a New Year's Eve family bash.

5.

Everleigh Davies, my dear girl.

I cannot help but notice that you are nervous, anxious to speak to him again. Your heart is not quite so glad and giddy, your heart isn't skipping so happily. You say, hello, Charlie, and you lean over the bar and kiss him on the cheek, not on the lips.

It is dead quiet in the pub, the after-lunch lull; old Joe is in the corner nursing his stout and reading the paper by the roaring fire. You finish polishing the glasses; your shift ends soon. Charlie swaggers about. He orders a pint and then offers you a cigarette; you say, no thank you, and he lights up and blows smoke in grey curling question marks. Charlie is full of hot air, he talks too fast about not much. So, what have you been up to? Not much. How was your Christmas? Ok, you? He keeps remarking on how you look and tells you that you look nice.

Everleigh, you do look good today. It is true, you are glowing, but you shrug and tell him, it's not for you, it's for Joe, and you nod over, and Joe gives you a toothless grin. You wear a black polo-neck jumper dress and knee-high boots. Charlie feels your curves through your clothes when he makes a big fuss of persuading you to come around to his side of the bar to hug him hello. It is not a good hug. He cajoles you and says, come here, grumpy, as he grabs at you. I'll take you down town, he tells you, you'll like that, that'll cheer you up. When he hugs you I vibrate with anger. I feel it, I hear his insecure heart; he smells of stale sweat, bacon grease and dishonesty.

When your shift ends it is already dark. You take the bus together from Kentish Town, through Camden down into Soho. You sit next to Charlie. He is not wearing a proper coat and looks cold and small in just his shirt sleeves in midwinter. It irritates you, he irritates you. This will be the last time you see him, Everleigh, you're holding in so much, but somehow you manage to be civilised, so you ask, how's your dad, how's the butcher's shop, how is Crowley, Crowley, Crowley? Good. Good. Good.

I Am Hagstone

China Town is busy. Red and green tinsel and flashing lights hang around the kitsch paintings of Chinese landscapes, mountains and lakes. You sit together at a table in the window. The rushed waiter interrupts things; you order your favourite, crispy duck pancakes and a bottle of white wine, since he's paying; he orders a dish of beef and noodles and a beer. There is a loaded silence between you. He is first to break it.

You alright? Charlie asks, you're a bit quiet, your time of the month is it? You shudder; you don't know how to say what must be said. You just know you mustn't cry. You shrug. Then he snaps brusquely, Everleigh, you may as well spit it out, I can tell you have the hump with me.

Well, the last time I saw you, you . . .

As you stop speaking you search his face for acknowledgement, for remorse, for shame, for guilt, maybe for an apology. The last time you saw him it was brutal. Charlie snorts as he quickly says, yeah, umm, sorry about that, I reckon I was a bit pissed. Then he laughs, hollow and loud.

Miss Everleigh, what do you tell yourself? Perhaps that it wasn't that big a deal, maybe it was all in your head, maybe it was just a role play, but without the play. You tell yourself you asked for it. You wanted Charlie. You went on that awful date at the cinema. You walked home after but when you got there he rang you and said, come over; he said, come over, come to my place, he said, you're being a silly girl, and he said, I'm waiting here for you, we're meant to be getting engaged. How you believed him when he said he loved you, oh how you wanted him to love you, to be loving, yes, you wanted that, you fell for it, yes, you wanted him, yes, but not like that.

Silence.

Now you're opposite each other in front of plates of glutinous beef noodles and chunks of greasy duck. You look at his shifty eyes, you watch his face, his chewing jaw. You focus on his dry flaky skin on his chin, a shaving rash, his dirty uneven chewed-up fingernails, the slightly thinning hair on the top of his straw-blonde head. How Charlie talks about himself, with an air of entitlement: he says, sometimes I need to do my own thing, you know, my freedom is important to me. As he says this he looks at you, puppy-eyed and wretched, his fork digging at the goo of his slimy beef chop suey. It is too hot; he shovels it into his mouth, it burns his tongue and he talks with his mouth wide open to cool it down.

I understand, you say.

Charlie continues, mouth open, churning noodles and meat; he tells you he has told his other girlfriends about you now, so it's all out in the open. Everleigh, I feel you, your heart is thrashing in your chest – he said *girlfriends* as in plural? He has told other people? Now you hurt not just for yourself but for all the other women he is stringing along, and it is then you realise that you are one of many broken promises. Now, the penny drops. Everleigh, you got it wrong and you got it all right; trust your gut, your fears are correct: he had no intention of marrying you. Everleigh, I tried to tell you, Hagstone is always right.

You tune out and then you tune back in. Charlie says, you know how I feel about you, he says, you know what you mean to me, Everleigh, and he squeezes your arm. Then he boasts, my other girlfriends aren't quite as insecure as you, Everleigh; I think you are so great, such a brilliant girl, but you're a bit old-fashioned, Everleigh, you can be a little needy, I need to be free, and then he pauses and says, it's not you, it's me.

Everleigh – you should get up and walk away. You should throw your wine in his face. You should stab your fork into his face. You should slash his throat and smash his face into his chop suey. You should slice his eyelids off and spoon his eyeballs out like a pair of sweet lychees. Do you want me to do it for you?

You are nauseous, faint, too sad to eat, too angry to swallow. You think, *I cannot eat this, this crispy duck, the plum sauce is too salty.* You hold it in; you will not let him see how you feel. Your jaw is clenched. You finish the wine, down it on an empty stomach, warm and sour. Words still spew from Charlie – now he talks about time. He repeats, it is not you it's me; fundamentally, he says, men are complicated. I need space and time, men need a lot more space and time than women.

Everleigh, your heart is racing. I feel you, how you feel used, chewed up and spat out. You suddenly see Charlie for what he is: an indulgent little boy, a mean man. It's not you it's me, he says for the third time; I mean what do you want, Everleigh? Charlie asks, what do you really want from me? He asks whilst chewing a bulging mouth of beefy noodles, what do you want from me?

Nothing, Charlie, nothing at all.

As you say this you get up and you walk away. You look back through the restaurant window, you flash Charlie a smile, then see his plate, visualise it, see it is all squirming with maggots and flies, see the fried beef and onion all sparkling pretty with shards of glass in pools of beef and blood, manifest it. See Charlie screaming, his nose bleeding profusely, he spits his hot food and blood out, spitting chunks of glass out, his cut tongue, bleeding lips, heat pustules, bleeding gums, throat jammed with glass, noodles as writhing snakes, coughing and spluttering, bleeding from the mouth, bleeding from the nose, blood, blood, white tablecloth, red everywhere, everywhere is suddenly Charlie's blood.

6.

I am Hagstone.

Me and my dear Miss Everleigh Davies have spent far too many hours thinking about Charlie. We have seen far too many evenings with my Miss Everleigh shivering in the cold hallway in a dressing gown, waiting by the shared house payphone. Now no more tears for Charlie O'Reilly.

You've wept far too much for that one boy. Now a

ripe fury consumes you. You avoid Charlie. You do not go anywhere near the butcher's shop now. You do not know what to do with this fury and anger. You have not spoken to him since that time: not since the cinema and the night you went to his house and saw your red dress torn and thrown onto his bedroom floor. Not since the bloody chop suey. Not since that whole miserable time. All the things he said, it loops in your head, all the things he did and all the promises he broke. Everleigh, you are in a thick dark treacle; you drink cheap red wine, you smoke and pace your room. You talk with Catherine and Yasmina until the early hours. They soothe you, console you and feed you. I feel you, your pain and isolation. You rarely leave the house. I see you search for Charlie in your mind and find him only in nightmares. I hear your fear and doubts, your grief swirling in your young body and mind.

The snow falls, thick and fast. Your period is late, I am growing in you. I show you the truth, I show you the way to your heart's true desires. Yasmina brings you tea and toast and gets into your bed. Catherine comes in from the shops with treats, chocolates, and the local newspaper. You see the front page.

Look! Charlie's dead!

You look at the picture of the butcher's: it is cordoned off, the smashed-up O'Reilly's sign hanging off the shop front, Charlie's motorbike jutting out of the broken front window, broken glass in the road. The headline 'BUTCHER SHOP SMASH!' Charlie is dead, his father is dead; a head-on collision into the front of the shop, an explosion. The newspaper calls it a freak accident and a community tragedy.

It is so creepy, do you think it was us? Do you? Yasmina gasps. Do you think it was the Hagstone that made this happen?

I dunno, I mean, he was probably drunk driving, Catherine remarks; he was probably driving like a maniac. But we did say death to the butcher's boy.

Yes we did. Fuck.

What can I say? I only do as I am bid, mistress. I want to please you. I do what is necessary.

When you are alone in your room, you light a circle of candles and stand in salt and sage; you hold me in your hand and look into the mirror. Now see how we see each other, look at me, look at us, look past your own reflection. You look me in the eye: I am Hagstone, horned beast, winged demon, in the mirror, beside you, behind you, become you, inside you, coming through to you from the other side of the mirror, the dark side of the mirror, an ever-present devil. You stand still and fearless. Now you ask the right questions and now you get the big answers. You speak in the language of flame, a multitude of multiverses, in our reflection in the mirror; you know the answers before I can swing . . .

Did WE kill Charlie?

Yes.

Did Charlie ever love me?

Stop – still I stop, still.

I Am Hagstone

I know what you are thinking so I make a tiny circle anti-clockwise.

7.

At the funeral, see all the family and friends wearing black, see how they say the right words, they say it is all very sad, he was so very young, he was too young, it was so sudden, so tragic, he had so much to live for. At the crematorium people whisper and gossip and stare. You stand in your power with your belly full of a devil's bastard. How they talk and gossip, how they love to spread rumours and lies, hear them all murmuring under the music . . .

Motorbike accident.
Yeah! Tragic!
So bizarre.
Who chose this song?
Charlie loved it.
He was too young, too young.
He was so young.
Everleigh is over there, look!
Yeah, but the family wants nothing to do with her.
I mean, she's clearly grieving, but changed, look at her . . .
I mean just look at her . . . look!
WITCH!

Ramona appears from the back of the room and yells it loud and clear.

Everleigh Davies, you are a witch! EVERLEIGH DAVIES IS A WITCH!

Ramona Barrow stands alone there, her shaved head, her pale face in a grimace, a half-drunk bottle of Jameson's in one hand and a lit cigarette in the other.

EVERLEIGH DAVIES IS A WITCH!

Ramona yells and points at us. Everyone stares at Ramona swaggering about, and then back at us again.

EVERLEIGH DAVIES IS A WITCH!

They gasp and mutter and nudge each other; eventually Ramona is gently led away. The congregation all mutter that word, witch, witch, what does she mean witch? The word vibrates in the walls and hangs in the air. The mourners wear judgements, excuses are made, guilt is passed along with the hymn sheets, the blame is hanging heavy in the air. Ronald O'Reilly is dead. Charlie O'Reilly is dead. Father Johnson gives a cloying speech about Charlie, the one and only beloved son of Mary and Ronald O'Reilly, and when he says *sin* he looks directly at us, Everleigh. That ugly-hearted priest stares down from the pulpit in judgement. Catherine holds one hand and Yasmina the other; you three are standing united. You want to see it, you need to see Charlie burn. People stare and whisper. All of your uncried tears are hard inside of you. A bitterness and anger where once was all soft, a weight of sorrow and grief where once there was a carefree mind.

You have taken me off the silk ribbon and put me in a dark place which I now know is your warm coat pocket.

I Am Hagstone

We take a train and travel south, back to the coast. You shiver and walk alone on the beach, the beach where you first found me. Your face is buried deep in your scarf, your hands shoved into your coat pockets, and your thumb is on me, feeling me. More snow is forecast. It is a bitter cold and wintry afternoon; the sky is empty and grey as rope above a churning brown sea. Frothing waves rush to shore, the sound of the wind, the pounding weight of seawater on the stones, wave after wave, the crash of water, the pull and draw, drag of rocks and pebbles, of salt and stone.

You sit on the sea wall and swig from a bottle of vodka. You cry one tear; it stays in the rim of your eye until the wind snatches it. Then you drink another slug from the bottle. As you drink it burns; you gasp and then drink more. Your feet in black leather boots, your legs swinging, the back heel of your boot banging, drumming against the sea wall. You fiddle in your coat pockets and find a cigarette and light it inside your coat collar; the wind is against you. You hold me in your hand. You rub me with your thumb.

I am Hagstone.

You tip your head back and swallow me whole, Hagstone, you chase me down with vodka.

Now we're united and we are truly one, Everleigh, our child grows strong inside you. We are timeless and forever. And the sons of men that will hunt us, that burn us, that only mean to hurt us, will one day be no more. We watch the wind change, we wait for the tide to turn.

BOG PEOPLE

NOTES

1. There was a black-and-white photograph of this Christmas party in the Folklore Library. *Christmas* is scribbled on the back, and the names of all four women present: *Everleigh, Ramona, Yasmina, Catherine*. And if you look closely at this black-and-white image there is an extra person, a black shadow, a spectral figure behind Everleigh at the table that night. The Folklore Library was torn down and the site made into a shopping centre and car park.
2. Charles O'Reilly and Ramona Barrow were seen arguing outside the Junction Tavern in Kentish Town; witnesses report that she attacked and scratched his face in a drunken rage. When Charlie's body was retrieved from the wreck, he was ten times over the alcohol limit. When he lost control of the vehicle, the motorbike smashed directly into the window of his father's butcher's shop and exploded into flames. It was inspected post-collision and the brake lines had been cut, and there were signs of extensive tampering. This led to further investigation and a conclusion that Ramona Barrow and/or Everleigh Davies were possible suspects, but the evidence was circumstantial. The case went cold.
3. The butcher's dog Crowley was named after Aleister Crowley. During the furore following these events, some said that the O'Reilly family worshipped Crowley's dark arts and followed the teachings of Thelema

I Am Hagstone

and that they had practised blood sacrifice. Since this incident this entire section of Kentish Town high street has been torn down and developed.

4. Some say that if you say or read the name Crowley three times a demon will appear in your mirror.
5. Shortly after the funeral Father Johnson was found dead with broken glass in his mouth.
6. Not all Hagstones are possessed by demons, most are lucky and friendly.
7. Local Sussex folklore says that Aleister Crowley cursed Hastings. 'The wickedest man in the world' died in Hastings in 1947. To some, when you find a Hagstone on Hastings beach it means you are 'protected' and to others that you are 'cursed' to always return there. Crowley's Hastings residence was called Netherwood, where he spent his final days in poverty.
8. The secret ingredient in Nan's batter was a pinch of turmeric.
9. Records show that Everleigh Davies had a healthy baby girl, born with a birthmark on her shoulder shaped like a Hagstone's 'O'.

It Fair Give Me the Spikes

TOM BENN

Tom Benn is an award-winning author, screenwriter, and associate professor in Crime Writing at UEA. His essays and fiction have appeared in *Granta* and the *Paris Review*. His horror film, *Real Gods Require Blood*, premiered in competition at the Cannes Film Festival, and was nominated for Best Short Film at the BFI London Film Festival. His fourth novel, *Oxblood* (Bloomsbury), was longlisted for the Gordon Burn Prize, the CWA's Gold Dagger, and won the *Sunday Times* Young Writer of the Year Award.

Last night I had such a peculiar dream, but oh, it fair give me the spikes.

I dreamt of the place where Old Nick lives, you know, just to see what it was like.

So, I lifted the latch and walked in; The Satan, to me, gave a shout.

'We've not got a seat in the pit or the stalls.'
So, I lifted the latch and walked out . . .

—Northern music hall song

To reckon Borges was right and to imagine some secret shape of time, coarse cuts of repeating lines: then to hear without sound the coal-and-iron chug of the nighttrain crossing the valley as a beginning, a service entry to the female heart of these sorrows, and one which permits **you** circular travel around a fixed point of a kind—a phonograph spindle—with **you** revolving outward, riding vibrations, before returning along a spinning disc of brittle shellac forever skewered upon this locus. Its pattern, a grooved vortex, steadily degrades with each revolution;

with each journey forward and back **you** reach other local beginnings, open wounds like playholes, bleeding through to someone, somewhere, as forgotten music.

[1896]

Follow the nighttrain: stone deaf at the sleeper carriage window as it rumbled across gloomy viaducts, rugged crests of moorland, while sulphurous light broke to reveal a horizon where first light fattened like a dying star and formed the signature of an industrial town already at toil predawn, its factorystacks belching the new day black, the mills dyeing the forked-tongue river sterile inside that Hellmouth north of Halifax where paternal cotton kings had housed their workers in spoked rows of blind back-to-backs quick to tilt and rot.

Within the passenger cabin, **you** found two half-clothed lovers, a handsome Chinese man, Ching Liu, and Lanfen, his doomed wife, who unstitched their lips long enough to glance at **you** in umbra through the steamed cabin glass—a shade kicking swiftly through time, sexed without form like a voyeur's shadow—but they paid **you** no mind.

The town's flame caught Lanfen on one side, striking her skin, hair, teeth. Her husband, using zhezhi papercraft, fashioned a tiny brimmed hat from a banknote, then hung it on his wife's left nipple, at which Lanfen looked down, laughing, as flat daylight replaced her glow.

On the station approach, they saw from their window

the dank morning wash the run of posters along the depot yard fence. Each bore their illustrated faces: *Chinese Sorcerer with Juggling Bride Acrobat! Directly from the Celestial Empire! One Night Only! SOLD OUT.*

A rap at their cabindoor. Lanfen made her husband's nose a hatstand while she concealed her breast. With the banknote balanced, Ching Liu, now hatted and buttoned and coated, lifted the latch and opened the door wide to the young steward. In good morning, Lanfen raised a leg toe-to-ceiling and held it there without breaking a smile or the tension. The young steward coughed and shrank from her display of strength, balance, poise. He stammered for forgiveness. Ching Liu took the banknote off his nose, pressed it warmly into the steward's waistcoat, and walked out after his wife, following the music of her laughter, a music unheard by **you**.

A twinhorse coach unloaded onto a narrow thoroughfare. Stagehands carried the luggage into the Tailored Pig boarding house where an imposing landlord—broomtashed; belly and braces held in fustian—passed a room key to one who took the bags upstairs. The landlord welcomed Lanfen open-armed. It was not their first stay. On his walls: framed portraits of music hall stars and playbills from bygone seasons. Male and female impersonators; grinning ghouls in minstrelface; local talent; touring oddities. Illustrious guests of the trade, all.

In the atticroom Ching Liu stalked the foot of an unmade bed in mock dress rehearsal. His was a solemn conjurer's act. His warmth vanished into Eastern caricature. Lanfen timed him from the bed, her limbs casually knotted over her neck. Ching Liu released a dagger from a flowing sleeve. It rattled in the headboard –

almost skinning Lanfen's toes.

She hooprolled her spine, unwinding herself, then vaulted into his arms: a fearless nightly receiver of her husband's blade.

Soon the mills let out onto day dark as night. Then the workers packed the music hall for tumblers racing gleams of ignited gunpowder; otherworldly visitations; trick daggers to the heart. Coloured lamps leaked over rows of pulledtooth grins, calloused hands fluttering like hellfire in a soundless thrum of applause.

After their act, they smoked Woodbines with other travelling performers at the Tailored Pig. The landlord held a lock-in and poured homebrewed sloe gin. Two Lancastrian clogdancing sisters drunkenly attempted to teach Lanfen their routine. But Lanfen's feet were too small for their clogs, and she accidentally kicked one off. Ching Liu ducked as it flew through the inn window and into a passing muledrawn coalcart. Even the landlord laughed. Then the clock struck above a cold fireplace and the clog sisters snored in a single chair while the others had retired to their rooms. The landlord had collapsed on his floorboards, drink glasses arranged in close outline so that when he twitched in his stupor, wetting himself, the glasses tinkled. Lanfen stepped over this music, tugged by her husband's hand.

Tipsy, they embarked on their nightwanderings, past witching hour. Kissing up broken cobble lanes, wearing shadows to duck a bobby on the beat. They reached the top of the town, where the night had no temperature and a naked moon shone daybright, and the paved paths broke into rural tracks, and Lanfen chose one that led to a stone-walled cemetery on the border of black hilltop and sky.

Angelwings parted and spotlit the gate like a stage prop. Lanfen skipped to it and found her light, arching her body on instinct to receive her audience, up in the gods and along the lane –

where **you** remained in impossible time and motion, a shivering scratch of ten thousand faces, as **you** lunged and jabbed at a silhouetted woman with **your** razor shard of shellac.

Mute figures, which Lanfen watched pull together and twist apart, approaching her in a stumbling dance.

Ching Liu touched Lanfen's waist. He looked at her and he looked at **you** and he saw nothing. Even as **you** rushed **your** quarry, almost knocking Lanfen over with fright as she threw herself against the cemetery gate while **you** tore townward, driving the woman out of the light, tripping her and stabbing and slashing, until she had passed and dropped from sight.

Lanfen trotted down the lane, following phantoms, ready to cry out. Already **you** had returned unnoticed from another direction of time, and **you** watched Ching Liu comfort her.

She was not trying to understand what she had seen, how or why; was agitated only by the effort it took to recall witnessing *herself*—another Lanfen—doubled and terrorised without form or sound. Seeing that dart of recognition on her own shouting face when this other her had crossed her light. The harder she thought about and felt for this noisy afterimage, the more degraded was its retrieval, till her mind buzzed and cracked and emptied. And when the noise faded from her expression, Ching Liu, relieved, claimed her hand and led her inside the beautiful silences of that cemetery, where Lanfen, dazed and forgetting fully what she had felt and witnessed, could see only by the white fingers of moonbeams as they fucked on an ancient grave hooded by enormous bramble. Tickled by bolting spiders and beetles, roaming leverets and hedgehogs, she slowed to peer up beneath the spiralling canopy of thorns, plucking blackberries to eat in osculation. As she climaxed the moon went out and they slept close until a freezing twilight showed their breaths.

When Lanfen awoke, she woke hurting, shrieking.

Ching Liu rose in sore confusion, and tried to console her, warm her, lift her to stand –

only for her to collapse on her skinned frostbitten toes.

Ink-blotched, swollen crooked, her feet dark and dead. Like the night itself had taken her flesh, and her career.

Nearby, the cast clog from the Tailored Pig was arrowed in fresh gravesoil, at which Lanfen screamed her sadness.

It Fair Give Me the Spikes

[1897]

Echoes of her pain played as music corroding across a phonograph 78, as brass notes, sour jokes and local patter, as barmy warnings and queer turns of phrase. Her blackened toes and dawn cries transmuting into comic song.

Heard
>   now
>>   by
>>>   **you**

on the return thereabouts to that beginning—a shade slowing through time, a year after, under another discus moon revolving, a circle of showing—when at the music hall a chairman announced the night's dancers, singers, curiosities, as **you** lifted the latch and walked unseen through a young comic pacing to go on. Trampcostumed, weakchested, heavily madeup: this Lancastrian lad, billed as Jim Cornet, had already collected many names onstage and off-, and so kept poor track of who he was now, would later be, and last week had been.

Martha knew he lacked polish and timing, but saw charm in the way he tripped over his lyrics and feet. His slapstick and woe received scattered applause. But sod the house: from the wings Martha liked what she saw and whistled to let it be known. Distracted, he turned his head and was thrown further off his mark, but played it to his advantage:

Cough-cough. 'A lass up in the gods says to me the other night, I ought to cadge a lift straight back to sunny

Manchester. I says, "Nay, lass. See, Jim Cornet's going far." She says not far enough.' A few laughs, under Martha's. 'Ta-ra for now! Be good!' Jim fled stage left, by mistake or design, then stage right, passing Martha in the wing. A shy grin. He wouldn't meet her eyes.

'Oi, Lancashire! You was alright by the end. But no cornet. Need a new name is all.'

'I'll think on it. You on next, are you?'

'Aye. What would you give to be above me?'

He coughed a fit. She got him a drink of water and he sipped it and waited with her, trading daft faces, then watched her get introduced and go on.

Martha greeted the stage on rubber hips. 'Settle down, settle down, while I sings you one of me own funnies...' Her voice she knew on a good night was halfway grand: stronger and sweeter than it needed to be. And when she skipped off stage to fattening applause, her eyes were buzzing for Jim backstage. She tapped a stagehand readying props for the headliner. 'Not seen that lil' Lancashire lad fussing about, have you, love?'

Before he could answer, Ching Liu appeared in costume and makeup, ready to be announced. Daggers secured under his flowing sleeves. His stagehand lit a long pipe issuing curls of tinted smoke.

The chairman recounted: '... and now, returning right the way from the Celestial Empire; please, my dear folk, the cruel dragon sorcerer himself; the master of black arts of the deadly Far East; he who speaks no word of English...'

It Fair Give Me the Spikes

Ching Liu winked at grinning Martha: 'Not a word.'

'... he who claims he can impale any lady's heart by blindfolded dagger toss and compel spirits to mend it, and afterward her blood shall remain on the blade. I give you Ching Liu, the Great Chinaman!'

He strode on stage robed in pipe smoke. Martha lingered awhile, then spotted Jim further back, hopping and turning but forever in someone's way. She smiled, willing him to see her, until he did.

Soon, over the skin of Martha's shoulder, Jim sneezed once, twice. 'Make a wish,' Martha said, within the broom cupboard chalkmarked *Private-Dressing-Room*, with its short bench and single stool below a lamped mirror; enough space for a costume case and a tin washstand, but tight enough for her to hold each wall as they made standing love in their stage garb, before the mirror. Jim finished, hacking and wheezing into her hair, sweating out the last of his powder makeup, and Martha laughed a dirty laugh, and Jim shut his eyes, and she kissed them and took his waist and didn't let go. He braced against the dressing bench that held a carton of Woodbines, two open envelopes with Chinese logograms, and a miniature paper hat. Applause reached them from the house. Martha hadn't room to bow. Jim curtsy-bobbed instead. She laughed; he turned his head in time to cough away.

'Right bad chest on you for a young lad.'

'Been bad with me lungs since I were kneehigh. Me mam made us kip out by the coalbunker if she was in entertaining her fellers.'

'Forgive her. You made it this far.'

'Our Lord's job, forgiving; not ours.'

'She had you out singing for your supper, I'll bet.'

'She was little, you know, me mam. Four foot summat.'

'Was?'

'Our Lord give me two bandy legs, right for acting the fool and right for running from home to find me fortune.'

'They ran you right into me.'

Ching Liu returned from the stage, shutting the dressing room door before his assistants could follow. The three performers regarded each other, damp-hot and without shame, their bloods coursing with clannish goodwill. Still Martha wouldn't let Jim go. Jim shielded and tidied her, as Ching Liu began to uncostume while he smoked a Woodbine. The small windowless space filled with roiling smoke. Jim buttoned a cough.

Ching Liu told them: 'I have toured England twice with my wife, Lanfen, a dancing contortionist of great skill and beauty. The truest talents, no tricks' – dropping a dagger into the case. 'Last year we performed here, together. My Lanfen caught frostbite and lost her foot. Still she rests at home.'

'I *am* ever so sorry,' Martha said.

'Home?' Jim said.

'Limehouse, London,' Ching Liu said at the washstand.

Jim said, 'Aye, no wonder you tell this lot you don't speak English. You're safer being foreign than southern round here.' He coughed. 'Once knew a London feller of the trade called Clegg. Pinched a load of offcuts from a fabric shop to make one of them China robes. Painted his self up, then started going by Mr Wu. Did better than he ever done as Clegg.'

Ching Liu dropped his Woodbine into the basin. 'A mighty conjurer, this Mr Clegg.'

'A mighty swindler more like.'

'I was his loyal apprentice, I'm sure ... or was he mine?'

Martha giggled.

To her he said: 'Is this one your apprentice?'

'Why, this is Jim Cornet from Manchester. Though I reckon he ought to go by John Willie from now on. John Willie. The next emperor of Lancashire.'

Ching Liu bowed solemnly in his undergarb to John, then, imitating his accent, declared: 'John Willie, King of the Mancs, Emp of Lancs. And you are Martha, his queen?' Without effort, he continued the conversation while he changed his shoes, put on pants and shirts and sackcoat. There was an urgent knock and he barked at the door in Cantonese, then smirked at them. Martha straightened his bow tie. He showed them an envelope from the dresser.

'My wife Lanfen and I, we write our poems. A verse for each town, each stage.'

Martha opened it, breathed its perfumed scent, studying this love code under the lamp. She pointed to a logogram. 'What does this mean? This one?'

Ching Liu whispered in her ear; she whispered in John's ear, who coughed again.

'Give her our love, won't you?' Martha said.

Ching Liu said, 'I will sow your pleasures into my next poem.'

Martha and John saw Ching Liu back to his lodgings at the Tailored Pig. He went in only to return, handing Martha a bottle of bramble gin. 'The landlord's own brew.'

Each of them was already plenty drunk. Martha gave John the bottle to admire.

'Ta, Mr Liu. Love to your missus. Now mind how you go.'

'I like this expression: *mind how you go*. Mind not where but *how*.'

John bowed and Martha pecked his cheek and Ching Liu smiled at them both and mimicked perfectly, 'Ta-ra! Ta-ra!'

'I do hope his missus likes our poem,' Martha said. 'Ay, they'll lock you out too, won't they?'

'I'm more mithered about who'll see Queen Martha home to Mother and Dad.'

'I'm already in for a belting. Might as well suffer dree with them thieves and lunatics of the night. If I'm lucky they might cart us away; show us the world; give us a new act.'

Martha and John, hip-to-hip, roamed town, swigging themselves unsteady. The night dream-quiet, theirs; humpbacked lanes of shattered cobble bound by mellow halos of gaslamp.

'You really sing your own songs?' John asked her.

'Course. Why? Who sings yours?'

It Fair Give Me the Spikes

They passed the toffee shop selling round tins from the sweetfactory.

'You've a voice on you like boiling black treacle,' he said.

'You've treacle for brains. My doing.'

'How long've you been at this game?'

Martha held up seven fingers.

'Seven years? And you've never left this town? That's longer than I've—'

'No. It were me seventh time up there. The chairman, ol' Percy, got fed up of me mithering to go on, so he give in last month. Me mam and dad reckon better to have no daughter than a stage performer. I can't blacken their door any darker.'

John coughed; she slapped his back, put an ear to his heart: 'Poor love. I'll scare the sitting Devil off your chest, so help me.'

'You could and all. We could sing him some smut not even fit for Mr Liu and his Limehouse wife.'

Martha steered them over a country lane, composing as she sang and swigged, heelpatting the cobbles for accompaniment. Then she kissed John the words and melody, and already she knew that this had the makings of a terrible love.

'Fast learner, you,' she said.

'You're the fast cat. Where am I taking you?'

In the freak daybright dark the lane went high enough for them to overlook the gasworks, the sweetfactory, a matchstick mob of chimneystacks rowed and partitioned like the music hall seats at full house.

'Seeing this?' Martha said to the roofless sky.

John coughed. 'I said there was summat queer in Mr Liu's pipe.'

Martha laughed. 'Don't let me go. Swear.'

'So swears John Willie, Emperor in waiting.'

'You shan't be waiting long. I know it.'

'Be long after you've lived your dreams twice over. That I can know.' He passed her the gin and they went on.

They arrived at the stage apron of the old cemetery, and its spotlit gate, under which Martha pranced until she saw **you** approaching –

up the lane, in a dumbshow of three, in which **you** tore at two silhouetted women, pricking their knuckles as they gripped the hems of their skirts to run. Let the women twist free, trip ahead, stagger closer to Martha without footsteps or voices, without human music.

Martha tried to call to them, but for John Willie the dark stayed still. He saw nobody. Heard only Martha's shallow breath beside him. When she shook him to get him to see, the gin bottleneck slipped from her fist, emptying uncracked onto the lane.

Stagelight shone in the expanding gin pool; a frightened Chinese woman emerged when she stepped through it silently to pass Martha, arching her back too slow for **your** razor shard of shellac.

Freckles of hot blood stamped Martha's face. She felt each splash of pinheat, then saw them repeated for a moment on the turning profile of the second woman chased, as she too crossed Martha's light.

It Fair Give Me the Spikes

She was another Martha, another double.

But **you** stabbed and drove the two women back into silhouette and down the track, townward, gone.

Puzzled, John kept Martha there, turning his body into her. 'What's to do?'

She looked to him to confirm the blood. John gave her nowt. She bent to find herself in the pool beneath them, only the gin had soaked away. Already she was forgetting what she had seen.

John took her through the gate, awed as she fed him blackberries from neglected graves. They made love among the insects, above the rested, after which John pillowed his coat and she wrapped them together in her wools and calico and they dozed awhile.

'I worry for your toes,' he whispered, gone shy. Another kiss put him right. His and her hands to her belly. 'I dreamt I'd me a son what grew up to tread the boards.'

'Our son? Oh aye.'

'It's true,' he said.

Martha laughed her dirty laugh and bared her belly to the moonlight, its train of matted hairs. '*A little peach in my orchard grew. A little peach of golden hue. Grown by Mother Moon and wet by Father Dew. It grew and grew . . .*'

Later, his snore woke Martha to grey morning, birdsong, shivery damp, migraine and scratches, aches and cramps. His breaths showed.

She felt to fix her skirts; they were tattered and stained at the back. Sticky blood on her fingertips. She rose to examine herself, cloudshadows moving over John. The gooseflesh of her thighs ran with drips, but she could find no wound.

'Blackberries. Be the bramblethorns.' He coughed, squinting up at her, half-awake, then saw she was unsatisfied and finally got to his feet, buckling under the weight of gin. 'Don't know about you, lass, but I slept like a top.' He knocked twigs and living things from his clothes, noted a lost waistcoat button. Then held his sore head, making sure that it had not been lost either. Martha's chapped cheek he brought to his chest.

'Count me toes,' she said.

[1938]

From there **you** caught an old song of circular ruin playing within the pillowed skull of a young woman asleep in her widowed father's house in that Northern milltown in the hills. Feeling the pulse of this music, **you** saw the dimensions of her dream in auditory vibrations, reverse waves which carried **you** into her ear. Down and down **you** fell, to another beginning, until **you** lifted the latch and took a seat in the stalls of her dream and took **your** pleasure from the fourth row of a local music hall of yesteryear, not true to life but far truer, one just as the dreamer dreamed it be, and tonight an empty house save **you**.

Timid was this dreamer, alone and on stage: a tired factoryhand of twenty-three, unwed, lotus in profile, innocent of any audience when again her music began –

inside a moonpale cone of spotlight, a shellac record

It Fair Give Me the Spikes

span on a dusty phonograph tabled before her. The live recording played tinny applause. Painful fidelity: shrill, distorted.

May was staged half in shadow, sitting on a worn, moth-bitten hearthrug. She wore her sweetfactory uniform: haircap, blue collared smock dress. She leaned forward and her sallow cheeks hollowed under the halo. Without taking her eyes off the phonograph, she filled a confectionery tin with wrapped toffees from a sagging pile of sweets in her skirt lap. When the tin was full, she reached over the rug for the disc lid. A scraping as she tried shutting the tin. The sound stabbed her ears. But she kept pressing and turning. The record jumped. May blinked tears until finally she lifted the lid and saw the tin was now empty – just as a reedy, male, Lancastrian voice sang a cappella on record:

Last night I had such a peculiar dream, but oh, it fair give me the spikes. I dreamt of the place where Old Nick lives, you know, just to see what it was like.

Flat vowels gave way to a stronger, wittier, female voice, and a tuneless piano walked through their duet.

So, I lifted the latch and walked in; The Satan, to me, gave a shout. 'We've not got a seat in the pit or the stalls.' So, I lifted the latch and walked out.

May swayed to this ditty and began refilling the tin from the endless pile of foil toffees in her lap. She repeated this ritual as the song ended and the applause returned, even when the female singer spoke to May through the phonograph horn while the needle ran:

Ee, never mind, our May. Sick to death o' toffees, I bet. Packing sweets all day in that factory. But soon you'll be clocking off; then you can come down and see me. That's if your dad lets you out the house. Us lasses have the same trouble with men as we do with toffee. Open our mouths too often to either and we risk having no teeth.

May twitched and **you** smiled as recorded laughter blared ugly from the horn.

Now, I might not be as sweet as May's toffees, but I can still give you belly ache. So, ay – forget your northern sorrows, all yous, at least for now. Have y'selves a right good laugh. Go on; it's on me. Put it all on Martha. Your Martha. Martha Maria Salter – a local lass, as you well know. And if you don't, well, how do you not? I mean, how do you do?

More ugly laughter.

An offstage door creaked and slammed.

Oi. Quick, May! Quick, love!

'What?' May stopped packing her toffees.

It's your dad. Back from the Tailored Pig. Be wanting his bit o' supper, and the rest o' your factory wages, and summat else if you're not careful.

A drunken, polio-stricken man hobbled across the stage, silhouetted on crutches. May never turned to see, not when he dropped a crutch and it clattered and he muttered, louder and louder, for her to aid him into the light, or when he went on without it.

Now mind how you go, May. Scream murder, if you have to. Ta-ra, love!

It Fair Give Me the Spikes

He reached the phonograph and flung the shellac disc into the stalls. 'What you listening to this barmy old muck for?'

'Stove's warm, Dad.'

'Then bring a daft widower his supper. Go on, May. Away.' He stooped, shaky with effort, to whisper against her ear: 'Be a good lass.'

And May flinched from his mouth, from those words, cupping her ear to keep them out, but it was too late and her ear bled and it poured between her fingers, down her neck, her uniform. Blood tap-tapped the tin lid.

Then May's dad was gone. The tin empty again; the record revolving on the phonograph for Martha's duet: its sound muffled, ringing, heard through a perforated eardrum. Tired May swayed regardless as she refilled the tin and bled.

At this, in **your** seat, **you** polluted her dreamhall and then lifted the latch and walked out. By daybreak **you** would drain from her head, trickle down the sinuses to crust her philtrum, to be mistaken by her in the mirror for cold mucus; **your** spend a salt-rind in the shells of her ears for her to attack with a wrungout flannel at the wash-stand while she readied for work, hurrying to be dressed and out the door before her dad had fully risen, when he would wave a crutch and beckon his daughter from the landing to perform further duties.

After clocking off, Gertie dragged her through the old streets, a sealed world in afternoon dark, and mounted a dogshat doorstep to a sunken terraced cottage so slanted with wear that she had to hop down again to avoid the mess. When Gertie kicked from it a lump of coal with her factory shoe, May saw the small run in her stockings. Gertie looked over her shoulder sharply: her strong face, the dead front tooth, a fortnight-old blackeye the colour of smoked haddock. A stubborn tenderness showed the longer she fixed on May, that tenderness an *apple of golden hue. Warmed by Father Sun and wet by Mother Dew. It grew and grew.* 'You coming or what? We're here.'

Still May lingered, shy in her overcoat and headscarf – as cranked sound blasted from within, shaking through the rotted frontdoor.

'Gertie, listen. That music.'

'Oh, just wait . . .' Gertie flashed a brass key from her handbag, opened the door and yanked May inside.

They had to shout over the old music, uncoating in the dim warren of the hallway. 'Place is a bloody midden, I know. But it's a cheap room to call ours after five, Wednesday afternoons. Landlady's no telltale. She's a right one. She makes out she was on the stage. Would have to have been donkey's years ago. No truth to it, I reckon. But she's blinking barmy now.'

'She'll hear you!' May said.

'She won't. She's gone deaf.'

Awaiting them: a 78 labelled *John Willie 1907* turned

on the gramophone, a dull needle doing damage. But no music was heard by Old Martha, singing and prancing in her girlish rags. Just a tactile resonance which buzzed around her small backroom with its notched and blackened mantle and little misframed portraits of wildlife and mythic scene nailed up all over to no design. A broken tile fireplace, spitting unguarded, threw the shadow of some great breathing animal. The buzzing was how Old Martha experienced this recording; its constancy kept her spirit and house standing. Hipswaying over to the fire, she took a squished blackberry from a saucer of curdled milk on her mantelpiece. She stained her lips with it, smacking them together to even the colour, then admired herself in the warped reflection of the gramophone horn. Behind her lay the hulking mastiff, docktailed and brindleblack, with drooped eyes of burning moonlight. Old Martha bid it, then shouldered the front paws, and waltzed about the room with her huge dog.

Gertie and May had already entered, wincing at the music. The dog dropped to the hearth corner to watch them. And Martha sucked more blackberries off her fingertips, rocking before the gramophone, drinking its thin sound. She acknowledged the women opaquely before returning to wherever this music took her.

'Hullo, Missus Salter! Hullo, Martha! S'only me. S'only Gertie. This is me lil' sister, May. She works with us at the factory. We've come straight from there . . . Martha, love? Watch me lips.'

Old Martha turned again, squinted at Gertie and

bobbed closer, looking to May in the noisy gloom like some once splendid bird, cramp-caged and neglected, till she carried barely a feather. In her sixties perhaps, or far older or far younger.

She sang-spoke her words: 'That eye's bit better, I see. Bit better. Giving it a rest, is he? Bit better than you *getting* the rest of it, ay?'

Gertie, unfazed: 'I said I've brung me little sister with me. From the factory. This is our May.'

May smiled in polite terror, untying her headscarf, revealing to Martha a short tight-curled bob, her ears bare.

Gertie raised a folded envelope from her handbag. 'And this'll see us through the fortnight.' She held out the money only to be ignored. The seconds stretched until the mastiff leapt up, snatching it from her hand. 'Weeping Jinny! Ooh! Bloody nearly had me fingers!'

Martha was in no hurry to retrieve the envelope from the dog. 'Ay, if she's your sister then I'm still young, plump and sweet, with two working ears and a full season of bookings. Up you go, loves. Fuck as loud as you like. These are the old houses, these are. They hold on to what they hear . . .'

May squeaked with shock.

Martha laughed a dirty laugh and daubed her fingers on her neckline, staining her tatty frock. '. . . Was me mam and dad's, this. And I were made and born up there . . . We get stuck, don't we? Stuck in our blood.'

Gertie said: 'Do you . . . hear yourself . . . when you speak?'

It Fair Give Me the Spikes

May elbowed her.

'No, never.' Martha pointed to the gramophone. 'Only when our poor John sings me songs.'

'*Your* songs?'

Before Martha replied, Gertie had winked ta-ra with her yelloweye, and tugged May towards the stairs. Over the banister they looked down at Martha's wet grin singing at them: 'Don't break me bed!' – as the mastiff chewed on Gertie's shillings.

The front bedroom was curling wallpaper and a bare curtain rail; a tarnished brass bedstead and mouldy mirror above the washstand. Bizarre trinkets and bibelots ran the skirting, sill, bedtable. A tall wooden chest filled an alcove. Gertie locked the door behind them, a key already in the lock.

'Your Francis won't know?' May said.

'Will he buggery. Costing us next to nowt and all.'

'That I'll believe.' May eyed the damp. 'Just, what if somebody sees us? Just, what if—'

'Just get here.'

A half hour and Gertie and May shared a cigarette across the sagging bed, their uniforms hung over the curtain rail with their slips and stockings illumined faintly by the gas torches of older streetlamps.

'Time's it?' May said.

Gertie ashed a chipped ornament balanced on May's thigh. It was shaped like a halved stonefruit. 'There's plenty time. Time for another Chesterfield, maybe two. Don't worry the minutes away.'

'I'm not. Forget what I said before. I'd be glad if we moved in.'

'You'll be home on the hour to play fetch-me-carry-me for your poor dad.'

May moved the ashtray to cup Gertie's belly. Sixteen weeks; just showing. 'Same with you and your Francis,' she said.

'This is me fourth time expecting. Fourth. Not once did he give us any say. Me mam said that it's his right. That I should've given a husband three before I turn twenty-five. And just like him she says I'm to blame. By tomorrow, this'll be the furthest along I've ever gone.'

'Your Francis never touches you of a night when you're expecting?'

'Reckons it's indecent. About the only time he leaves us alone. So, you might as well thank him for today, for this, not God.'

'Don't talk wicked,' May said, taking the cigarette.

'We're all going downstairs in the end, aren't we?'

'Gertie and May. Together. Hand-in-hand when they meet Old Nick.'

Gertie smiled lovingly, pinched the cigarette and smoked it down as another record finished under them. May slipped out of bed, heard the 78 begin again.

'From where is she picking blackberries? It's November.'

Gertie shrugged.

May went: 'Does she really spend day and night cranking these maudlin ditties?'

It Fair Give Me the Spikes

'It'll be how Old Martha went deaf, I reckon.'

May tried the wooden chest. Inside was a mildewy crush of music hall costume: crumpled frocks, bloomers, bustles, headpieces, veils. Crusty letters, lyrics, and a small shoelaced stack of photographs. May went through the circular portraits carefully, checked the inked dates on the back of each.

Young Martha, resplendent in stage dress and makeup.

Young Martha's updated playbill picture, with her now beside a male stage partner.

Young Martha, the spirited bride, with her partner the bridegroom.

'Forty year ago.'

Gertie matched another Chesterfield and inhaled, then came over to inspect the creased wedding portrait, turning it to check the date. 'Well, I'll be. So, Martha *was* on the stage.'

'Looks like they both were.'

Gertie dropped the photograph back into the chest. May set down the rest, then unrolled a tattered playbill: 'Look at her. A singing comedienne. Queen of the hoi polloi.'

'Had them rolling in the aisles, I bet.'

'Been all over, she has.'

Gertie unrolled another, showing Martha low on the billing. 'About as far as Scarborough from what I can tell. Wonder how she ended up back here for good?'

'Widowed? Like me dad. Perhaps she come back to mind her folks. She said this was their place.'

From the chest Gertie pulled out a plum Victorian dress and matching petticoat. 'Here, May. Chuck this on.'

'Give over. I daren't.' Somehow the fabric had an odour of wet soil and leaf and insect. Then for a moment May tasted the scent of weathered limestone.

'For me . . .?'

'No. Not on your life.'

Their chilled sweat drew the whirling dust as they each fought their way into one of Martha's stagefrocks. May sneezed twice, snapping the ash from Gertie's cigarette, which stayed between her lips. In the bad mirror May caught themselves doubled, quarter-costumed, bizarrely transformed.

Gertie wiped away ash, flicked the cig like a tiddlywink into the washstand, then talked to her in the mirror: 'Sneeze twice; make a wish.'

They shared a long stillness before breaking into giggles and Gertie span her round and around until they fell over the bed.

Downstairs, Old Martha put on another record. The song soaked up the laughter from the room:

I dreamt of the place where Old Nick lives, you know . . .

'. . . *just to see what it was like.*' May sang to herself, finishing these lyrics without knowing how she knew them, trying to remember her dream.

Gertie's cigarette had gone out and she plucked another match from her handbag. She looked again at Mirror May, who blushed and stopped singing. But as the song played, something else called to May. She spun again in the ruined frock, fanning the skirts, agitated to find the source of this second song, hidden under the first.

Dragging the chest from the alcove, May uncovered a large damp-mulched hole. May reached in, to her elbow, and pulled out a small filthy coalsack. May started to reach into the sack but stopped. When Gertie touched her, she jumped. Whatever force had been compelling May to find this thing had vanished. So, Gertie took the rancid sack and turned it over above the costume chest: a battered sweet tin fell out, its disc lid shut tight.

'It's one from the factory,' May said.

'From well before our time.'

May held it and half-remembered, her eyes watering. She was cowed when Gertie took it from her.

Gertie got on one knee and opened the tin outward to May, like a mouth, as if proposing to her with an oversized engagement ring box.

'Well . . . ?'

'There's a fortune inside,' May said.

'No?'

'See for yourself.'

Gertie did. Fat, shoelaced wads of old fifty-pound banknotes. 'I know I said y'ought never to tie the knot. But I meant with a feller. How about with me? We could run off and be Lady and Lady Muck. With child.'

'They wouldn't know what to lock us up for first.'

'Not if we went abroad.'

'Gertie, she's deaf not daft.'

'You've seen her. What's she gunna do with this?'

'How'd you ever find this room?'

Her dead tooth showed. 'Advertisement in Hilly's tobacconist. These are old notes, these are. Still, money's money. I could be rid of our Francis. Leave your drunken dad a few bob to square with the tallyman, then he can get pickled in the Tailored bloody Pig for bloody good.'

'Anyroad, your Francis'd never give you the divorce.'

'No, he'd sooner string us up; keep his pride in one piece.'

May twitched and the cash tin fell from Gertie's hands back onto the heap of the open chest. May looked away. A hollowing dread returned. They shared another stillness, a numb kiss; then Gertie started to strip while May retrieved their clothes from the curtain rail.

At the window May saw a flatcapped man on the doorstep. She ducked a heartbeat before he looked up. 'Good God, it's your Francis.'

He went at the frontdoor with boot and fist.

Gertie shrank with each braying thud, still not out of Martha's bustle skirts. She hoisted the frock back up, flinching to the window before May pulled her down.

'Hilly at the tobacco shop. The advertisement. She must've seen you, said summat to him.'

Gertie gripped her. 'That busy boss-eyed cow.'

'Might've been someone at the factory. That Florence? She's always suspected. Or, or, Ivor, in the office? He's a right nark.'

Downstairs the dog barked, alerting Martha to the caller.

It Fair Give Me the Spikes

'She's about to open her door to him,' Gertie said.

But May stopped her from letting go. 'He can't know for sure we're here. And if you call down she won't hear you, but your Francis will. And then we're for it.'

The frontdoor was opened.

'Listen,' whispered May. 'Listen.'

They crawled to the bedroom door but through it the gramophone gave its shout, making it impossible to hear what was said between Old Martha and Francis. Helpless, murmuring prayers, May watched Gertie turn the key in the lock.

'Wait . . .' Fiercer now, May wrapped herself around her.

But Gertie shucked May off like a coat and opened the door and dashed downstairs and May turned and raced to the window and saw Francis soon step out – lowering his cap, raising his coat collar, setting off at not-quite-a-run.

May began to follow Gertie down, but spotted Old Martha's money now fanned over the top of the chest. As she stuffed it quickly back into the tin, the tin into the coalsack, she felt something else there and pulled a mildewed newspaper.

> *November 1922.* JOHN WILLIE, FAMED SINGING COMIC OF THE MUSIC HALLS, DEAD AT FORTY-TWO. LEAVES BEHIND WIFE ELIZA, FOUR SONS AND FOUR DAUGHTERS.

Stuck behind it she unpeeled a handscribbled letter but lost much of the ink to the newsprint. May read on, connecting broken carriages of words into a train of mawkish comedy:

> *Forgiv[e] me sw[eet] Martha my [l]ove for my dre[a]dful aban[don]ing [o]f you all them [y]ears ago . . . I took your hear[t] . . . [y]our songs . . . [y]our spark . . . None knows . . . am still bound to you under [o]ur Lord . . . I sh[all] be [d]ead and b[u]ried soon enough . . . It is [jus]t like you would always tell me – it is not the [c]ough that carries you off but the c[off]in they carry [y]ou off in! . . . [B]ut at l[east] rightly t[he]se earnings [n]ow run back to you . . . [Y]our scoundrel hus[band] John [Will]ie*

May finished and glanced through the open door at the aftersound of a continual silence. Old Martha's music had stopped.

Down she went, still in her plum frock. The mastiff lay beside his mistress; the short fur of its shoulderblades rowed back and forth like dark oars. It whined in May's direction, taking no notice of Gertie, who stood over the body, by the wash of blood leaving Old Martha's head where her skull had cracked on the hearth edge.

May pulled Gertie away and shook her gently. She was weightless and cold, pliant but unseeing. May tried getting her to say what had happened. But Gertie stayed mute, her eyes blank on Martha's body, whose image seemed to alter subtly with every thin flame of draining firelight. May could smell floss-ends of hair starting to singe.

'She just had a do and she tripped and she fell? It

wasn't your Francis? It wasn't, was it? What about the money? Will they think *we* did it? Gertie, *will* they? We shouldn't even be here! What will me dad say? It's getting on now; I've-I've to be back; he'll want me home.'

Gertie stared through her and repeated in a tone missing all colour: 'He'll want me home. Francis. Francis' – then turned and went to the hall. May followed her; the dog followed May.

'What you doing?'

By the frontdoor, Gertie calmly put on her coat over Martha's dress. Unable to button it at the belly, she touched her bump, then lifted the layers in stages. From her thigh Gertie scooped a clot of blood into her palm. Rivulets trickled her bare leg. And May saw that and steadied herself awhile, before putting an arm around Gertie to guide her back inside. 'Let's sit you down.'

'That's another one I've lost . . . me own doing . . . but I must tell him . . . Pray he'll forgive me . . .' Gertie showed her the clot. Up close, it looked like a crushed blackberry and May gasped and let her go.

So, Gertie lifted the latch and walked out.

May wanted to chase her, but the street was an abyss that drank Gertie up and left May with nothing to pursue. Gertie was gone from her sight without footstep or voice, without human music. And this stopped May from crossing the threshold. When she looked round, the dog was watching her, expectantly. She shut the frontdoor and returned to the backroom, where Young Martha now stood, awaiting her audience.

Old Martha's body seemed to remain by the hearth, but her features to May were now blurry, her lines tremulous, vibrating.

'Is that not you?' May said.

Young Martha gazed narrow at this murdered woman. 'Me? No, I'm dead but I won't lie down.'

Young Martha paced before May, beaming: 'Right. Well, I reads and writes better than some. I still lives at home with me Godfearing, stage-shunning, honest-days'-toiling father and mam. But if I can keep this gig up, I'll pay twice me keep. See, behind our dinky house, great chimneystacks belch a dye which holds onto every stitch of sky I've ever dreamt under. But I *know* I were meant for more. *More? More?*' Young Martha hiked her skirts in bold increments. When she dropped them her face fell too. 'I was nice and plump, wasn't I? I wasn't a bad voice. I wasn't a bad act. I wasn't too bad a daughter or wife. Shame I couldn't be a mother. No sooner did he put one inside me I'd lose it. But unlike our John, like *magic*, soon as I'd get on stage, I'd always, always, have them laughing . . .'

Not even a thin smile from May to ease the terrible silence.

'. . . on a good night.'

May swallowed to keep from fainting.

Young Martha dismissed the silence and resumed: 'See, me and our John met backstage one night. When I was climbing the bills and he was dropping down

It Fair Give Me the Spikes

them. But he convinced me to put our acts together. And in no time we was wed. Course, he left me quick for a clog dancer from Wigan. Married her still married to me. Common in them days. Ah well. She give him a full litter of sons, I read. Then he went and recorded all me songs and all me routines and he went and made a mint.' Young Martha put her back to May, to the body, and faced the gramophone. 'But they've all forgotten him now, haven't they? Like they forgot *me* . . .' She took off the 78 and turned. 'Now listen. Would you like to hear how I lost mine?'

'Lost *what* . . .?' May whispered.

Young Martha bowed, pointing to her own ear: 'Exactly.'

With clowning effort, Martha snapped the brittle shellac into jagged triangles. The sharpest points she held to her ears.

'Don't!' May leapt at her.

Confusion masked the pain, until May saw that Young Martha had gone, and she was standing in a buzz of sound, holding two razor shards of shellac, having harpooned her own eardrums.

May's ears bled down her, stains eaten by the plum frock. Drops joining the pool on the hearth, where Old Martha's body had never lain.

Only Gertie's.

And May looked and saw her truly. Having known it before she knew it. Having witnessed Francis from the window, fleeing after murdering his lavender wife. May having witnessed too, poor Gertie's ghost, bleeding home to her husband, losing another baby.

Now the coals were burning out. May waited over the body long after her tears and blood were spent, until she felt the hot tongue of the mastiff lapping her hand to comfort her.

The dog led her to the backdoor, which let onto a plot choked with weeds and junk, ending in a deep coalshed. May raised an oil lamp over it, lit by one of Gertie's unspent matches thought lost in May's hair. She opened the coalshed and peered in; the dog started digging through the heap. The hours and a shovel May used to give Gertie her burial, that bruised yellow-eye the last bit of her showing between the coals. May drove the shovel so it stayed, then she lifted the latch and walked out.

In the other room upstairs, May found an aged corpse, supine over the bed, with a sleeved 78 under her crossed boneskin hands.

John Willie's comic song. Martha's song.

Old Martha's real body had wasted there three years and more, flesh perishing into stagecloth. Any pride on her skulled face hidden behind a bouquet fit for a music hall queen at curtain call: cheeks of blazing wildflower and bramble, blackberries fruiting and dying and fruiting, with spores and fungus blooming from her empty sockets.

It Fair Give Me the Spikes

    May's dawn shadow reached for Martha's record and took it downstairs –

    ending another beginning that pealed in reverberant loops of shellac

                                         through

                              which

                    you

              retreated

        triumphant

to

the

alcove

    a shapeless witness, looming unnoticed by the living or the dead, the human or animal, with only the walls vibrating to acknowledge **you**, having been vitalised by **your** presence, empowered as all places are by grief's irruptions, braced by this forgotten music of agonies and bloodshed and the long littleness of a woman's lot endured and whose inverse echoes halt the rot and slow subsidence into shallow foundations.

    May as Martha restoked the fire, playing the old song on the gramophone again, again, again. And the dog lay by the warm gorestained hearth, watching the deaf woman dance:

Acknowledgements

This anthology was picked up by Rose Tomaszewska and I am enormously grateful for her dauntlessness and enthusiasm, as well as for early guidance. A huge thank you to Molly Slight and Asia Choudhry: I have learnt so much from your insights and working alongside you has been a gift. My appreciation, too, to Jessie Spivey for invaluable expertise. I particularly wish to thank Becky Hardie and the wider Chatto & Windus team for embracing and administering the *Bog People* unpublished writer competition, and to all the entrants.

Many thanks to my agent, Joanna Swainson, for her wisdom and support. The online folk community is an encouraging and collaborative space that is constantly supplying me with new fascinations; I am so thankful to be a part of it. All the contributors to this collection, of course, have my immeasurable gratitude for their participation.

Thank you to all my yellowbelly family, blood relations and otherwise. As ever, thank you to Michael for an embarrassment of encouragement. When I was a kid, my mum would lead my brother and I in endless rounds of Consequences, a game where each player adds blindly to a narrative so that a surreal story is revealed at the end. Our combined efforts always tended towards the weird and grisly. So, thanks most of all to Mum, for mashing my developing brain into the service of storytelling, surrounding us with library books on mysteries and ghosts and myths and monsters, seeding my love of lore and being the keeper of ours.

Hollie Starling

Copyright notice

Introduction and 'Yellowbelly' © Hollie Starling 2025

'The Ossuary' © A. K. Blakemore 2025

'Perpetual Stew' © Daniel Draper 2025

'Carole' © Emma Glass 2025

'Eldritch' © Mark Colbourne 2025

'The Spit in Your Mouth and the Bile in Your Stomach' © Mark Stafford 2025

'The Hanging Stones' © Jenn Ashworth 2025

'The Keepers' © Natasha Carthew 2025

'I Am Hagstone' © Salena Godden 2025

'It Fair Give Me the Spikes' © Tom Benn 2025

Credits

Vintage would like to thank everyone who worked on the publication of *Bog People: A Working-Class Anthology of Folk Horror*

Editorial

Rose Tomaszewska
Molly Slight
Asia Choudhry

Copy-editor

Hayley Shepherd

Proofreader

Jane Howard

Managing Editorial

Graeme Hall

Design

Julia Connolly

Publicity

Jessie Spivey

Production

Eoin Dunne

Audio

Nile Faure-Bryan
Hannah Cawse